**Copyright Info**

This novel was first published
Butterfly Books Publishers, County



This book incorporates data and information provided by www.visitroscommon.ie

Editing, Formatting, and Cover Design by Nicola Kearns at leitrimwritingcottage.com

ISBN: 978-969-569-221-9

Butterfly Books Publishers

# Going Home

CATRIONA BYRNE

# Dedication

This book is dedicated to my mother, Breda, who gave me my love of reading.

# Acknowledgements

I would like to thank my family for encouraging me to finally finish my novel, especially my daughter who acted as a proofreader and has been my constant motivator.

A big thank you to the Irish Writers' Centre, The Arts and Culture Office at Roscommon County Council, and my Editor and Publisher, Nicola Kearns, at Butterfly Books Publishers, for her unwavering professional support to the end.

# Table of Contents

# Chapter 1

Olivia woke with a jolt in her new surroundings, the unfamiliar sound of downpipes crackling in the Mediterranean heat ending her afternoon snooze. Sitting up slowly, she took in her surroundings of white-washed walls, a wrought iron bed, a pine chest of drawers and plain white bed linen. The blank wall was adorned by a simple colour splashed print and an earthenware pot of vivid red geraniums. Slowly stretching her long limbs, Olivia lay back in the shuttered, peaceful room. The simple décor was soothing, with none of Betty's bric-a-brac collections. A slow sigh escaped her, the drama of the day suddenly assaulting her thoughts. At last, she was on her long-awaited holiday. After six years of planning she was finally here, but instead of arriving as a couple with her husband, she was alone!

Throwing the light sheet off, Olivia swung her legs over the side of the bed, the humiliation coming back. Glancing at her watch she saw it was after 6 pm. Sighing, she wondered how it had all gone so wrong. She had got up this morning at seven, anxious, but excited for the boys starting First Year in Boarding School. Parting with them would be tough, but she would have to get over it. The excitement of going on holiday with Tom would be the perfect distraction. Every bone in her body craved sunshine and a change from the everyday routine. Not even twelve hours later, her plans had been turned upside down. She had arrived without her husband, disappointed and frustrated.

How could her bubble of excitement have burst before her holiday had started? She could hear her sister moving around in the living room, without doubt anxiously awaiting the full story. Better get this over and done with as soon as possible. Olivia lay slowly on the bed, cradling her head. Closing her eyes, she tried to calm herself. It was no good. Her mind still raced. How did her plans get so messed up? How did she not foresee them going so wrong? She tossed and turned, the day's events churning through her brain. Surely, she should have noticed something was amiss. Olivia thought back to this morning, slowly trying to dissect it all.

At 7.30 am, Olivia had reached over and turned off her long awaited alarm as it beeped urgently. She had been tossing and turning since before seven and when Tom got up, was unable to settle down again. Going over the plans for the day for the hundredth time, she was still undecided if it was excitement or anxiety she suffered from. It was a big day. Her thirteen-year-old twins were effectively leaving home to begin their secondary education in a Boarding School, about seventy miles away in Galway. She would no longer be seeing them every day. She wouldn't be allowed to see them until the mid-term break at Halloween. An acceptable settling-in period for students according to the school.

Olivia groaned aloud. Mentally chastising herself, she vowed not to start the day in a maudlin mood, not wanting to spoil the day for the boys by getting overanxious. She had decided to value her last day with them and make it a pleasant and memorable time. Forcing herself into action, she swung her legs over the side of the bed and shrugged on her dressing gown. Pulling back the bedroom curtains revealed the usual cloudy, unsettled sky. Feeling optimistic, her eyes rested on a patch of pale blue trying hard to break through but seemed to be fighting a losing battle. Was it just the Irish who had a fixation with the weather or did the world over do the same, but with better results, she wondered?

With eyes fixed momentarily again on the growing patch of blue, she decided the sun would win through and be a good omen for the day. In the shower, she mulled over the final checklist for the boys. Bags and schoolbooks were packed, all paperwork had been forwarded to the school, the boy's phones had been topped up with credit - very important. However,

Olivia was unhappy with the ban on all calls to and from parents during the settling-in period, except for emergency calls. This was another of many objections she raised with Tom, but he agreed with the school's stance on this one too.

He thought it best to let them settle in. They will be fine. If there is an emergency, of course, they will be allowed to call. Stop raking it over, she berated herself. Tom had made the decision. The boys were going today and that's it. Towelling herself dry, Olivia hastily brushed her mousey blonde, bob length hair.

Not great, she thought, glancing critically at her hair in the full-length bedroom mirror. Her hairstyle was dull and serviceable, functional. It was just past her shoulders and overdue a good trim but would have to do. There was no time now to toy with the idea of a new look and anyway, Tom kept reminding her he liked it as it was. There was no doubt about it, Tom was a creature of habit and didn't like change.

Olivia quickly dressed in the clothes she had left aside last night - her cream safari jacket and matching trousers, together with a coordinating olive green, camisole top. Tom had given her the outfit the previous Christmas. Giving it a scan in her full-length mirror she thought it looked okay, if a bit overdressed for dropping the boys at their new school. But there was no time to dally. It was seven-thirty already, time to call the boys and get them out of bed.

Andrew and Jonathon were already in overdrive mode when Olivia opened their bedroom door. Instantly, she was overwhelmed by the waft of Lynx body spray. It was hard to think her boys were now thirteen and could still be as hyperactive as three-year-olds!

'This room stinks of body spray and you haven't even had your showers yet,' Olivia shouted from the bedroom door.

'Mam, he robbed mine last night, so I'm getting rid of his now. Fair's, fair,' Andrew piped from under the covers.

Jonathan, who was not to be outdone, responded by landing a perfectly aimed pillow at his brother's head.

'C'mon, lads. We need to be out of here by nine, so no dallying about. You know your father is a stickler for timekeeping. Straight into the shower now. Jonathan, you use the shower in my bedroom. I left your uniforms on the bed. I'm off to make a proper Irish breakfast to set you up for the day,' Olivia cajoled, sneakily dragging the duvets from their beds and dashing for the stairs.

'Great, Mam. Four sausages for me,' Jonathon shouted.

'I'll have five, seeing as I'm bigger than him, Mam,' Andrew yelled.

'Yeah, you've got a fatter arse and belly alright!' Jonathon guffawed.

'Yeah, yeah. Enough of the comments. Get up and going now!' Olivia called in response from the bottom of the stairs.

Downstairs, the rashers, sausages and pudding hissed under the grill, the homely smell filling the kitchen. Listening to the boys bickering from upstairs, Olivia knew she'd really miss them. She enjoyed cooking and cleaning up after her sons, including all the ferrying to hurling and football matches. Most people would think her completely mad to voice such an opinion, but that was how she felt. Her whole life revolved around her children since moving from London eight years before. She hadn't worked outside the home since then and was a full-time mother. They were her whole life and filled her days. She got them up and ready for school. At lunchtime, they cycled home and all three sat down to lunch every day.

Every evening, the whole family including Tom's mother, Betty, had dinner around seven. Olivia usually enjoyed this routine, the exuberance and energy of the boys' company and their friends, even the noise, mess, scuffles and usual demands of teenage boys. It gave her life structure and purpose. Now they were going to Boarding School and she would miss them terribly. Reminding herself not to think about it, she was determined to be happy and positive for them.

Breakfast was almost ready and waiting with tea just about to be brewed. At a quarter to eight, Olivia checked everything was prepared in the kitchen. It all looked fine. The table was set with its usual willow patterned delph. Eagerly taking their places at the table, the boys helped themselves to generous portions, each surreptitiously watching the other's plate. At ten to eight on the button, Tom's mother breezed into the kitchen.

Dressed in her customary matching twin set, navy with pearl buttons and coordinating tweed skirt, perfect make-up and perfectly styled hair, Betty believed she was the epitome of mature style. She was a generously well-built, handsome country woman, who perfectly represented the head of the local Senior Ladies Committee.

'Good morning, all. I dropped in to check on the plans. Are you ready to go boys? Have you checked everything, Olivia? We don't want to give a poor impression from the start,' she asked, easing herself into her usual chair, relieving the constraints of her knotted neck-scarf.

The boys nodded to their gran, confirming in unison they were ready to go.

'Are you sure now, Olivia? Did you check everything this morning?' Betty enquired anxiously.

She prided herself on her organizational and motivational skills, believing in addition to her excellent homemaking expertise, like bread making, crocheting, knitting, quilting and debating, that she was a wonderful homemaker and arranger.

'Mam checked everything yesterday and again this morning. So, yes, everything is fine, Gran,' Andrew replied, tightly.

Betty unimpressed by her grandson's tone, looked long and hard at him. On getting no response, she rolled her eyes in her customary Betty fashion, followed by a few short sniffs.

'Boys, I am just concerned all goes to plan. I constantly worry about you all the time. I'm afraid that's one of the perils of being a grandmother,' she said, miffed by Andrew's offending tone and dabbing her nose dramatically.

'Thanks for asking, Betty, but I have checked everything twice and yes, all is okay. Would you like some breakfast with your cup of tea? I have loads left over,' Olivia soothed in a conciliatory tone, aware of the importance of avoiding one of Betty's sulks that could last for days if the mood took her.

Betty shuffled irritably into her seat at the head of the family table, relieved Olivia had finally acknowledged her concerns and worries about the boys' preparations.

'Well, I had my breakfast at six-thirty, as you know I do every day, but I didn't sleep a wink last night worrying about the boys. I'll try a sausage and a couple of rashers if they are spare. Just the one sausage mind. I never have a big appetite.'

Olivia placed the prepared plate before her mother-in-law. The plate, laden with a full Irish breakfast complete with homemade potato bread lay tantalizing before Betty.

'Betty, eat whatever suits you. It was going to waste otherwise,' Olivia replied, tactfully.

'Thank you, Olivia. But your generation needs to work on meal planning and housekeeping skills. It's shocking the amount of wasted food nowadays,' Betty preached, feeling obliged to impart her ample knowledge as an experienced homemaker to her daughter-in-law.

As Betty tucked in, the boys exchanged a knowing look and excused themselves from the table. Just then, Tom entered the kitchen, also checking on the morning's plans.

'Good morning, Tom. Everything's ready to go here,' Betty assured him, as Tom gave his mother a perfunctory kiss on the cheek and took his chair beside her.

Olivia passed the generous plate of breakfast before him, with his usual mug of strong tea.

Having reassured Tom and Betty all was okay, the boys dashed off for a final check on everything. On the way, Jonathon nudged Andrew.

'Bet you a fiver there won't be a crumb left on Betty's plate,' he whispered.

'I wouldn't place ten cents on that bet. Sure, Betty has never yet left the table with anything on the plate,' Andrew sniggered in reply.

In the kitchen, Olivia finished off her breakfast after topping up Betty's cup of tea. Tom quickly tucked into his breakfast and as usual, had it polished off within five minutes. He pushed his chair away from the table, stood up and grabbed his jacket off the back of the chair. Pulling it on, he reminded Olivia he would be back at nine sharp to leave with the boys.

'Don't be worrying about a thing, Tom. I have everything ready, including our bags for this evening. We will really enjoy this trip, Tom,' she gushed, beaming at her husband.

Tom was a stickler for details and Olivia knew from experience her husband liked his plans to run smoothly.

'Well, we'll deal with one thing at a time. Talk later, okay. See you at a quarter-to-nine sharp,' he said, slipping out the kitchen door, dressed in his customary green, wax jacket and work boots.

'My poor Tom. He's rushed off his feet and never gets a minute for himself,' Betty sighed morosely, glancing at Tom's departing figure.

Olivia gathered the blue delph, loading them carefully into the dishwasher, mindful Betty was in prime viewing position over the handling of her precious crockery. The delph was a present from her mother-in-law, a set she had for years but felt needed to be used, being of such good quality. However, Betty didn't have the space in her own home, so gifted them to Olivia. Tom, anxious to please his mother, had decided the delph be used daily, so Olivia now had the privilege of looking at them morning, noon and night.

From the very start, every week, Betty did a quick, covert stock-take of her heirloom and was prone to states of agitation on discovering the odd chip or crack, or even worse, the odd complete fatality. Of course, all this very distressing news would have to be relayed by Betty to Tom, who in turn would relay it all back to Olivia, with a plaintive request to be more careful. In the beginning, Olivia appreciated Betty's well intentioned gift, but she finally figured out how to avoid Betty's sulks after weekly inspections by buying three additional sets of delph.

After every dishwasher mishap, she replaced the casualty with a new one, making life easier all around.

'Yes, we will enjoy our holiday away,' Olivia replied. 'I can't wait. Our first time abroad together in six years,' she sighed, in anticipation of her holiday.

'Well, don't be bothering Tom with all that carry on this morning. He's up to his eyes with everything. Indeed, just like myself this morning. I've no time to chat right now. I'll see you later,' Betty declared, hastily removing herself from the kitchen table after Tom.

Well, Olivia thought. That's a first. What did she say? No time to chat! Betty, who could sit and talk all day, every day. Olivia smiled to herself, content to do a final check on the day's plans in peace.

'Okay, lads! Clothes bags, schoolbooks and sports bags are all packed in the boot,' Olivia hollered, making her way into the hall and shouting up the stairs.

'Yeah, yeah,' the twins shouted in reply.

# Chapter 2

At quarter-to-nine, the boys, Tom and Olivia were all ready to go. As they were about to leave the driveway, Betty strolled up to the car, all dressed for a day out.

'Push over boys and make room for your gran,' she ordered, easing herself unceremoniously beside Andrew, handbag landing in his lap.

'I didn't know you were coming with us,' Andrew remarked, unburdening himself of her large, overstuffed bag. God, she must have the kitchen sink in this, he thought, thumping it onto the car floor.

'I wouldn't miss this trip for the world. I need to know you're settled in safely. Otherwise, I'll never sleep a wink tonight,' Betty sighed, taking up a very generous portion of the back seat and hemming the two boys into the far corner.

Over an hour and a half later, Tom drove through the school entrance, parking in the carpark of St. Joseph's Boarding School. After checking the boys into the school and inspecting dormitories and facilities, Olivia was immensely relieved to see the boys relaxed and quite excited at the prospect of starting in their new school. It was the official registration and start date for all first-year students. It was comforting to see all the other parents and students also seemed to be wearing the same slightly lost, but enthusiastic expressions.

They had previously taken part in a detailed tour of the school and its wide-ranging facilities, including research into the academic opportunities offered by the various boarding schools. Tom had decided St. Joseph's was the most suitable. Betty liked to expound on the virtues of a good education in life and believed that university was the way to go. She hadn't been fortunate enough to have such an opportunity, but felt if born in the right era, the sky would have been the limit for her. All through her life, people had commented on her sharp brain and she now felt with the wealth of life experiences behind her, it was her duty to point her grandchildren in the right direction in life. Tom had high hopes for his sons and liked to think his opinion was the deciding one in this case. The boys had been clever enough to play along and let him believe that too.

The parents and children gathered in the large auditorium where the staff and principal welcomed students and gave a detailed brief on school policies. A welcome pack was issued to all including the school curriculum, school sports activities, field trips and school calendar.

The principal introduced his staff and concluded his speech by reiterating the rule on mobile phone usage, requesting parents abstain from making personal calls to the boys until the mid-term break. The school found this policy allowed the students to forge better friendships with their fellow students, in addition to speeding up the whole settling-in period. However, both parents and students alike were to be reassured communication would not be limited in any way in an emergency. Parents could always phone the school secretary to enquire about their son's progress, or any other query they might have, between the hours of 9.30 am and 1 pm. Students were asked to say goodbye to their parents as classes would commence at 11.30 am. Olivia glanced at her watch. It was 11.15 am and the principal and staff were leaving the podium, awaiting their students for the first class of term.

Gosh, they don't waste any time, she thought! Bustling and shuffling set in as parents hugged goodbye. No final kisses here. It wouldn't look cool in this male environment of thirteen- and fourteen-year-olds. Jonathon and Andrew looked around as the tempo had suddenly sped up. Suddenly, everyone was in a rush.

Students were busy saying goodbye, anxious to get to know the form of the other students before they were down to the grindstone in less than half an hour. Better get on with things. Tom and Betty hugged the boys, followed by their Mum.

They were putting on a brave front, Olivia thought. Glancing at her sons, she studied them long and hard, amazed at how they had turned from boys to young men in one morning. Hugging her, Jonathon whispered. 'Don't worry. We will be fine, and we are lucky there are two of us.'

'Double trouble,' Andrew added, winking reassuringly at his mum.

Olivia noticed the principal and staff walk purposely towards the grand exit area, politely awaiting the prompt departure of parents. Tom, Betty and Olivia quickly walked to the door, the boys saying their final goodbyes.

'Well, you look very smart and grown up in your new uniforms, Boys. Be good and study hard. This college is awfully expensive you know. Your father has worked extremely hard over the years to pay for it,' Betty sniffed, fumbling in her handbag for a tissue.

'Yeah, Gran. Goodbye, Mum, Dad. Have a great holiday and don't worry about us. We will be fine,' Jonathon replied earnestly.

'Yeah, see you in eight weeks for the Mid-Term break. We'll have the place well sussed out by then,' Andrew joked.

'Lads, I want you both to study hard. And you, Andrew! You settle down and behave. I don't want to be getting complaints in the first week. Be good, okay,' Tom warned in a low, hushed voice.

'C'mon, Jonathon. We'll head to the classroom now. We don't want to be caught sitting in the front row for the year! Bye, all,' he called, grabbing his brother by the sleeve and steering him away.

As they made their way back to the car park, Olivia gave a last look in the direction of the school, realizing her life was going to change in a big way. The boys were only thirteen, but she knew being away from the comfort of their own home every day and having to be responsible for themselves meant they were going to do some serious growing up very fast. She hoped they were mentally mature enough to cope with all that was ahead of them over the next coming weeks.

'Well, that went great, I thought,' Tom said, starting the car and reversing for the journey home.

'It will do those boys a power of good. They need to grow up a bit and be more independent. There'll be no mollycoddling there. I think plenty of discipline will do them the world of good. Olivia, you have them spoilt rotten over the years,' Betty replied, manhandling her handbag into submission onto her lap.

'Well, thank you very much for that, Betty, but I'm happy with them as they are,' Olivia retorted.

'I think a few tough house rules in that new school wouldn't go amiss at all,' Tom muttered.

Olivia knew not to bother responding. Tom and Betty were a real force to be reckoned with when they got together. Experience had taught her that. While they continued to discuss the merits of their wise choices, Olivia daydreamed, watching the passing countryside and enjoying the rich autumnal colours of September. Summer was not quite over and autumn was just starting. The best of both seasons contributed to a riot of colours as they sped by. The wide ranging spectrum of autumn leaves ranging from palest ochre, yellow, vibrant orange and burnt red to earthy browns adorned the various shrubs, trees and hedgerows heaving with wild fuchsia. Their vibrant pink and purple flowers grew in wild abandon, fringing every road in the country.

In a few short weeks, autumn winds would scatter the leaves and blooms far and wide, providing a carpet of colour everywhere. It never ceased to amaze Olivia how abruptly the landscape could change. The colourful window boxes and pots on display in every house in the country looked so fine at this time of year. All the flora looked their most magnificent and blooms at their healthiest, blowsy, over mature blooms with their drooping heads of vivid shades, burnt reds, oranges and yellows and every rainbow colour in between. Olivia felt as though they were putting on their final best effort before autumn and winter kicked in, knowing time was running out. Well, time might be running out for them, but she was off on holiday and she smiled in contentment at the prospect.

'I see the weather is about to change again. More rain by the looks of it,' Betty moaned, as the first spatters hit the windscreen.

'Well, I'm hoping not to see any rain over the next ten days. In a few hours, Tom, we'll be basking in the sunny South of France. I can't wait,' Olivia crooned.

'Ten days on your own is such a long time,' Betty lamented, fiddling noisily with her handbag in the back seat and blowing her nose loudly into her tissue.

Olivia couldn't wait. The break wasn't half long enough she felt, but it would have to do. There was no point in rocking the boat now. It had taken six years to get this far.

# Chapter 3

'Look, I don't want to have a big argument about this. It's just not a good time at the moment to go away. I have a lot of work going on right now on the farm.'

Tom paced the kitchen floor repeatedly, explaining his reasoning to Olivia.

'Not good timing! We booked the flights last March. We agreed on it with Angie. She is expecting us at Carcassonne Airport in a few hours. We talked about it numerous times over the last few months. You know how excited I was about this trip. Remember the two of us discussed what vineyards to visit, wines to sample and places to explore. You printed off reams of paper for things to do, maps - you name it. We checked it all out,' Olivia cried, flabbergasted by his outburst.

'I just said the timing is not good at the moment. We could think about it again. Maybe in the Spring or next Summer,' Tom replied.

His voice was steely and determined as he placed his palms firmly on the kitchen table, stating his case to Olivia.

'I'm stunned. Just exactly when did you decide 'the timing wasn't good'? You have watched me pack our cases.

Hey, we were only talking about this yesterday. You printed off the tickets only a few days ago. When did you change your mind?'

Olivia couldn't sit still. She stalked from the counter, unable to tolerate Tom's levelled stare one minute longer.

'I felt pressured into this holiday with your sister from the start. It's not my thing. You know that. Look, we could take a few days off and head to Cork or Kerry. We could go this week if you like. Book into the Glen Eagles. You like it there. Betty might like to come too. She'd enjoy the break herself,' Tom wheedled as he ambled over, arms outstretched towards Olivia.

'Is this some sort of a joke, Tom? I have visited Cork and Kerry for my holidays for the past six years. Lovely though they are, I don't want to go there again on holiday. To say I'm slightly sick of them is an understatement. I want to go abroad on the holiday we booked. We'll change it to just one week if that's what you want,' Olivia implored.

'I'm trying to meet you halfway, Olivia. I said a trip to France doesn't suit me right now. We can go anywhere you like in Ireland for a few days. Check it out on the Internet. I've got to head out. Give me a call on the mobile when you have decided on something,' Tom said, bluntly.

Olivia's unaccustomed outburst was getting on his nerves. He reached for his hat and went out the door, slamming it hard on his way out.

Olivia looked in shock at the banged door, its echo resounding throughout the kitchen. What had just happened? Had all her plans for the last six months just gone up in smoke? This was surely only a blip and her husband was just getting into a panic. Tom, a creature of habit, didn't like change, but when he got to France, Olivia knew he'd be delighted. Angie had described it all in such detail and sent brochures of the area. They had looked for hours at pictures of the beautiful beaches of Cap D'Agde, the rambling streets of Agde and the magical Marseillan Ville.

The chance to explore the beautiful buildings, street markets and lovely street cafes, the quaint fishing port of Sete and its town set amongst stunning pink cliffs looked so appealing. Tom was just having a wobbly moment. They were going to France today. She and Tom would have a ball! They needed it!

Olivia reached for the telephone and dialled Joe Egan's mobile number. Joe was a self-employed carpenter and during the Celtic Tiger years travelled daily to work in Dublin like half the country did and never seemed to have time to be at home.

Now he focused on working on his small farm of about fifty acres and doing any other bits of work he could get. He also helped Tom regularly on the farm when needed. Olivia liked Joe. He was friendly and approachable, and she felt at ease with him. As the number rang out, she smiled, delighted with her quick thinking.

Joe was his usual chirpy self and after exchanging pleasantries, Olivia got straight to the point, explaining her dilemma with Tom. Five minutes later, Olivia hung up the phone beaming. Joe would look after their two-hundred-acre, dry-stock farm for the ten days Tom was away. He knew the routine inside out. Olivia was thrilled with her perfect solution.

Sitting at the table, she went through her final checklist. Passports & boarding passes printed, bags packed, one large bag and one cabin bag each. She couldn't wait to phone Tom and pass on the good news. A glance at the kitchen clock told her it was only half twelve. They could leave in an hour or so and have a quick bite of lunch on the way and a nice relaxing drink in the airport, with plenty of time to catch the flight. Olivia excitedly rang Tom's mobile number.

'Hi, good news, Tom. Everything's sorted. Joe's looking after the cattle, packing done, tickets checked in. We're all ready to go. If you hurry back, we can leave within the hour.'

'Yeah, listen, Olivia. Can't talk at the moment. I'll phone you back,' Tom cut in rapidly, before promptly hanging up.

'Yeah, okay,' Olivia replied, dejected at being cut short.

Never mind, he'll be back shortly, she thought, delighted with her arrangements. He'd have nothing to worry about for the next ten days.

Tom sat down at his mother's table, a mug of tea in hand and put the mobile phone back in his pocket. Betty had great sympathy for her son. Olivia could be very demanding at times. She didn't know which side her bread was buttered, but Betty vowed not to say a word against her. She didn't like to interfere and enjoyed this rare one-to-one time with her son. Tom understood her inside out. He was her only son and Betty was very proud of him. There was a daughter, but Tom was worth ten of her. Lilly had a selfish streak and would suit herself when to visit. With three kids and her life revolving around them and her husband, Betty was way down her list of priorities. She didn't appreciate Betty liked to be involved in her grandchildren's lives as a granny should be.

Lilly told her on the last visit it was not Betty's place to chastise or punish her children. As if a smack on the bum was any great punishment to a five-year-old. No, Lilly preferred 'time out' on the naughty step. Such rubbish, indeed. She tried to tell her daughter she had a wealth of experience behind her, but no, Lilly would do things her way with her children in her home.

She sniffed as she recalled the last visit. Lilly would need Betty's opinion someday, probably sooner than she thought and Betty would enjoy reminding her of the times she snubbed her advice in the past. Tom was completely different though, much more agreeable, understanding and appreciative of her advice as a good son should be. He understood her need to be involved in his family and always included her in his plans, aware she could be lonely. She was widowed for eight years and dedicated all her time to Tom and his family.

'Mam, I had best get home and set the record straight with Olivia,' Tom decided, rising wearily from the kitchen table.

'Indeed, it was a silly idea of hers anyway, this trip to France to her sister. You have her spoilt rotten as it is, Tom. Olivia doesn't know how lucky she is. We could all have a lovely trip to Kerry. I like that hotel in Killarney we stayed in last year. The GAA dinner dance is on in a couple of weeks. We always enjoy that, Son,' Betty crooned, as Tom made his way next door to face the music.

Olivia met Tom at the door, noticing it was just after half twelve.

'C'mon, Tom. You're cutting it fine. All is ready to go. Just grab the bags and load up.'

Tom sauntered into the kitchen; his eyes downcast as he dodged the luggage-laden hall with Olivia fast on his heels.

'Olivia, I already said this holiday is not a good option at the moment with so much going on.'

Reaching across the kitchen table he glanced leisurely over the front page of the daily paper.

'What's for lunch? I'm starving,' he added, looking expectantly around the kitchen countertop.

'Never mind lunch. We can pick that up on the way. I've left out a change of clothes for you on the bed. C'mon, hurry up and we'll have time to have a nice lunch in the airport before our flight, washed down with a glass of cooled Chardonnay to get us in the mood for our holiday,' Olivia trilled, bustling around the kitchen and hastily emptying the dishwasher of its final load for a while.

Tom looked at her in surprise.

'Olivia, did you not hear one word I said? It just doesn't suit me now. I'm far too busy.'

'Never mind that. I have it all sorted. I spoke to Joe a while ago. He'll keep an eye on things for us. So all is good on that front.'

Tom looked on in shock as his wife continued in her whirlwind of multi-tasking, tidying the kitchen, emptying the bin and doing a final clear-out of the fridge.

'Olivia, will you just stop for five minutes? I need to talk to you properly. What did you ring Joe for?' Tom asked, exasperation showing on his face.

'Joe is the perfect solution. He'll keep an eye on the farm as well as here and give you a call if there are any problems. Tom, it's all sorted. You'll have nothing to worry about. I only spoke to Angie an hour ago. She cannot wait to see us!' Olivia was delighted with her quick-thinking.

Tom slowly laid his palms on the kitchen table, exhaling in a slow, controlled fashion. Lowering his eyes to the table, he proceeded to clench and unclench his fists.

Olivia tensed at his sudden change in demeanour, previous experience alerting her Tom wanted her full, undivided attention.

'I'm only going to say this once more. I told you this morning. The timing isn't good. I have a lot on. We'll think about this again. Maybe in the Spring when things have settled down,' Tom muttered.

'The Spring? Nothing will be any different then. Everything's paid for and arranged. We're all ready to go now. We made these plans last Spring. Don't you remember? September was your choice,' Olivia answered, failing miserably to hide exasperation in her voice.

Tom leaned forward, picking his hat from the table.

'I'm off out. Why don't you go on a shopping day? Give Mam a shout for company. I'll see you later,' perching his hat firmly on his head, he casually walked towards the back door banging it firmly after him, confident the matter was finally sorted.

Olivia stared at the door after Tom left. His final parting words echoed in her head. Oh my God, she thought. He doesn't have a clue and cares even less. A wave of anger mixed with humiliation washed over her, realizing Tom had made up his mind and his decision was final. They were not going on holiday today.

Turning on her heel, Olivia ran to her bedroom, quickly changing into jeans, a t-shirt and low-slung sandals. Grabbing her cream safari jacket and handbag, she checked for her bank cards, mobile phone, charger and passport. Yes, all okay.

She hastily threw the other passport aside on the bed. No need for that. She was ready to go and would have plenty of time to browse in Duty-Free before her flight at five. She was going on holiday!

# Chapter 4

Olivia swung her legs over the side of the bed and tried to calm her racing heart. Angie had picked her up at Carcassonne airport just a few hours ago and Olivia had filled her in briefly on Tom's absence. Within forty minutes they arrived at Angie's beautiful apartment at Marseillan Plage, a lovely coastal holiday location. At her sister's insistence, Olivia quickly refreshed and had a cat nap to calm her thoughts. After a half hour resting, Olivia looked at her watch, knowing Angie would be waiting anxiously for an update. I better get up and face the music, she thought.

'Well, hopefully, you are feeling a bit better. C'mon outside. I have a nice chilled white wine spritzer waiting for you. Better grab your sun hat. The current temperature is 26 degrees!'

Olivia made her way out to Angie's courtyard, framed by frangipani and hibiscus. In the corner, a nicely pruned fig tree provided just the right amount of shade. Settling herself at the table, hands resting on the tabletop, she tried to unclench her hands. Breathing deeply, Olivia reminded herself she was finally on holiday. At last the long-awaited sunshine. Moving to the lounger she faced the sun, taking off her hat to feel the heat on her face. Wonderful! Her closed eyes were soothed by the sounds of chirping crickets and the distant sound of crashing waves. The aroma of perfumed flowers mixed with fresh, salty air assaulted the senses. Olivia felt she could drift away in bliss.

'Well, Sis. I'm delighted to see you. I know you're upset about Tom, but you're on holiday now. I know you'll enjoy yourself.'

Angie leaned forward, throwing her arms around Olivia. 'C'mon. Cheer up,' she continued. 'I want to show you the sights and give you the grand tour. The beach, Marseillan Plage, is only a five-minute walk in that direction. Some lovely restaurants are five minutes in the opposite direction. What more could a body want in life?' Angie sighed, pointing left and right at her courtyard gate. 'Tell you what. Let's have that chat and get things off your chest first and then we'll do our grand tour.'

Angie handed Olivia's freshly topped-up glass over before joining her on the other lounger, resting her own glass on the dividing glass-topped, wrought iron table.

'Well, what can I say? Tom changed his mind at the last minute. I filled you in on most of the details on the way from the airport. You know, I rang him when I got to Dublin Airport to say I was waiting for him, thinking when he had time to think things over he'd come to his senses. I was so shocked when he spoke to me. He was livid I had gone ahead without him, as though we seemingly agreed to change our plans to a few days down in Kerry. His ultimatum was I return home straight away and apologise for all the stress I caused him. I really couldn't believe his bloody tone and attitude,' Olivia hissed through gritted teeth.

Angie stole a sideways glance at her sister noting her barely suppressed rage, completely out of character for Olivia. Her drink was practically untouched and she was sitting completely rigid, tension etched in every bone in her body. Discussing Tom would be a very touchy subject!

'Look, c'mon, Sis. Let's enjoy your holiday. Tom didn't come for whatever reason, but I'm thrilled to have you here. Relax. Enjoy your spritzer and let the holiday begin. You can start by exposing those pasty white legs to the sun. They're long overdue a bit of Vitamin D,' Angie cajoled, handing the sparkling drink to her sister.

Angie wasn't overly surprised at Tom's non-appearance. As long as she knew him, she always felt he liked to be the decision-maker. They were harmless little things in the early days of their relationship, but since Tom and Olivia moved back to his home turf in Kildare, his controlling manner was very evident to Angie. No doubt the wonderful Betty didn't help the situation either. She casually tried to discuss it with Olivia a few times in the past, but every time Olivia just laughed it off before subtly closing the subject. She felt Tom had chipped away at Olivia so much over the years, that she had become resigned to the role of peacekeeper in the household.

'Hey, I know you're right. It's just I thought we had the same plans, but Tom had other ideas. He may have calmed down, changed his mind and be out here on the first flight tomorrow!' Olivia mumbled, stretching her legs satisfyingly.

'Absolutely, but for now, lie back and enjoy the afternoon rays of sunshine. It's only half-six. We'll head out for dinner around half-eight. Perhaps we could take a quick stroll to the beach shortly and walk along the seafront to our restaurant overlooking the ocean. What more could a girl want?'

'He's still not answering his phone. I'll call again later. Maybe he left it at home again,' Olivia sighed, disappointedly staring at her phone.

'You are here for ten days, so I think you can take it he's not coming out. He's pretty much giving you an ultimatum. Either go home and apologise, or continue on holiday. I don't want to pressure you, but it's Tom and Betty against you again. Put it in the back of your mind,' Angie suggested, concerned for her sister's woes. 'Enjoy the last few days of your holiday and chill out. Have a stroll down to the beach, clear your head and remember you are on holiday! We'll meet back here in an hour or so and head to Marseillan Ville for lunch. I'll introduce you to the wonderful Stefan.'

'With an interesting offer like that, how can I refuse? I can't wait to see what the big French attraction is,' Olivia laughed in reply, dragging out Angie's yellow beach lounger and the ever-ready beach bag. 'See you later. I'm off to soak up some sunshine!' Olivia called on her way to the nearby beach.

Lying back on her lounger on the Marseillan Plage, she surveyed all around her – couples, grandparents and young families, but also several single men and women topping up their tans after spending their day at work, office jackets folded carefully to one side. Others expertly played *petang* without a hair out of place and looking professionally chic as only continental Europeans can.

Olivia topped up her legs and arms with her suntan lotion, very pleased with the lovely golden sheen achieved over the last few days. She felt ten years younger already and considered a sun holiday the best mental and physical therapy ever. Completely relaxing, she realized there were only a few days left before her holiday was over. She'd have to return home to Tom and Betty and endure endless sniping over the holiday debacle that could last decades. Olivia knew she would just have to suck it up and get over it, but it wasn't all that bothered her.

She felt she had very little purpose at home now the boys, her allies, were gone. Her eyes had been opened wide about her marriage as she covertly studied Angie and Stefan's relationship. They were besotted with each other still. Angie positively glowed in his company and looked at least ten years younger than her forty-five years. Her sister and Stefan had been together almost five years and still, the spark between them was undeniable. Their easy relaxed conversations, the little knowing looks and kisses between them were almost sickly compared to her relationship. Tom's endearments usually consisted of, 'What's for dinner?' and 'Don't forget to pay the ESB bill!'

Rolling onto her tummy and slathering on some sunscreen, Olivia reminded herself to enjoy these last few days in paradise!

# Chapter 5

'The three cottages are yours for the taking. Mum and Dad left them to the two of us. But honestly, I can't see myself leaving here to settle in the West of Ireland. I don't know exactly what state they are in, but Dad had done a bit of work on them. The one they were living in was quite nice, rustic, but nice. That was two years ago and I haven't seen the cottages since. Maybe consider taking a trip there. It'll give you something to do with your spare time. You don't have to make any definite plans. Look at it like this. You're only thirty-five and you've no commitments because the boys are gone till Christmas.'

Angie tried to encourage her sister as she hugged Olivia goodbye at the airport.

'This blip with Tom is probably only minor anyway. Regardless of whether he came on holiday or not, you'd still be in the same situation at the end of the week. You're at a crossroads in life now and you have the opportunity to do something new, get a job, or do anything you like.'

Olivia reached forward and embraced her tightly.

'Hey! I've had a ball. I feel much clearer-headed and refreshed. They say absence makes the heart grow fonder, so I'm very hopeful in Tom's case,' she said.

'Good for you. Love you to bits and I'll be in touch. Now go, or you'll miss that flight!' Angie gushed as they parted with a final kiss and Olivia headed for the Departures Lounge.

Olivia didn't plan it. She just desperately wanted to get away from Dublin Airport and couldn't bear to be anywhere near there anymore. Before realizing it, she was on the M50, having made an instant decision to head for the West. A slight drizzle started and she had the heater turned up to the max to keep the windscreen clear, but somehow the heat was adding to the confusion in her brain.

Olivia knew she couldn't take any more. She had texted Tom the evening before with her arrival time at Dublin Airport and spent over two hours excitedly waiting in Arrivals, before finally receiving his long-awaited text.

*Busy. See you at home tonight.*

Still refusing to register the tone of his text message, she phoned him, only to hear him reiterate his text message word by word, his anger and rage filtering down the phone. Olivia had visibly reddened with shame and humiliation as Tom's indifference and complete lack of interest towards her finally hit home. And so, she had made the snap decision not to go back to

Kildare. She couldn't face him with the surge of rage rushing through her and knew she had to stay away.

Eventually, the traffic snaked past the slip road to Lucan and keeping her foot on the accelerator, she picked up speed, driving into the wide-open countryside. The verdant trees, cattle filled fields, sleepy towns and villages lifted her heart rate. That would serve him right, she thought. Feeling stress and strain leave her body, she finally released a slow steady breath, the tension gradually easing away with the knowledge she was not going back to Kildare.

Just over two hours later and after seven o'clock, Olivia cautiously drove her car down the boreen towards Doon Shore and overlooking Lough Key in Boyle. Her car bumped and groaned at this unfamiliar territory. She slowly moved along, soothed by the myriad of autumnal colours of the overhanging fuchsia and elderberry bushes laden with over-ripe purple fruit.

She continued driving, passing the other six cottages on her way. Nestled at the end of the laneway, her parent's three cottages slowly came into view, all painted a rich honey cream. Olivia swallowed the lump in her throat, recalling the last time she visited here nearly three years ago.

She, Tom and the boys had spent the day with Mum and Dad. They loved the area with its beautiful unspoiled scenery and loads of space to run around. Dad had even managed to rig up two fishing rods and there was such excitement going off in his little boat, returning later with a single fish. It was a very small perch that didn't diminish the excitement for Jonathon landing his first catch. Tom wasn't in favour of staying overnight. The cottage was a bit rustic to his liking, so they only stayed the day and headed back to Kildare that evening. Olivia had left that day with every intention of making regular trips with the boys back to this idyllic retreat her parents were creating. Regrettably, that didn't happen, unfortunately allowing other unimportant things in everyday life to get in the way.

Olivia turned off the engine and stepped out onto the gravel driveway, slowly turning and surveying all around. Her parents had been here for two years after returning from England for their retirement. The scale of the project in trying to put three very dilapidated cottages back to life seemed to spur them on and both had gotten completely caught up excitement of the development. They spent days and nights at work on them. Their weekly telephone conversations with Olivia relayed all the work carried out the week before – putting in windows, replacing bathrooms and installing a heating system. Nothing seemed to phase them. Their response to any anxieties raised concerning all the hard work was always the same – they got caught up in the excitement of the refurbishment.

Little did they know their stay in their new home would be so short-lived. Arriving in June, Breda had her heart attack in September the following year and died just before Christmas. Her dad, Matt, had lived only four months after her. Unsettled after his wife's death, he would visit Olivia for a few days but was always restless, returning to his cottage to continue tinkering away. Without the companionship of his wife, he neglected himself and soon lost interest in taking care of his health, surviving on tea and ham sandwiches and losing the will to bother cooking a proper meal.

Olivia crunched along the gravel, made her way to the front door and eased the key into her parent's last home. The stiff lock gently squeaked as she slowly turned the key. The yellow painted, peeling door opened grudgingly with a tired groan as she eased it wide open and got her first full view since her last visit. All the evidence of their hard work was there. The terracotta, tiled floor had been repaired in places where a few of life's accidents had occurred over the years. The walls were painted white and Olivia was choked with emotion on seeing her old paintings framed and displayed on the walls. Family photos of her boys, a large wedding photo of herself and Tom -

even older photos of her and Angie were propped on the mantelpiece over the large, stone fireplace.

Opening the stove door she saw the fire had been set, stacked with kindling and sods of turf. Even the turf basket was filled to the brim, a box of matches nestling on top, in anticipation of someone restoring life into the cottage. The scene looked as though her parents had just popped out for a message and would be back shortly. Olivia took it all in, acutely aware they were not coming back. Despite this, the overriding feeling was one of welcome, with fond memories of the good times her parents had creating their retirement haven.

Giving herself a mental shake, Olivia went to the stove and struck a match to the kindling. It was only September, but she felt the flames would dispel the air of the autumn chill. Within minutes, the kindling was alight, its leaping flames casting an instant cheery glow to the room. Glancing around and taking in her surroundings, she made her way through the cottage. It had the traditional layout of Irish cottages, single storied with a bedroom on either side of the main living room.

She opened the door from the living room into her parents' bedroom. The terracotta tiles continued in here and her parent's bed, adorned with her mum's cream-toned crochet throw pulled at her heartstrings, picturing her mother ever busy with her crochet hook. The walls were wallpapered in sky blue paper, but ravages of time and neglect were taking their toll as it peeled away from the walls at the corners. She continued into the other bedroom, originally one large room with two windows on opposite walls. Dad had split it up into two smaller, cosier ones, each with their own window.

Again, the walls were wallpapered in swirls of lemon and yellow. While the paper was still intact, the musty smell of dust and lack of fresh air was overwhelming. As was the fashion in the '70s and '80s, a bathroom and a kitchen, or scullery as it was called back then, was patched onto the back of the cottage to improve life by bringing sanitation and benefits of a so-called fitted kitchen to rural dwellers. Olivia made her way to the back hall linking the extension to the old existing building. She smiled, thinking back on her mother's comments about the extension.

While the building work was done reasonably well, there was no money to spare on an architect's advice on any of those extensions back then. Design, layout and function were never a consideration. Just build it as quickly as possible. Generally, the kitchen was about the same size as the bathroom - about ten feet by fifteen feet, way too small for a kitchen. Unfortunately, the builders never considered when kitchen cupboards and appliances were installed, the roomy kitchen very quickly became a limited galley kitchen, with just enough space for one person to work in, instead of accommodating a large Irish family. Of course, they used the same dimensions for the bathroom.

Mother complained bitterly about it. It was far too big and always cold, summer and winter alike. Factors like insulation, double glazing and a heating system weren't high on the agenda back then.

Olivia smiled as she surveyed the bathroom now, white tiled floor to ceiling, jazzed up with accent tiles on the walls displayed flamboyant rambling roses in varying shades of pink and peach, with a background of verdant foliage. No doubt, it was all the rage in the eighties and possibly the nineties. Any discerning follower of current interior design where cool greys and minimalist interiors were in vogue would have ripped off the tiles instantly. Olivia was aware her parents were very practical people and flowery tiles would not have bothered them. In their opinion, those tiles were functional and did the job, so they were going nowhere. However, Sheila liked her comfort and Olivia was delighted to see they had two large modern radiators installed.

She gave it a final assessing glance; it needed a good clean to rid it of resident spiders and their vast empire of embroidered webs stretching from corner to corner on the ceiling. Otherwise, it looked pretty good. Fortunately, the white bathroom suite looked in good condition, if a little dated. Olivia thanked her lucky stars her ancestors had not given into the fad back then for avocado or brown suites. That would have been completely impossible to live with. But giving the wall tiles another quick appraisal, she felt their chintzy charm slowly beginning to grow on her.

# Chapter 6

'Well, fill me in on all the news. How are you settling in now you've been in Boyle for two weeks?' Angie asked eagerly.

'I'm in a bit of a quandary. I am surprised I've settled in so easily. I've only been here a fortnight, but I've met more people and had more visitors than in the last few years in Kildare!'

'There you are! Told you they're a friendly bunch. Dad always said they were a bit wary of strangers at first. They like to sus you out a bit in Roscommon and get the measure of you. But, they're generally a decent straight-talking lot,' Angie laughed.

Olivia chuckled in agreement.

'You could say that again! I was a little worried the first few days. I had callers with varying comments such as, 'Just checking there wasn't a break-in. I noticed the door was open.' 'Did I buy the place?' and the best had to be, 'Exactly what relation was I to Matt and Breda?' They don't mince their words. When I gave them my pedigree, history and proof of ownership, they cautiously accepted me. After that, they couldn't have been more helpful. Two bags of turf were dropped off.'

Olivia looked at the sods now stacked next to her stove.

'You remember that couple Mum and Dad were very close to, the retired couple, Sheila and Mick? Mick had a stroke six months ago and it affected him very badly. He totally lost his walk and is in the Nursing Home here in Boyle. Sheila visits him every day, but after the busy life they had, she's at a loss for what to do with her time. So, she is now a regular visitor of mine. Sometimes twice a day! But you know, I don't mind. I enjoy the stories about Mum and Dad, what they got up to and Sheila knows everyone. I mean everyone! She's a good laugh. We usually have lunch together either here or at her place at the top of the lane. I'm not lonely. She has organised a card-playing session for autumn at my house. She thought it would be a good way for me to get to know everyone.'

'You have been busy,' Angie broke in, amused at her sister's description of her neighbours.

'Anyway,' Olivia continued, barely taking a breath. 'I had the first session here last Thursday night. Just a gathering of the neighbours. There's a young couple around my age, Suzanne and Gerry, Conor – the very shy lad that dropped off the turf and an English couple, Liz and John - their son, Mark and of course, Sheila. We had a few glasses of wine to break the ice a little. Conor needed a lot of coaxing to get a few words out of him, but the others were great craic and it was a very nice easy night. We are already making it a regular night out every Thursday. So yeah, things are working out great.'

'Well, Olivia, it sounds like you have one very busy house. You are not short of company and certainly seem in great form. Any further developments with Tom?' Angie enquired tentatively, mindful of her disappointed sister on holiday only weeks before.

'Yeah, you know I phoned him when I arrived at Dublin Airport. I believed he might have been waiting for me. Instead, he left a voicemail to say he was too busy and would meet me at home that evening. He was still as angry as ever that I went to France. His non-appearance confirmed my decision not to go back to Kildare.'

Olivia sighed resignedly, recounting the continuing sorry situation between herself and Tom.

'So yes, the cold war is continuing. I phoned him a few times the first week and he finally answered after the third phone call. He's still livid over my non-attendance at the GAA dance with him and ranted again about my so-called,

'Gallivanting to France.' The conversation was very short. He finished by saying he expected me home the following day. So as you know, I'm still here and presuming his mood hasn't improved.'

Angie listened in surprise.

'No plans to return in the next week or so?'

This reaction from her sister was out of character. She had been with Tom since her teens and her whole life revolved around accommodating Tom and her boys.

'None at all. Betty has phoned about five times and left numerous agitated voicemails to say how life is hard on them both now. Tom has to get his dinner in the local pub. She's doing a little housework and keeping him company. He's paying for a cleaner to call twice a week and of course, Betty got her dig in how she wouldn't dream of letting her son down. I didn't ask her to elaborate, but I'm sure they're managing just fine. Besides my mind and energy are preoccupied elsewhere. I'm busy painting and decorating, rearranging furniture and trying to declutter, but you know, I'm loving it.'

'Good for you,' her sister interjected, happy Olivia was keeping herself occupied.

'I'm doing it all without the scrutiny of Betty and Tom's critical eyes. I know the standard of living here would be considered basic compared to what I've left behind in Kildare, but the peace and tranquillity more than make up for it. I'm enjoying trying to put things back together. Mum and Dad had some amount of stuff stashed in the sheds, chests of drawers - bits of beds, light fittings, mismatched rolls of fabric. They couldn't pass up on a so-called bargain, could they?' Olivia laughed.

Angie was so relieved to hear her laugh. Her newfound enthusiasm for the refurbishment project was working as the perfect distraction for any Tom-related negativity. And to think she left a very stylish home with manicured gardens for a shabby, dilapidated '40s cottage.

'And you won't believe it, but in the middle of all the stash in the shed, I found a load of my old artwork - paintbrushes, easels, the whole works! I never knew Mum had kept it all. The shed is like entering a charity shop – full of surprises, mostly goodish, but a few dodgy bits as well. There were two dead mice and Dad's collection of motorbike helmets in varying states of decay. One perched up on a shelf is now a bird's nest for the swallows. They looked so good in it, I couldn't evict them!'

Angie howled with laughter down the phone.

'Dad was convinced those helmets were worth a fortune. He would turn in his grave if he saw their fate now, splattered in swallow droppings! You seem to have your hands full with painting and DIY, but considering you worked for years in property management and showhouse fit-outs for the estate agents in London, pulling those cottages together should be a doddle for you!' Angie chortled.

'Thanks, Angie, for your questionable faith in me! You know, it's eight years since I finished up in London. It seems like a whole lifetime ago since I worked outside the home and made my own money and decisions. Being away from the workplace knocks your confidence. I'm living on the €150 weekly payment Tom pays into my account. When I think back to the generous budgets and expenses I had in London for the showhouse fitouts, my present budget is non-existent. But I like a challenge. I think if I put some serious thought into this, I could make a possible living from renting the cottages.'

'That's the attitude, Girl! Mum's sewing machine is hidden there somewhere too. You were always creative in your student days. Put all your experience and creativity to the test. You've been out of the work scene far too long and were good at marketing and selling. Remember the huge commissions you earned in London, selling all those trendy apartments?' Angie encouraged, delighted with her sister's enthusiasm.

'I know and I loved my job back then. I've been doing a bit of market research in the area. I rang a few auctioneers and rural properties are going pretty cheap. There are still a few of them around and because the three cottages are on one plot of land, even when upgraded with new kitchens and bathroom suites in two of them, they're still going to be very small rustic rural cottages. At best, I'll get about 180k to 200k for the three of them.'

'Gosh, that's not great, Olivia,' Angie replied.

'They will always be just bog-standard country cottages, no matter how chic or cosy you make them. In current times, people have much higher expectations of what a family home should be, so I'd always have a very limited sales market for them. However, they did mention there's a big demand for rental property, especially holiday lets and I can completely understand that. Boyle and the surrounding areas are completely unspoiled with the majestic Lough Key and acres of woodland walks in the Forest Park. I hopped on the community bus, 'Local Link' last week and travelled from Boyle in the northern tip of the county, all the way to

Roscommon town. We went via Tulsk, Strokestown and Roscommon town. About twenty-five miles in total. The bus driver gave me an impromptu tour noting all the historic points for me on the way.'

Olivia swung her feet onto the couch, excited to tell Angie all she had discovered.

'Tulsk has the Queen Maeve burial site and caves listed as a UNESCO World Heritage Site. There is Strokestown House and grounds that date back to the 18th Century housing the famine museum as well as providing guided tours of the house. It hosts regular poetry and musical festivals. Roscommon town has pretty much everything you'd need - hotels, hospital and cinema, an annual Lamb Festival promoting the local farming produce and is a creative magnet throughout the county. The icing on the cake has to be the River Shannon, running from top to bottom of the county through numerous towns in between.'

'It sounds wonderful,' Angie replied impressed.

'I never knew County Roscommon had the longest stretch of the River Shannon,' Olivia continued. 'When I have a better handle on my projects here, I'm hoping to spend a couple of hours in all the local tourist spots to get a proper feel for the area. The long-term plan is to do holiday lets. I hope to draw up a synopsis of each location for my tourist guide and of course for my website, when I'm marketing the cottages for rental. I'm looking forward to spending some time assessing all on offer in the county.'

'You can stop there! You've sold it to me!' Angie squealed. 'I'm not overly surprised. Mum and Dad were always raving about their jaunts around Roscommon County. 'An undiscovered gem,' Dad used to say. Though, I used to think he was biased as it was his home county. No matter what you decide to do with the cottages, they have to be maintained and habitable. I'm delighted you took on the challenge. To keep you motivated and on track with your DIY projects, I'll give you a call on Sunday evenings to get the lowdown on everything. Keep up the good work! I've got every faith in you. For now, I've got to go. I've got a date with Stefan at seven. I'll chat to you next week!' Angie trailed off, full of good spirits as always.

As the phone rang off, Olivia considered all they'd chatted about. For the past eight years, since the family returned from London, she had spent all her time looking after the boys and the house. What with school, soccer practice and matches, her life seemed to revolve around driving them from A to B, dropping them off at school for nine and collecting again at three. There was football training on Monday and Wednesday evenings, Karate on Tuesday evening and to finish off the week, usually a match on Saturday morning.

Tom was always too busy to do any of the running around. Now that part of her life was over with the boys in Boarding School, it was time to occupy herself with something new. Anyway, it wasn't as if Tom was madly missing her and hot tailed here to join her. No, it was time for a diversion.

Olivia didn't want to dwell on her marital mess right now. Picking up her paintbrush again, she surveyed her partly finished handiwork. The open plan sitting-room cum dining room was beginning to look well. It's amazing what wonders a fresh coat of paint can do, she thought.

Time to find Mum's old sewing machine and put it back in use. The tired faded orange, flowery Eighties furnishings were screaming for a makeover.

# Chapter 7

Liz glanced at the clock. Yes! It was half-past-two and she resumed her daily position beside the front sitting-room window, the blind positioned to enable a perfect view of all that passed up and down the lane. She stood to re-adjust the blind again, blocking out the glare of the autumn sun so she could feast her eyes on them. Hearing their excited shouts before they came into view made her heart swell with joy. Such happy children, dragging schoolbags along the road, pushing and shoving each other as only siblings would get away with. Their mum coaxed them along gently as they passed by her window. Liz smiled, admiring the three redheads going their way.

After her daily fix of window viewing, Liz lay back in her armchair and closed her eyes, allowing her mind to wander to the past. She had just turned fifty-three and lately her mind drifted to the past a lot. She reflected on the busy lifestyle she had even as a young girl, growing up locally about fifteen miles away on a rural farm. Indeed, as all children had in those times living on a farm in the 1970's. Summer holidays were a particularly busy time with turf to be cut and saved.

That job could take months as you were reliant on dry weather to cut the turf, then build it into stacks called 'clamps' to dry out. This work was done on your knees and finally, when it was eventually dry, it had to be handled again and tossed into a trailer to bring home. Liz piled up behind her dad in the tractor who drove the turf home and they then unloaded the turf by hand into the turf shed. Depending on the weather, the turf could be cut in April. If you were unlucky to have a bad summer, as you very often did in the West of Ireland, the turf might not get to the shed till September!

As well as turf, most farms had some tillage, about a half acre of vegetable garden containing spuds, carrots, parsnips, turnips, cabbage, beetroot and salad. They'd often have another acre or so of either oats or barley, to feed livestock in the winter months. Liz smiled, thinking back to how self-sufficient farms were back then. Fuel came from the bog and practically all food was supplied by the farm. Pigs and chickens roamed in the back garden. The bread was baked daily by Mum. All food was organic, but such expressions were unheard of back then. It was literally from farm to fork.

Saving the hay was another Summer chore. When the meadow was cut, it had to be walked through and any thistles and poisonous ragweed removed. It was then turned by pitchfork to dry out and finally forked into cocks of hay secured by hand-turned hay ropes. Liz laughed, thinking of the so called 'summer holidays' of non-stop work tending either the hay, turf, or weeding in the vegetable plot. All of this was interspersed with plenty of churchgoing, their only social activity. Monthly Confessions, Holy Day Mass, First Friday's Mass, Benediction, weekly choir practice, and of course, Sunday Mass, including attending every funeral within a twenty-mile radius.

Looking back on it now, it was probably a hard life compared to the carefree days of children nowadays, with no bouncy castles or play dates back then. Everybody in the countryside had the same routine of hay, turf bog and tillage every summer holiday, to be followed every night by a decade of the rosary on bended knee by the kitchen chair. Nobody gave it a second thought. They just got on with it.

Because of the eight-year gap, Liz and Joan were never particularly close as sisters. Joan, being the oldest, always tended to be in the role of telling Liz what to do, where to do it and how precisely things should be done. She was always mature and sensible, and had a close bond with Mother, always by her side.

By the time Liz was eight and Joan sixteen, Liz felt she had two mothers. Mother always described Joan as a 'steady level headed girl' and did not hold back in wishing Liz would follow in her older sister's footsteps. However, Mother's wishes were all in vain. She and Joan were like chalk and cheese. Liz was carefree, giddy and loved having fun.

Their father, Paddy, was Liz's ally. Throughout her life, she felt Joan and her mother were on the other team. Life was happy, but Mother was the boss in the house and had the final say in all things. Joan joined Macra, the only social hot spot for people back then. At seventeen she met Jack, her husband-to-be. Jack was twenty-four, a farmer, a teetotaller, an only child and considered a very good catch. Mother very much approved and soon they became a steady couple.

Jack tended to be a man of few words and seemed happy to fall in with Joan's plans, so all went well. Joan was engaged on her eighteenth birthday and walked down the aisle at nineteen, delighted to have bagged her man and have her future mapped out. They settled in Jack's home in Boyle. As Jack was their only child, Jack's elderly parents welcomed Joan wholeheartedly into the home place. Joan mellowed and relaxed in the love of her husband and new home, but about eighteen months later, tension slowly crept in as all eyes were on Joan for the eagerly awaited grandchild, but nothing was happening. Subtle and notso-subtle hints were regularly dropped by her in-laws and neighbours.

Indeed, even Mother mentioned it at every Sunday visit and Joan must have been demented by the complete lack of subtlety by all. After two years of marriage, the strain was showing. A coolness had set in with the in-laws, with no further mention of babies. The disappointment showed on Joan and Jack's faces. Mother carried the cross for her daughter's woes and in sympathy adopted a permanent dour expression. On Sunday evenings, Mother insisted Liz make every effort for Joan's Sunday visit, to make her feel special. She made her favourite dinner and ensured the place looked spick and span, as Joan had high standards. Mother danced attendance on her every whim. Dad and Liz were expected to do the same.

Joan revelled in the attention and did not hold back in telling how unfair life was living with the in-laws, the devastation and sadness she suffered because she couldn't get pregnant. Long private conversations took place between Mother and Joan where she lamented her life. Dad and Liz would be shooed out of the kitchen so they could whisper 'women's talk' in earnest. At thirteen, Liz was considered only a child and excluded from these intense *tete-a-tetes* between Mother and Joan. Dad always gave her the knowing wink to leave the kitchen as soon as possible.

They used the Sunday evening to escape the weekly ongoing saga by hopping on their bikes and heading off for a spin to the local bogs, or the river for a bit of fishing. They'd have a wander along the spongy turf banks, taking in the lilac and mauve heather interspersed with bog cotton. The only sound heard was the occasional call of the curlew and corncrake. Walking in companionable silence for a half hour or so, Dad would slowly spill his weekly domestic frustrations, confiding he found Joan's visits exhausting. He felt truly sympathetic to her predicament and tried to advise Mother to step back from the situation, encourage Joan to spend Sunday afternoons with her husband and his family and try to soften the rift with them. Dad said Mother knew better as always, insisting Joan needed the support of her family and the subject was firmly closed.

And so, Dad and Liz settled into a pattern of escaping to the bog, fishing, or even saving the turf. Their relationship was easy and unstrained. Both spoke their minds, cracked a joke or two and listened without interruption in the haven of the bog. Liz thrived with confidence every Sunday evening. She had her dad's undivided attention and wasn't the 'child' in his eyes. She had a voice and opinions. He listened. Life was good.

At sixteen, Liz met John who had recently moved to the area. Aged seventeen, tall, dark and handsome, he was a breath of fresh air. His father was a sergeant and his family moved into the local Garda Station. John had no farming background, so his conversation went beyond the usual tractors and engine size. Liz smiled thinking back to those days. John was such easy company. Within weeks, she and John were inseparable. They both attended the local secondary school and had such a good time together. He was the perfect diversion, enabling her to escape the tension at home. Mum wasn't aware of John as she was preoccupied and Dad was delighted to see Liz happy.

Four months after meeting John, Liz discovered she was pregnant. John was very supportive and suggested telling her parents immediately, but Liz panicked and kept putting it off, preferring not to think about her predicament. Despite her slim frame, at six months Liz knew she couldn't keep her secret much longer and confided in her dad. Shocked, he reassured Liz he'd break the news to her mother, who no doubt would be mad for a week or two but come around in time. Liz recalled the relief of sharing her secret, crying and apologizing repeatedly for disappointing her Dad. He hugged her, saying he would talk to Mum and everything would be okay. A tear slid down Liz's cheek recalling Dad's earnestness and belief he could make everything alright with Mum.

She shuddered, thinking how wrong he had been in gauging Mum's reaction. She completely lost her mind, repeatedly shouting about the shame and disgust brought on the family.

Liz and her dad pleaded with her mum that she and John planned to go to England. He had relations over there who would look after them until they got sorted and able to set up someplace on their own. But no, Mother decided enough shame was caused by Liz already and hereafter she would make all the plans for her future. The topic was not up for discussion. Despite Dad's best efforts to engage on her behalf, the subject was closed. Liz was banished to her bedroom with minimal contact with everyone. Dad later told her Mam informed the neighbours that Liz had pneumonia. This excuse justified the complete lack of contact with school friends and neighbours. Mother remained very angry, believing it was best for Liz to move away as soon as possible, arranging for her to stay in a mother-and-baby home in England run by a Catholic organization. She allowed no interference from John's family. Within a fortnight of receiving the news, Liz was ensconced in a mother-and-baby home in Liverpool.

They were the loneliest months for Liz as she waited for her baby. Unknown to her mother, she kept in touch with John who reassured her he would join her when the baby was born. The three of them would make their way without her mother's input. John's loyalty sustained her during the last few weeks, his plan keeping her sane through those dark and lonely nights. Two weeks before the expected due date, her mother came to visit Liz. Liz thought she might have come around in time, but she was as distant as ever, refusing to engage or discuss the baby.

Two days after her arrival, Liz went into labour early and was terrified. Sr. Angela was the kindest and most attentive midwife ever. Mother stayed with Liz but kept her distance. Her beautiful baby girl was born within hours. Liz cried with joy when Sr. Angela placed the baby in her arms and presented her with a photo from her Instamatic Camera, a present from John.

Liz was overjoyed as mother and baby gazed intently at each other. Her baby's golden-red eyebrows and downy strawberry-blond hair were picture-perfect. Mother even smiled as she lifted and cradled her new grandchild. Liz slept well that night thinking the worst was over, looking forward to her life ahead with John and their beautiful baby.

The next day, Joan and her husband arrived. There was much excitement over the new baby. Liz tried to explain to Mother all would be fine. John had plans in place and apologized for the trouble they had caused. However, Mother reassured Liz she had already made plans, to focus on resting and making a good recovery after the birth. Liz explained that John was travelling over the following day with his parents and felt confident of their continued support. Birth registration and paperwork had to be filled in. Mother insisted she comply as the baby home had treated them very well. Liz questioned none of this, not giving the paperwork a second glance, happy in the knowledge she would be starting a new life with John and their baby soon.

Things seemed to happen very fast after that. The following morning she was moved to a dormitory ward with other mothers whose babies were kept separately in a nursery. Questioning this with the Sister-in-Charge, she assured Liz it was normal practice as the babies in the home were usually for adoption and Liz had signed all the relevant paperwork. She frantically questioned this repeatedly and was reassured that yes, she had signed the paperwork.

The new adoptive parents were Joan and her husband. Her mother had finally made them parents. Mother had left a note saying Liz was a minor and not in a position to provide. Her sister and brother-in-law would be excellent parents and she strongly advised against contacting the family again. The very sight of Liz brought her nothing but terrible shame. £200 was enclosed with the note. They left with her baby, without saying goodbye.

# Chapter 8

John closed the door gently after him as he entered the sitting room. He spotted Liz hunched over, studying the familiar well thumbed photographs.

'Liz, stop tormenting yourself. You are only getting yourself more upset dwelling on the past,' he said, patting her shoulder gently.

'I can't help it. Every day I see her out in the laneway walking with her kids. It breaks my heart.'

'I know! But, you have the power to change all this. The whole reason we moved here is to put matters right, is it not?'

'John, you know it's not as simple as that,' Liz replied.

'We have been here a year now. Mark and I have been waiting patiently for you. We are completely unsettled. I don't know if you want to stay here or go back to London. With this stalemate, it's proving to be hard work and affecting all of us, Liz,' John exclaimed, dejectedly.

'I know. I'm sorry, Love. I think we could be very happy here permanently, but I can hardly just knock on her door and announce myself. Can I?' Liz pleaded.

'Well, maybe that's just what you'll have to do. Mark is also getting frustrated. He would settle here quite happily if he knew the long-term plans. Please, Love, think long and hard about it. You know I just want us all to be happy,' John begged, stroking Liz's shoulder sympathetically.

'But that's just it. Would she be happy with me launching all this at her?' Liz implored, biting the tip of her nail anxiously.

'I'm sure she'd be delighted with the truth. Isn't everybody entitled to that at this stage? Listen, I'm heading out again to finish that job with Mark. Don't forget it's cards night up in Olivia's. You'll enjoy that. See you later,' he said, bending to perch a parting kiss on Liz's cheek.

Liz gathered up all the photos received from her dad over the years. After the baby's adoption, Liz and John moved to London aware they couldn't return home. They started a new life for themselves and ten years later had their wonderful son, Mark. Dad kept in touch with John's family with letters and photos. She had ongoing glimpses into her beautiful daughter's life.

Photos of the Christening, First Communion, Confirmation, family get-togethers, first birthday, through to her 15th birthday when the correspondence suddenly stopped. Dad died of a heart attack. John's parents phoned to let them know.

Mother had organized for him to be cremated in Glasnevin. No doubt, to minimize the possibility of a scene at home in case they turned up. Liz and John went to the cremation but kept well away from her family. They went to grieve for Dad. It wasn't the time or place for a scene.

John saw his daughter for the first time in his life. His expression was a combination of awe and heartbreak. Suzanne was fifteen, slim and tall, with an abundance of golden-red curls. She seemed to be so sad at the funeral. Dad and she had been very close, but he never disclosed the family secret to his granddaughter.

It was hard for them not to comfort her. They knew this wasn't the right time, contenting themselves with the knowledge

Dad said she was a very happy girl and Joan and John adored her.

Observing Mother from a distance, Liz could see she hadn't changed. Her controlling manner was still evident as she controlled the group throughout the service. Purposely avoiding Liz's gaze, it was evident Mother was ruling her family still. Liz and John left immediately after the service, grieving for her father, but content to see Suzanne was as happy as they could hope for.

# Chapter 9

Conor scrambled back up the lane and quickly let himself into his grandfather's cottage, his home for the last six months. It was after half-eight and he had just dragged the two bags of turf, leaving them outside the newcomer's front door, fleeing as quickly as possible. He didn't knock on the door. Sure, she couldn't miss the turf bags on her front doorstep. His heart raced and his breathing was coming in short, ragged bursts with the effort of dragging the load. Lowering himself into the nearest chair, he kicked off his scruffy runners and held his head in his hands. It was probably just over a ten-minute quick walk, but he had probably made it in less than five in his haste to avoid meeting anybody. He hadn't been out of the house since Saturday, five days ago. He had no plans to be out today either, but that bloody woman up the road had knocked three times earlier to remind him to drop off bags of turf to the newcomer, Olivia, at the end of the lane.

Sheila had started knocking at the door before one this afternoon. He ignored her at first, thinking she would eventually take a hint. But no. She then went to the front windows and started knocking on them too. He had no choice but to get out of bed and answer the door. Straight away, she went into a big spiel about the newcomer who was arriving later that day and to drop off bags of turf. Sheila reminded him the fuel he was burning was courtesy of Olivia's family's turf bank and it was only good manners to oblige Olivia. She rattled on and he muttered something in response, closing the door as quickly as possible. He had just been sitting down to lunch and jumped up on hearing her call through the open window.

'Now Conor, don't forget that turf. She's coming today.'

The final reminder came an hour later, with her pouncing on him in his back garden saying she just happened to be up this way and again, and not to forget the bags of turf. So, to avoid any more visits from his stalker, he dropped the cursed turf off, praying that was the end of the visits from her and anyone else, for that matter. Jumping up, Conor locked the door to be sure. He wasn't going to be ambushed by his over enthusiastic neighbour again. All he wanted was to be left in peace. He wasn't bothering anyone and in turn, didn't want anyone bothering him.

He had moved down to Boyle in March over six months ago after suffering the rantings of his mother for three months. He'd had enough, packed his bags and headed to his grandfather's home place. He glanced over at the sideboard and the collage of photos representing his life before last Christmas. Life had been so good then. Everything was working to plan.

Ashling and himself had been together since his first year in college when they instantly hit it off. They both became secondary school teachers and were lucky enough to get jobs in schools in Dublin. Ashling was very easy-going and they fell into an easy pattern. They had the same hobbies and goals, shared the same ideas and worked well together. They had a life plan. Last November they had looked at several apartments with the idea of moving in together in the New Year. Then Christmas came.

On Christmas Eve they went for a drink and Ashling blew Conor's whole world apart. She blurted out that things were moving far too fast. She felt pressured to move in together and her life was being planned out. What she wanted was to live a little while she was still young. She said she had been in a relationship with him since she was eighteen. Now she was twenty-five and did not want to settle down with a mortgage and two kids in tow a few years later. She had decided to go travelling on her own and enjoy life before she hit thirty and have some fun. She was going immediately after Christmas, unwilling to prolong the upset. He remembered looking at her, completely flabbergasted.

Conor couldn't believe what he was hearing. He asked why she had not mentioned any of this before and was astounded when Ashling said she had tried, but he had chosen not to hear her. He was twenty-seven, having spent the last eight years with his soul mate who he thought had the same dreams and goals as him, now telling him she wanted to live life and travel. It felt like he was looking at a stranger. To add insult to injury, Ashling reached across, squeezed his hand and said she would always love him as a friend, but she needed to spread her wings and one day he'd realise she had done the right thing. She got up, grabbed her bag, gave him a quick hug and left. On Christmas Day she phoned to say she hoped he was okay and wished him good luck for the future. Conor had to tell his parents on Stephen's Day that Ashling was going travelling on her own. She left on the fifth of January.

He believed she would cop on and realise how good they were together and come back to him, but it never happened. Conor knew he should put the photos away. Their presence continually mocked their good times in the past. One of them was taken at a friend's wedding, another at a party. His favourite photo was of the two of them sunbathing on holidays in Spain, smiling and happy as he thought they were. Groaning, he flipped over the photos angrily, thinking how bloody blind and stupid he was. Another photo was only taken in November and less than two months later, she had dumped him! Bloody relationships! Who needed them? After Ashling left, he was naturally upset and did not particularly want to discuss the breakup, but his mother felt otherwise.

As an only child, he had the full attention of his parents and his mother wanted to talk. He explained Ashling wanted more from life than he could offer and wanted to go travelling without him. He did not want to discuss it any further. Suddenly, his evenings and weekends were empty. He didn't know what to do with himself and spent his time in his bedroom. His world had revolved around Ashling. He had no close male friends he wanted to talk to. His thoughts were running over time, trying to analyse where he had gone wrong. Sleep evaded him and he returned to his teaching job in mid January, but couldn't focus as his mind kept wandering.

After two weeks of sleepless nights, he knew he couldn't keep up the facade and packed in his job in the school. The Principal had a chat with him, put him on sick leave due to stress and told him to come back when he was better as he would be sorely missed by staff and pupils alike. However, Conor didn't believe any of this small talk. Why would he believe it? If his girlfriend of eight years hadn't, 'sorely missed him' why would anyone else?

He explained to his mother he was taking time off from his job for a few weeks. She smothered him with hot dinners, endless cups of tea and name-dropping of lovely single girls who were daughters of her friends. That was the final straw. Conor knew he needed distance from his mother before he lost the plot. And so, he hatched his plan to go somewhere where no one knew him, where there'd be no questions asked about Ashling. He made his escape to Boyle.

# Chapter 10

Sheila's knock signalled it was around eleven. Turning the key in the front door, she eased it open, making her way in laden with her brimming basket.

'Sorry, Olivia. I am just back from the Nursing Home. Mick is not in good form again today. He keeps telling me he has been in the Nursing Home for months and made a good recovery since his stroke. He's fed up and itching to get home. He was content for ages with all the distractions of the Roscommon Football Team. When they beat Galway I thought he was going to burst with excitement. All aches and pains were quickly forgotten,' Sheila sniffed. 'When the team were doing so well beating Mayo, then Mayo coming back and trouncing them, the dissection and discussion of those matches were a great diversion. They kept him preoccupied and he seemed quite content in there.'

Sheila placed her basket heavily on the table, sighing wearingly.

'But now the football final is over and Roscommon's chances of ever winning the Sam Maguire Cup are well and truly quashed, the discussion and easy banter with the men has fizzled out. They seem to have nothing left to talk about. His only conversation now is, 'When am I getting home?' I don't think he's fit enough to leave the Nursing Home yet. Any ideas?' Sheila asked, dejectedly.

'My first idea is to get onto the Manager of the Roscommon Football Team. Tell him to get his act together. The team's performance is having a very poor effect on the wellbeing of the patients in the Nursing Home. What do you think?' Olivia laughed in reply.

'Very funny, indeed. I couldn't even joke with Mick about that suggestion at the moment because he might well take me up on it. No, I was thinking of something more practical concerning him, rather than the football,' Sheila replied, eyeballing Olivia in despair.

'I know, Sheila. I just enjoy winding up Miss Fixit'

'Miss Fixit! Why would you call me that?' she queried, frowning at Olivia in confusion.

'You are joking, I hope?' Olivia asked in shock as she patted Sheila's arm. 'Well, where do I start? I've been here a matter of weeks and you have been such a help giving me bits and pieces. You organized getting the electricity reconnected to the other two cottages, gave me the names of tradesmen and introduced me to the neighbours. I have made many friends in the last two weeks. My house has become, 'the go-to place' for a weekly drink and game of cards. You are like a counsellor to that depressed lad at the end of the lane and best friend to so many people around here. They all sing your praises. After all that, I'm sure you and I will be able to help your Mick as well,' Olivia smiled.

'Oh, Olivia. You know I love helping you out. I like to be busy and have something to fill the day with. All those bits and pieces are nothing. Most of it's from the charity shops here in Boyle anyway. The paint is rescued from the County Council Recycling Depot, so you're more than welcome. Anyway, I appreciate your company and love our chats. To tell you the truth, I've been a bit lonely since Mick went into the Nursing Home, so you're a godsend really,' Sheila acknowledged, welling up with emotion.

Olivia jumped up, put her arm around Sheila and hugged her tight, tears pricking her eyes, 'Aw, Sheila thank you. You know the feeling is mutual. I love your company. You've made me so welcome. Please, stop upsetting yourself. You and Mick have been wonderful to me. I could not have settled in here without all your help. Mick has even given me so much business advice from his Nursing Home bed. I haven't been this content in years, so it's now my turn to help. Tell me, Sheila, is Mick walking much now?'

'Well, he has improved an awful lot since the stroke. He gets physio twice a week in the Home. He's much stronger, but I'm worried he might go backwards without physio when he gets out,' Sheila mumbled anxiously.

'Come on! Don't get all maudlin on me, Sheila. You could arrange to have more physio sessions for him through the GP. You could also check out some Home Help for an hour in the morning and evening to help with getting him out of bed and dressed. Anyway, I'm living right here beside you whenever you need a hand,' Olivia soothed, as doubt crept across Sheila's face. 'What do you think, Sheila? It's worth making a few enquiries, isn't it?'

'I would hate for us to be a burden on you, but I know he'd be over the moon with the suggestion of getting out. You know the staff up there in the Home are lovely and know his moods and ways inside out by now. Megan, that lovely nurse he has, mentioned he seemed to be losing motivation with the physio and exercises. She suggested considering the home option, so I'll take your advice, Olivia. I'll check it all out first before I mention a thing to him. If he gets a hint about coming home, it'll be like dealing with an over-excited child on Christmas Eve. 'Is it today? Is it tomorrow? What day am I getting home?' I won't mention a word to him yet. I'll make enquiries first and put a plan in place,' Sheila mused, rhythmically tapping her fingernails on the table, options and plans racing through her mind.

'That's the spirit, Sheila. You have a great circle of friends who would be more than willing to help. John, Liz's husband does some volunteering in carpentry work at the Men's Shed in Boyle. To break up the day he could take Mick down there for a few hours' break for you.'

'The Men's Shed! Sure, my Mick and three other fellas set up that place a few years back. It proved a godsend for many local men who suddenly found themselves with a lot of time on their hands when the recession kicked in. It hit this area very badly. Mick would love visiting all his old buddies. Oh, Olivia, you're getting me all excited now. You know I love a challenge,' Sheila exclaimed, a spark of excitement lighting up her eyes. 'Now that we have a plan, I better get a move on. Things to do and phone calls to make,' she added, jumping up and clattering her mug onto the table.

'What about a top-up before you head off?' Olivia asked, hastily pouring tea into Sheila's mug.

'Okay, make it a quick one. Tonight after the card game we'll celebrate our plans with a leisurely glass of wine instead,' Sheila quipped, with her usual sparkle and enthusiasm.

'Perfect! That's a date,' Olivia agreed, clinking Sheila's mug to seal the deal.

Sheila gulped her tea while quickly rebuttoning her jacket. Hastily putting her empty mug back on the table, she then dashed out the door with a newfound pep in her step.

Now she had a plan, nothing or no one would get in Sheila's way, Olivia thought, clearing up after their unusually hasty elevenses.

# Chapter 11

Olivia leaned her bike against the bank wall and rearranged her carrier bag full of messages in the front basket of her bike. She was feeling happy with herself knowing she had once again bought her groceries within her weekly grocery budget of fifty euros, even splashing out to throw in a bottle of wine for the card game on Thursday night.

She was living on what most would probably consider a frugal diet of porridge or brown bread and a poached egg for breakfast every day, two packs of chicken fillets in varying stews or casseroles, and salads five times a week. She had fish twice a week from the reduced section, if lucky enough to get it on offer. All of this was supplemented by Sheila's weekly supply of free vegetables, exchanged for the bountiful supply of apples, raspberries and blackcurrants growing profusely in Olivia's back garden. Her lunch was usually homemade vegetable soup or salad.

After six weeks of a revised diet, Olivia was pleasantly rewarded with a lot less bulk around her waist. She was always bordering on a size 14, even if she insisted on buying size 12 and squeezing everything in! To minimize her costs and conserve her petrol bill, the car was getting a bit of a rest and she used her bike practically every day of the week. Rummaging in her purse she extracted her bank card. She needed cash for petrol.

Olivia keyed in her PIN and entered her withdrawal amount. 'Insufficient Funds' bounced onscreen. Re-entering her €70 withdrawal figure again, the same message re-appeared. Olivia frowned in annoyance and checked her balance. €12.25 popped up. This couldn't be right. She logged out and in again. €12.25 was her current balance. Glancing at her statement, she instantly realised Tom had forgotten to lodge her weekly shopping money of €150. He always managed the money and had set up a weekly direct debit years before from his account to Olivia's to cover the grocery and petrol money. He managed all the other bills directly from his account and believed he was particularly good at money management.

As Olivia dialled Tom's number and listened to it ring, she felt calm and collected. There was obviously some glitch with the bank. The tone changed to voicemail. Olivia asked Tom to give her a call regarding her weekly payment. She put her purse back into her backpack and headed into the coffee shop in Boyle for her weekly treat of a cuppa and scone, and a good old chat with the owner. Afterwards, she pedalled home, leisurely taking in the beautiful autumn colours along the banks of Lough Key. Tucking her bike into the shed, she felt the familiar throb of her mobile in her pocket, signalling a message. Stealing a glance at the phone, she let herself in, pleased to see Tom's number on the screen. She flipped open the cover, blinking in confusion as she read and reread the message.

*As you're still away, I had to get in a cleaner and pay her €60 to clean and tidy up every week. I get my dinner every day in the pub. Your €150 weekly payment just about covers it.*

Olivia could feel the anger rush through her body as she dialled his number. He answered on the second ring.

'Hi, Tom. I'm trying to figure out your text.'

'Yeah, well, I'm spending probably maybe a bit more than €150 a week on cleaning and dinners and really, I'm just not able to continue paying your weekly allowance on top of that as well.'

'My weekly allowance, as you grandly call it, covered grocery shopping for five people as well as petrol money for my car. Yet you can pay sixty euros for weekly cleaning and pub grub and think it's okay to stop paying me any money. May I remind you that I contributed very generously to the house and farm you bought eight years ago. I'm astounded we're having this conversation,' Olivia hissed, feeling a flush of rage wash over her.

'If you just came home, I wouldn't be paying for a cleaner. Nor would I have to go to the pub for my dinner. I'm finding all this nonsense a right pain. I'll have another look at the finances this evening and see if I can manage sixty a week. How does that sound to you?' Tom suggested.

He wasn't at all sure how to handle this unexpected aggressive attitude from Olivia. Why couldn't she cop on and come home?

'Well now, Tom, what a very generous offer you make. I'm sorry about all the inconvenience I'm causing you. But you know what, I think I'll manage without your pre-conditions. As for your weekly offer of sixty euros – here's a suggestion for you. Stick it where the sun doesn't shine,' Olivia shouted in response, before promptly cutting Tom off.

How in God's name had she married such an ass? They say love is blind, but right now she was blind with rage at the arrogance of her so-called husband of fourteen years.

Half an hour later, Olivia hastily let herself into the cottage, plonking in a chair, aware she needed a plan and fast. She was confident of having no problem renting the cottages as holiday homes, but she needed to get all three properties up and running as quickly as possible. She had pittance left in her current account. After buying two new fuse boards, paying for their fitting and buying, and fitting a replacement stove, she would be down to less than €200 of her €3,000 renovation funds.

Sighing, she scanned through the purchases and labour costs jotted in her notepad. With cost comparisons online and making a few phone calls to replace the fuse boards, Olivia knew whatever way she tweaked the figures; it wasn't going to add up. Her concentration was broken by Sheila's knock and Olivia rose dejectedly to answer.

Sheila bustled in, laden as usual with a gift. This time a freshly baked apple tart. She was making great use of the continuous supply of cooking apples from Olivia's back garden. In return, Sheila was keeping Olivia stocked with rocket, spinach and onions from Mick's now overgrown greenhouse, heaving with ripe produce.

'C'mon, Olivia, put on that kettle and let's put a dent in this tart. It's just out of the oven,' Sheila trilled, gingerly laying it on the table. 'I've made great progress with Mick's plan. The GP was so helpful. She gave me the physio's number and the public health nurse's too. I spoke to both and the nurse said she'll try and organize home help for me for the first few weeks when Mick gets home. Afterwards, she'll assess his progress on an ongoing basis. Thanks so much, Olivia. I would never have checked things out without your suggestion,' Sheila beamed.

Olivia promptly clicked the button on the kettle and it was soon hissing away. Wearily, she took two mugs from the dresser and placed them on the table. Returning from the scullery with the filled teapot, she placed it on the table and sat down heavily.

'Sheila, I'm delighted with your good news. You'll have Mick back home in no time now you have a plan in place.'

'Absolutely! What's up?' Sheila asked, scanning Olivia's browbeaten expression.

'Nothing! Why do you ask?' asked Olivia in surprise, passing Sheila her mug and plate.

'I've been coming in here every day for weeks. Trust me, I know when something is up. C'mon! Spit it out!' Sheila tutted, noticing the overflowing paperwork and calculator on the corner of the table.

Olivia wasn't her usual breezy self. There was something on her mind.

'If you must know, I'm trying to sort out my finances. I have my nest egg allocated to sorting out the major bits in the other two cottages and was living off €150 weekly payment my husband puts into my bank account. However, today he's decided as I am no longer 'providing housekeeping duties' at home, he's stopping the payment until I return to resume normal service. His whole attitude has confirmed I don't plan to return home, but I cannot live on fresh air, so I must come up with a moneymaking plan fast. Any ideas?' Olivia laughed hollowly into her mug.

'Hm, I'm glad you're not willing to sell your soul for €150 a week. The cheek of the man! But never mind that. Of course, a smart, attractive woman like you will be well able to get a job. No problem!' Sheila grinned, tucking into her apple tart.

'Well, I'm flattered by your confidence in my abilities, but I'm only new to the area and wouldn't know where to start looking.'

'There's no time like the present, Olivia. You mentioned you worked in London in an office. Fill me in on that.'

'Yes, I did, but that was years ago. I spent eight years selling expensive property over there and enjoyed every minute,' Olivia replied excitedly, reminiscing on the good days of working in London.

'What exactly did your job entail? Tell me all the details,' Sheila questioned, scanning the table for paper and a pen.

She quickly grabbed Olivia's notepad, flicked to a new page and began scribbling her notes.

'Sheila, you're putting me on the spot. I sourced property in the right place and at the right price, as well as selling properties for clients. This also involved preparing the property for sale. It could be a major job to include refitting the kitchen and bathrooms, painting and decorating throughout, or just fitting it out with carpets and curtains and furnishing it. Showcasing was the term the business used. I had a database of clients, sellers, buyers, potential sellers and buyers, contact details for tradespeople and furnishing suppliers. I prepared quotations and invoices, and even assisted with mortgage applications as the company also sold mortgage and life insurance services,' Olivia replied, with Sheila scribbling furiously.

'Were you good at your job?' Sheila asked, her pen poised midair.

'Without being big-headed, I was appointed Executive Salesperson after six months. I was lucky because I loved every minute of my job. I got a real buzz out of it. All those commissions on my sales gave me a healthy wage,' Olivia sighed, remembering her pleasure in buying and selling property.

'I'm impressed! So, you're a dab hand on the computer, experienced in buying and selling and able to work with people. Get started on that CV today. I'm sure with all your experience you shouldn't have a problem picking up work locally,' Sheila proclaimed, studying her notes.

'I don't know about that. I'll put a CV together and give it my best shot,' Olivia ventured.

'That's the attitude. I'll put a few feelers out and have a chat with Mick. He knows who's who. You never know, he might have a few ideas himself. Cheer up Olivia, getting a job won't be a big challenge for someone as experienced as you. It'll be a great way to get to know a few more people in the area,' Sheila added.

Rising to her feet, she carefully folded her scribbled notes into her purse.

'It's a lovely day out there today, Olivia. A great day for a walk in the Forest Park. The sun is cracking the stones. You should make the most of it while it lasts because days like these in October are few and far between,' Sheila suggested, buttoning her light jacket.

'Good idea, Sheila. I might do the very thing. I need to clear my head. It does look gorgeous out there and would be a waste to pass up on such a rare, good day,' Olivia replied wistfully, glancing out the window, appreciating the autumn sunshine on the dappled russet leaves on her beech trees. 'Good. You'll enjoy the walk. Don't worry about the job front.

We'll sort something out. While you're out and about, if you get a chance would you mind picking some blackberries? The brambles are full of them at the moment. I heard it's a great year for hazelnuts as well. There's a bumper crop this year. If we don't get there early, those flaming squirrels will clear the lot of them in a week,' Sheila blurted, fishing enthusiastically in her trusted woven basket and producing a handful of plastic bags.

'With a subtle offer like that, how could I refuse?' Olivia laughed, taking the proffered bags, thinking Sheila never missed an opportunity. She was always two steps ahead with her planning.

'Ah, you're great. I'm getting a bit long in the tooth for scrambling in the brambles for blackberries and chasing squirrels. You can't beat blackberry and apple crumble with toasted hazelnuts on top,' Sheila wheedled, a broad grin spreading across her face. 'I'm off for now. Looking forward to our card game later. Cheer up. Between the lot of us, we'll get everything sorted. See you around eight.'

'Thanks, Sheila. I don't want to worry you about my predicament. You've enough on your plate.'

'Not at all. We're a good team,' Sheila replied, giving Olivia a reassuring hug at the door.

'Just one more thing, Olivia. Is all the usual gang coming tonight?' Sheila enquired.

'Yeah, Liz, John, Mark, Gerry and Suzanne, Conor and you and me. That makes eight of us.' Olivia counted the names out on her fingers.

'Conor is coming along?' Sheila asked in surprise

'Yeah, he's been dropping in and helping me out. I think the promise of a hearty dinner does the trick. He and Mark are coming for dinner at seven. Mark said he'll get Conor to hang on for the game of cards.'

'Well, Olivia! You certainly have a way with the boys,' Sheila winked mischievously.

'Sheila, I might be good, but I'd say you're even better with the boys. Poor Conor was shamed by you into helping me in the first place,' Olivia replied, eyeing her friend suspiciously.

'Oh, you found me out,' Sheila stuttered shamefacedly. 'Let me explain, Olivia! That lad has been cooped up there on his own for months on end. Actually, nine months now. I know the history there. I got chatting to his mother last March when she came to visit him. He didn't allow her in, even though she had travelled from Dublin. She made several attempts to call to him, but he completely blanked her. One day after another failed visit, I brought her in for a cup of tea and we had a long chat,' Sheila explained. Putting her empty basket on the floor, she continued.

'To make a long story short, she asked me to try and keep an eye on him. Seemingly Conor went into a deep depression after his long-term relationship broke down. He shut everybody including his parents out of his life and escaped down here to the country. To give his poor mother some peace of mind, I try and keep an eye on him and report back to her. He's an only child you see. The fact he's finally mixing with people will mean so much to her. I'm sorry about misleading you, but my intentions were good. I knew the lure of a young attractive woman was bound to have success with any man that had a pulse!' Sheila winked, a crafty smile spreading across her face.

'Oh, Sheila you'd charm the devil himself. I'll admit my first few meetings with Conor were a bit strained to say the least. We had a few uncomfortable silences and rather difficult conversations early in our acquaintance. I think in a matter of weeks we have come to an agreeable understanding. He won't kill me with conversation when he drops in, but we work comfortably in silence. He is a woodwork teacher, so is brilliant at carpentry. He told me he's a rubbish cook but loves his food, so fortunately we have a good balance. He's coming for dinner at seven with Mark. We will see you and the rest of the gang here at eight.'

Sheila rushed forward and threw her arms impulsively around Olivia.

'Oh, you're such a good girl. I'll give his mother a shout later. You don't realise how much this will mean to her. Don't worry. I'll be extremely discreet from now on. I won't mention a word to him,' Sheila promised as she buttoned up her coat and made her way to the door.

'I hope so. I don't think he'd appreciate being spied on. See you later,' Olivia warned, wagging her finger mischievously at her friend.

Sheila nodded sheepishly in agreement and Olivia closed the door after her, thinking that must have been the longest goodbye ever. She was going to take Sheila's advice on board before the weather changed its mind. Grabbing her raincoat, an essential clothing item for every season in Ireland, her strong umbrella, essential for pulling down hazel-laden branches and finally retrieving her car keys from the key rack, she stuffed Sheila's plastic bags in her pockets and headed off on her trip to the park.

# Chapter 12

As Olivia turned into the main entrance of Forest Park, she was bowled over as always with the scale and beauty of the treelined entrance. On either side, majestic beech, oak, ash, sycamore and pine trees towering more than thirty feet kept her company. Shades of ochre, russet red and burnt orange interlaced as the last defiant green leaves billowed to the ground in the gentle autumn breeze. Beneath the giant trees, rhododendrons and holly grew vigorously, their shining bottle-green foliage glinting in the afternoon sunshine.

Driving slowly to appreciate the view, Olivia continued along its tree-lined avenue until the beautiful vista of Lough Key and its splendid castle placed majestically in the centre came into view. As always, its fairytale beauty stopped her in her tracks. Parking her car beside the lake, she reached into the back for the bag of stale bread. Grabbing her raincoat and stuffing Sheila's bags into the pockets, Olivia made her way to the edge of the lake. Within seconds, the haughty swans glided into prize position up to her, scattering the waterhens and ducks in their wake. Feeding the greedy swans first, Olivia strategically aimed the remainder of the bread at the ducks, happy she had hoodwinked their ever-greedy neighbours.

Standing on the pier, Olivia scanned her surroundings. To the right was the castellated tower and to the left, moored at the dock, lay the kayaks and rowing boats, the mooring bay decorated with an array of barges and cruisers of varying sizes. Overlooking them sat the restaurant and gift shop, together with the children's indoor activity centre, all set in the most idyllic wild forest setting, dominated by giant red cedars immense girth and height, big enough to house the most wonderful games of hide and seek for adults and children alike.

Olivia breathed in deeply, the overwhelming serenity and beauty of her surroundings washing over her, instantly restoring her inner calm. Turning away from the view of the Castle, she made her way to choose a path among the hundreds of acres of woodland with endless walking and cycle trails. To the left, rising into the sky sat the Moylurg Tower, occupying the location of the former impressive Rockingham House built in the 1800s. From the Tower down to the shore of the lake were the underground tunnels, still accessible to this day.

The cool autumnal air increased her speed and Olivia continued her way to the bog gardens, still lush with varying species of giant ferns and rhododendrons splendid in every shade of pink and mauve. She paused to lean over the twohundred-year-old limestone fairy bridges adorned with gargoyles, now softened in appearance from the centuries of rain showers. Staring at her reflection in the brackish waters below and looking upriver at the near skeletal overhanging trees adorned with their lichen, ivy and moss combined with the autumn sweet scent of a decaying summer, it was easy to feel transported back to olden days.

Olivia had already visited the park several times since September, but every time she visited, she was overwhelmed by the gentle beauty of the place and felt she discovered a new charm on every occasion. Shaking herself out of her dream world, she stuffed her hands into her pockets and rediscovered Sheila's bags. Yes, she knew just the perfect place two minutes' walk from here to go hazelnut picking. Better get in there quick before the squirrels took the lot or she'd have a very disappointed Sheila to deal with.

Olivia surveyed her group of new friends, her neighbours from the lane, chatting easily to each other in her basic, but homely house. She, Conor and Mark had dinner earlier at seven o'clock. Mark proved to be the perfect guest, chatting easily and entertaining them with stories of his travels in Australia where he spent over two years working and travelling. He had then moved to Boyle with his parents, Liz and John, a year ago. He had grown up and trained as an electrician in London where he joined his dad's maintenance and renovation company and resumed working with him on moving to Boyle. He joked there were the odd few off days in the first year working with his father, as in all father and son working relationships, but now they generally worked very well together. Mark did plumbing and other DIY, thanks to expert instruction from his Dad. Olivia smiled, remembering him patting his belly appreciatively after her chicken casserole, followed by apple crumble and custard.

His easy-going attitude seemed to relax Conor, who hadn't left a crumb on his dinner plate and even managed to crack a joke or two! Conor had enquired if Mark was planning to move again. Mark surprised us both as he slouched on the couch, saying his original plan was to stay in Boyle for a maximum of three months or so while his parents settled in. He was surprised at how well he adapted to the area and was enjoying the easy going way of living. No traffic jams, plenty of work and the bonus was spending free time on his boat. So, he was definitely planning to stay.

Olivia was pleased to hear this news. She found Mark's company easy. Glancing discreetly again at him, she thought he was very easy on the eye too. He had dark curly hair down to the collar of his red sweatshirt, a nice broad cheeky smile, tanned and toned arms, lovely long jean-clad legs - what was there not to like! He had generously offered to install an electrical shower in the three cottages at a reasonable price. An instant hot shower would be an absolute godsend, she considered.

Olivia refilled the teapot that was under a lot of pressure as Sheila raised her teacup for yet another refill, the third. She needed a final cup to wash down the last bite of apple tart, she said. Downing the final cup of tea rapidly, she summoned everyone to order around the table as she stood up to update everyone on her news.

'Mick is doing great, now he knows he's getting out of the Nursing Home. I'm hoping he'll be home in two weeks as I now have a home care plan in place, thanks to Olivia's suggestion,' Sheila smiled over at her neighbour.

Everyone cheered at Sheila's good news and congratulated Olivia. She flushed in response, saying it was a pleasure to help in any small way. Sheila had been a godsend helping her settle in.

'I know it'll be a lot of hard work, but the thought of getting home has lifted Mick's spirits so much. He's now getting out of bed and trying to do the physio exercises at last,' Sheila laughed.

'Well, if you need a hand when he gets home, don't hesitate to call either John, Mark, or myself. We're only next door to you,' Liz smiled back encouragingly.

'Absolutely, Sheila. Just make sure you have some of your homemade apple tart ready. That'll have everyone calling around,' Mark joked.

'Ah, you're all very good. I'll be taking you up on your offers, at least until Mick is a bit steadier on his feet. Thank you all. Enough about me. Olivia, tell us where you're at with the renovations,' Sheila urged, settling back into her chair.

'I'm doing okay. As you know, Mum had a stash of fabric stowed away, so I'm at the sewing machine morning, noon and night making up bed linen and curtains. The budget is unfortunately very tight, so I'm trying to upcycle what I have in fabric and furniture. The plan is to live in this cottage, but I'm hoping to renovate and furnish the other two cottages and rent them out as holiday homes, to provide a regular income for myself. Mark is connecting the other two second-hand stoves Dad had stored in the shed. Most importantly, he's installing an electric shower here for me as well, so happy days. A big thank you to Mark. Things are looking up. I'm on the hunt for work to subsidise my improvements, so if anyone hears of anything going, give me a shout. Anything at all would be appreciated,' Olivia said, encouraged by the ease and friendliness of the group.

'Olivia, I've just started to do voluntary work in the charity shop. Thanks to Sheila, for suggesting it. Anyway, there are some nice bits of furniture, curtains and bits and bobs left in. I could keep an eye out for you and keep some things aside if you're interested. I wouldn't want to be offloading them onto you. I just thought, you being so handy with the sewing machine, you'd have them altered to suit in no time,' Liz ventured timidly, anxious not to offend her new neighbour.

'Thanks a million, Liz. I need pretty much everything! I'll drop down to you tomorrow and have a good rummage. As you can see, my style is very much shabby chic. A bit too shabby now, but I'm hoping to bring in a bit of chic as things develop. I'm going to keep the décor simple and bright in all three cottages. White-washed walls throughout to maximise the light, as unfortunately Irish cottage windows were very much designed to keep the maximum heat in. Lots of daylight wasn't a priority back then. I have two generous-sized couches and I'm going to make removable cotton covers for them,' Olivia said excitedly.

'Today's your lucky day. I took in two bags of Donegal woollen blankets. Remember the ones from years ago that lasted forever, with two candy stripes at the top in blue or pink? They're in perfect condition. Two of them still have the shop labels attached. The lady who dropped them in told me she was clearing out her deceased mother's hot-press. She had them stashed on top of the hot-press, with two brand new sets of striped flannelette sheets - kept especially in case any unexpected important visitors stayed over. Those woollen blankets were used before duvets came on the scene about thirty years ago. Would you be interested in them? I know from previous experience in the shop there was a poor demand for them,' Liz asked, a little more confidently than before.

'Liz, you're making my day. That's exactly the style I'm looking for. Good old-fashioned comfort. I'll be into you first thing tomorrow for an hour. I'm short on many bits and pieces. I'll be absolutely delighted to call in. Thank you so much,' Olivia grinned in anticipation of tomorrow's visit.

'Sorry to interrupt you, Olivia, but could you just tell us exactly what items you're short on and how much more work you have to do? This could be a mutual favour as we're trying to redecorate and need to offload a lot before we start,' Suzanne asked, taking her phone from her pocket in anticipation of a list.

'Gosh, you're putting me on the spot, Suzanne. I don't want to sound as though I'm begging. I have only known you all a couple of weeks. I'm sorry. I'm doing fine. Thank you,' Olivia blustered, feeling uncomfortable with all eyes focused on her.

'Not at all, Olivia. This could be a mutual favour. We need to offload furniture in a bedroom in the process of being redecorated. So no, please trust me. You would be helping me do a proper clear out at last. My seventeen-year-old son is way past sharing a bedroom with his twelve-year-old brother. I have his new room ninety percent finished. I just need to repaint the skirting boards, give the walls a final coat of paint and remove the existing furniture. I'm hoping the move lends to a more peaceful household for everybody! Shoot with your list,' Suzanne urged, her phone poised in hand.

'Seeing as you put it like that, here goes,' Olivia replied, hastily rummaging through her handbag for her weekly updated checklist and slowly reading aloud.

'Beds, headboards, mattresses - two doubles and four singles. Eight bedside lockers, four wardrobes, chests of drawers, sheets, curtains, lamps, standard and bedside. Two couches, two old-fashioned dressers or sideboards with display shelves on top. Two kitchen sinks, fridges, cookers, bookcases, cushions, rugs and throws, delph, glasses, and cutlery. You did ask, so that's it,' Olivia sighed, folding her checklist carefully and replacing it in her bag. 'Dad had a lot of the work done in this cottage. The other two have the flooring practically finished but need replacement kitchen and bathroom fittings. The lot really,' she added.

'That's been a great help to me. Off the top of my head, you can have two single beds, mattresses and headboards. You can also have that wonderful bargain my husband bought on Done Deal two years ago for seventy euros, a beautiful, cream leather couch. It's lovely, but doesn't fit properly in my living room and has been parked in my cramped hallway since. It'll fit perfectly into one of the other cottages. You're more than welcome to have the lot,' Suzanne offered.

'I wouldn't dream of taking them without paying. At least for the new couch,' Olivia pleaded.

'Not at all. Take it all. I'll be grateful to you. I'll finally be able to declutter. Jack can move into his own bedroom and I'll get my hallway back after two years. It's a win-win situation all around. Thank you, Olivia. I'll have a proper check around the house, attic and shed. I know I'll be passing even more stuff your way. Oh, one more thing. How are you getting on with the painting and decorating?' Suzanne asked, her red curls ablaze and bobbing frantically with the energy offloaded by their owner.

'It's a slow process. Lots of timberwork needs sanding and varnishing, walls need refilling in places and painting. Luckily, the floors in all the living rooms and bathrooms have been tiled with terracotta tiling and still look good. But all the bedroom floors have a touch of woodworm, so need treating and sanding before I paint them with two coats of hard-wearing paint. Plenty of work to be done. I'm getting there slowly,' Olivia smiled.

'If you're interested, I could offer the services of my reluctant transition year student. Jack's seventeen and doesn't want to go back to school. All summer he was supposed to be arranging work placement for a minimum of two weeks. Despite our best efforts to secure something for him, nothing suits him. The excuses so far range from, 'That place would be boring,' or 'There are weirdos working in there,' or the more regular response is, 'I wouldn't ever want to work in a kip like that.' Suzanne rolled her eyes, before continuing.

'I have asked him to come up with a few suggestions himself, but I'm a realist. If we don't arrange something for him, it'll never happen. What do you think? Would he be any help to you? I'd love to say he's a fabulous worker with a wonderful personality, but the truth is he's sometimes bone idle, with poor social skills. We probably haven't had a proper conversation together since he was thirteen, so he won't kill you with chat. I think he'd enjoy this 'hands-on' kind of work, rather than office or factory work. What do you think?' Suzanne asked hopefully, her fingers crossed discreetly under the table.

'Oh, wow! You're selling his good points to me! I don't have much experience with seventeen-year-old lads. My two boys are only thirteen and haven't started that downward teenage personality slide just yet. I don't frighten too easily though. I'd be delighted with the help. I wouldn't want to be wasting his time if he wasn't learning anything useful with me. After day two of sanding and painting and more sanding, he'd very quickly get fed up, and probably run for home rapidly,' Olivia worried.

'I'll be in and out to you, Olivia, over the next couple of weeks, installing electric showers and putting in the stoves. I could teach him a few things. Maybe you might show him the basics in carpentry, Conor, when you're replacing that skirting and refitting the doors?' Mark rushed in to reassure Olivia.

'I suppose I could show him a few things,' Conor said reluctantly, wriggling uncomfortably in his chair as all eyes swivelled towards him expectantly.

'Sure, you'd be great at that sort of thing, being a teacher. You'd have no problem. So that's sorted. Between the three of us, I'm sure we'll keep him occupied for the next couple of weeks,' Mark suggested to Olivia, who nodded appreciatively at his quick-thinking plan.

'That's perfect. Thank God, I have that sorted at last. You don't know what a relief that is to me, Olivia. I'll get him to ring the school first thing on Monday to let them know,' Suzanne sighed.

Sheila rose from her chair, surveyed the group and smiled, clapping her hands in delight.

'We all came to Olivia's rambling house this evening for a chat and cup of tea, but this has been the most productive two hours I've had in years. Michèal Martin could learn a thing or two from us. Firstly, thanks to you all for offering your help with Mick when he gets out of the Home. It's a great comfort to me, knowing I have your support.'

She looked appraisingly around the room, then continued.

'Secondly, Olivia's cottages will be getting furnished and decorated. Finally, young Jack will be sorted with his work placement. I propose a toast to everyone here. Cheers, to the best neighbours in the county!'

Sheila raised her teacup as the group cheered in response.

'Now, come on, Olivia. Get out that pack of cards for a quick game of Twenty-five,' Sheila urged, the self-appointed chairwoman, as she instructed everyone to clear the kitchen table.

Rounding up the gang under her skillful instruction, the group had the delph washed, dried and put away in the dresser within minutes.

# Chapter 13

Olivia rolled over in her bed, woken by her mobile ringing. Squinting at her bedside clock, she saw it was only ten-past-eight on Saturday morning. She had been painting walls and ceiling in the bedroom until nearly one in the morning and every muscle in her body felt stretched to the last. Seeing her caller was Sheila, she answered it.

'Hi, Sheila. What's up? Is there a problem with Mick?' Olivia blurted anxiously, rubbing the sleep from her eyes.

'Not at all. He's fine. Sorry for the early morning call. I had to catch you as early as possible. Mick had a visitor at the Nursing Home last night. Paddy Murphy, the auctioneer, in Boyle. They were chatting about business and Paddy said things had picked up with sales and rentals. He started lamenting about how worn out he was trying to manage the office and arranging viewings. To make a long story short, Mick remembered me telling him you're on the lookout for work and mentioned this to Paddy. Paddy is a bachelor in his mid-sixties and very set in his ways in work and business matters. Mick had it hard to convince him he needs help and to consider you for a job. He eventually agreed to have a chat with you today in the office at eleven. Go down there this morning and knock him dead with all you've got,' Sheila said excitedly.

'Oh, Sheila, you're both very good. I'll be straight down to him for eleven. What exactly do you mean - knock him dead with all I've got?' Olivia enquired cautiously.

'Olivia, he's an old-fashioned, middle-aged bachelor, but still has a pulse. Use your youth, charm and feminine wiles on him. Convince him he needs urgent help and wouldn't manage another day without you. Fill him in on your experience. You'll have him hooked,' Sheila recommended.

'I'm a bit short on interview clothes, but I'll give it my best shot. I loved working at property. I'm sure it would be no different working in Boyle either,' Olivia replied, a spark of determination running through her at the prospect of finally earning some extra money.

'That's the attitude! Best of luck. Make sure to give me a call on how it all went,' Sheila requested.

Jeez, Olivia thought, hopping quickly out of bed and hitting the immersion switch for a shower. It would take at least a half hour before the water would be hot enough, so she strode to the kitchen and made her daily porridge breakfast. Three weeks later and there were still enough Oatlets left for another week's breakfasts. At €1.70 a bag, it was the best value and healthiest breakfast ever Olivia decided appreciatively, putting the porridge bag back in the cupboard.

Five minutes later and porridge ready, Olivia sat at the table to consider all her interview clothes choices. Unless Paddy was into paint-spattered shorts or jeans and grey-tattered tshirts, her options were limited. Spooning the last of her porridge, she knew this was not a time for dithering. Racing into her bedroom, Olivia opened her wardrobe to assess the contents of her holiday suitcase. On the wardrobe floor lay her paint spattered jeans and t-shirts, a bit too casual. Three pairs of shorts, five various coloured t-shirts, two floral summer dresses, a safari jacket and the linen trousers she had from her holiday two months ago.

Her shoe selection consisted of three pairs of sandals in varying styles, one pair of flip-flops, one camel-coloured pair of wedges and suede cream sling-backs, as well as her very tired looking runners. The only addition to her holiday wardrobe was a pair of skinny Penney's jeans she had bought two weeks ago for the princely sum of €11.00. Nothing for it, she decided, but it would have to be the linen trousers and cream safari jacket. It was a quarter-past-nine. She dashed for the shower, confident a plan was in hand.

Twenty minutes later, with hair dried and make-up done,

Olivia grabbed her freshly ironed, linen trousers. Standing in front of her full-length mirror, she pulled them on, zipped them up and closed the belt. Something wasn't quite right. She pulled the belt another notch. No difference. She pulled another notch and the trousers still hung like a bag. They were always loose fitting trousers and usually looked well on her. She loved them for travelling as they were flattering as well as comfortable.

She'd been aware of losing a few pounds, but the mirror didn't lie. In this outfit, she had neither hips nor curves and looked like a bag of rags. Oh my God, she was to meet and impress this man in less than an hour. She was in trouble and panic set in. These trousers were not a runner and it was too late to call Sheila. Mind you, Sheila's size 16 flowery dresses wouldn't be much help anyway.

Racing to her wardrobe, she yanked the door open again, taking out one of her flowery dresses, wedge sandals and safari jacket. She pulled the shift dress over her head, struggled into her sandals and looked at the result. A few inches were off her hips and bum, but also disappeared off her chest. The final look wasn't great. Grabbing the belt from her trousers, she gathered it around the middle, pulling it tight. At least she had a waist now. No obvious chest or bum, as the dress billowed out from lack of curves and excessive fabric. On the plus side, she knew now size 14 was too big for her. She pulled the belt a little tighter. Lifting the dress more flatteringly above her knee, Olivia studied her physique. Still too much billowing fabric. My God, she looked like a kid who had borrowed their mother's dress! Panic began mounting within as time was moved on.

Bolting to the kitchen, she grabbed her sewing box, rooted out a few safety pins and took off the belt. Grabbing the dress hem, she pulled it over her head, becoming entangled in her panic. Finally, she wrestled it off and turned the dress inside out. Ruching up some pleats of fabric in the chest and waist areas, she carefully positioned safety pins to create subtle tucks in the dress. Forcing herself to breathe slowly to avoid the possibility of a wayward safety pin, Olivia gingerly popped it back on, secured the belt and admired her handiwork in her bedroom mirror, with less bulging fabric all over.

It was not fabulous, but certainly better. Anyway, it was going to have to do, as time wasn't on her side. Olivia quickly retouched her makeup, brushed her hair and finished with hairspray. It was nearly half-ten. She wanted to be there in plenty of time. Grabbing her jacket, bag and keys, she dashed for the car, scowling at the heavy drizzle and chill in the air.

'You're very welcome to Boyle. Mick tells me you're new to the area. Come in. Take a seat in my office,' Paddy exclaimed when she finally arrived at the auctioneer's office.

He extended his hand as Olivia shook out her wet umbrella and accepted his welcome. He led her through the reception area into his office. Olivia scanned the reception area, noting the untidy paper-strewn desk and overflowing bins. The weather had taken a turn for the worse by the time she reached Boyle. Even though she had parked the car only minutes away from the office, her feet squelched when she entered the office.

'Yes. I've been in Boyle six weeks,' Olivia returned the smile, easing her wet sandals under Paddy's desk, trying her best not to shiver with cold.

'Oh, six weeks. You're only a visitor then,' Paddy frowned, considering this information.

Olivia passed her three-page CV to him, hopeful its contents would impress.

'No. I'm definitely staying long-term. I am doing up three old cottages by Doon Shore and hoping to rent them out as holiday lets and in the meantime, acquire part-time work to supplement my income,' Olivia rushed, anxious to allay any fears she might leg it by tomorrow.

Paddy sighed. Surveying his visitor he scratched his head, unsure this arrangement could work.

Olivia could immediately sense his hesitancy and decided to take control of the situation.

'Paddy, as Mick has probably already explained to you, I have worked for nearly ten years in London, buying and selling property. I think I could be a lot of help to you here. Mick says you're very busy with sales and viewings and could do with help in the office,' Olivia intimated.

'Working in London is all very fine. But things are different working in a rural area like this,' Paddy said, standing and putting Olivia's CV firmly to one side on his desk.

Olivia sensing his lack of interest, immediately decided on a different tack.

'I can work in any situation. You're short on time and I have plenty of experience working in different circumstances. I noticed your reception area needs updating. A lot of your website sales and rental properties are not displayed in the window. I could sort that out in no time at all,' Olivia stated.

'How do you know they're not displayed?' Paddy asked, puzzled at the stranger's knowledge.

'I checked out your website this morning and had a quick look in your window before I came in. I'm presuming a lot of your customers wouldn't be experts on website use, so you should maximise the use of your window displays. You're on a busy street and would catch the eye of passing trade.'

'You've done your homework. I'll give you that. You're right about my customers. That bloody computer drives me mad. I take the photos but have an awful job uploading them. To be honest, I don't have time for that stuff.'

'That's where I could help you. I could do three or four days a week for the first two weeks to get your brochures and window displays updated and give the place a tidy-up. After that, two days a week should probably keep things ticking over for you,' Olivia suggested, mindful not to offend Paddy.

The place needed a miracle makeover and she desperately needed a job.

'I'm not sure. I'm a one-man show and used to doing things my own way,' Paddy replied, walking away from his desk towards the door, unsure of the pace of the conversation.

He wasn't a man to be railroaded and liked to think things over for a while.

'Maybe, you could put me on a week's trial. I'll sort out your website and the office. I'll give the reception area a tidy and arrange an updated window display straight away.'

Olivia surveyed his reaction as he swung around, sure she was winning. She had his attention.

'I'll even give the reception area and your office a lick of paint for good measure. Have we got a deal?' Olivia asked.

Standing up, she extended her hand to Paddy to close the agreement.

'You certainly know how to sell yourself. You must be able to do that in this business. Right so, we'll give it the week's trial and see how things go from there,' Paddy agreed, giving Olivia's outstretched hand a slow, firm handshake.

'Thank you, Paddy. Can we discuss hours and wages?'

Olivia smiled, knowing she needed to agree on a rate immediately. Best to strike while the iron was hot. Haggling over the wages at the end of the week could very well prove bad news for her. Better to get it all sorted out now.

'Well, what about €100 per day for eight hours? Half-nine to half-five?' Paddy suggested.

'€100 is just above minimum wage. €150 a day is more reasonable,' Olivia replied, determinedly.

'€150 is a huge amount. I can't afford that,' Paddy spluttered, surprised at her forthright manner.

'For €150 you're getting a cleaner, painter, receptionist and administrator all rolled into one. In addition to this work, I've years of experience in the property market. I think you're getting a pretty good bargain all around,' Olivia calmly replied.

'Since you put it like that, I suppose €150 is a fair deal. We'll give it a week's trial and see how things go. I'll see you on Monday. We can go through the paperwork and everything then,' Paddy agreed, as he shook hands to seal the deal.

'Perfect. Thank you. I'm looking forward to working with you,' Olivia said, standing to leave.

'Oh, just one more thing, Olivia. I think you can put away the strappy sandals for another year. It's the middle of October, you know. You'll end up catching pneumonia. According to the weather forecast, the first frost is due from next week,' Paddy added, frowning at Olivia's footwear, utter confusion etched across his features.

'Thanks for that, Paddy. What exactly is the dress code for me?' Olivia smiled captivatingly, glancing at her new boss's attire.

He wore well-worn tan corduroy trousers, a tired, fawn jumper, with a brown and cream checked shirt and a tie tucked inside. All set off with a good sturdy pair of comfortable looking, well-worn tan shoes. He was the best tribute to the 70's era she had seen in years.

'I like to think smart, casual works best. I've been wearing this style for the last thirty years and not had any complaints,' Paddy boasted smugly, proudly patting his chest. 'See these shoes. Clarks they are! I got them nearly ten years ago. There are ten more years left in them. An expensive shoe, but well worth it,' Paddy stated, struggling to bend down and stroke them.

'Lovely, so smart casual it is. I'll be off so. Looking forward to starting on Monday,' Olivia said, as they stepped outside and Paddy locked up the office.

'That's sound. We can go through everything then. See you at half-nine,' Paddy waved.

The heavy rain had eased off, but a persistent mist had rolled in. Olivia dashed back to her car, hastily letting herself inside. Kicking off her useless footwear, she turned on the engine and put the heater fan on full. Letting her seat back slightly, she massaged her frozen feet back to life.

Within minutes, she could feel the heat easing life back into her feet and legs and considered all that happened in the last half hour. It was one of the strangest and funniest interviews she ever had. Paddy was no walk-over by any means but he was a refreshingly straight forward man to deal with, unlike a lot of the arrogant, stuffed shirts she encountered years before in her work.

Smiling as she analysed the interview, Olivia laughed out loud at Paddy's troubled expression as he scrutinised her slightly steamy, damp summer dress and sandal-clad feet. She must check out some fawn and brown clothing, after all, smart casual and beige tones were the way to go! God, she couldn't believe she'd nailed it. Okay, the job was only on a week's trial, but she was determined to make herself indispensable. She knew she could do wonders for that office with a large dustbin. A lot of cleaning and a serious slick of paint would guarantee an instant makeover. She whooped with joy, overwhelmed with relief at the prospect of her money worries being over.

More importantly, she knew without a doubt her choices in life wouldn't be forced by Tom's withdrawal of her pocket money. It felt good to be in control again. With a quick look in the mirror, Olivia put her car in first gear and headed home.

# Chapter 14

Suzanne hummed contentedly, surveying the contents of the hallway. Thanks to Olivia's renovation requirements, she had accumulated quite a medley of items to give to her. In the back of the shed, she discovered an old-style kitchen dresser. It was storing years of paint stacked for a visit to the Civic Amenity Centre next week. The dresser was in good condition overall, but the woodwork was stained and filthy from birds' droppings after spending years in the shed. Suzanne had seen some of Olivia's handiwork and felt sure she'd do wonders with it. She smiled in anticipation of finally getting rid of all this clutter and to make things even better, she would be getting rid of her son too. Well, he'd be out of the house for a few weeks at least.

Following the visit to Olivia's house, Suzanne put the suggestion to her son about doing his work placement at their neighbour's home. She dressed it up as much as she could saying it was only a five-minute walk away, emphasising as well as learning about painting and decorating, he could also shadow the carpenter and plumber. He'd hummed and hawed, as only teenage boys do. Suzanne stuck her heels in, telling him he had run out of all other options at this stage. Receiving a petulant grunt in response, she took it as a reluctant yes. She wasted no time in contacting the school and getting the okay for Jack to work with Olivia. The school understood he had no interest in academic pursuits and agreed this placement might give him some insight into what work he might like to do later. As it was a transition year, they agreed to be flexible with his work placement hours. Suzanne couldn't wait to arrange dates and times with Olivia.

It was only six weeks into the transition year term, but the constant shouting every morning for him to get up and go to school was wearing thin already. At seventeen years of age, she thought things would be getting easier, but it was a constant uphill struggle. By the time Suzanne had called him four or five times, from 8 am every morning, listened to him grunt and groan and moan, do the daily hunt for his shoes, trousers and jumper, find his bag and coat, she was completely worn out listening to him when she finally bundled him out the door at eight-fifteen. The other three children aged three, twelve and fourteen, Aimee, Maria and Luke were a dream, by comparison.

Olivia changed from her interview outfit, delighted to shed her damp makeshift dress and wet sandals and hastily pulled on her only pair of jeans and a jumper. Strolling into the kitchen, she put the kettle on and was looking forward to a warming cup of tea when the door knocker rattled. She could hear Sheila shouting hello on the doorstep.

'Come on in. The door's on the latch,' Olivia called.

With a flourish, Sheila pushed the door open carrying her usual basket of home baking, its smell filling the kitchen with a pungent aroma of cinnamon and mixed spice.

'Congratulations! I knew you'd win him over,' Sheila squealed, rushing forward and wrapping Olivia in a congratulatory hug.

'Morning, Sheila. Thank you. I'm just in the door and changing out of my wet clothes. News travels fast around here,' Olivia laughed, hugging Sheila affectionately in return.

'Good! You've got the kettle on the boil. I made this treacle cake this morning. It's still warm. We'll have a slice with a cuppa to celebrate,' Sheila chirped, going to the dresser for mugs. 'Tell me. How did hear about my good news so fast?' Olivia asked, filling the teapot.

'Mick knew you were meeting with Paddy today, so he gave him a call ten minutes ago and got all the news directly from the horse's mouth. Paddy said you were a tough cookie but was impressed with you. He said it was only a week's trial, but Mick said to tell you if you play your cards right, you could very easily make it a permanent arrangement. He reckons Paddy is getting tired of trying to juggle everything. He does a lot of rentals as well as sales. While he understands the importance of the internet for advertising, he's never got the hang of that computer. The truth of the matter is this, Paddy is more of a social animal. He loves doing a deal with buyers and sellers one to one, but he's not big on paperwork. So, hang in there for the week and bowl him over!'

'Sheila, I have been doing some quick calculations. If this job works out, it will get me out of my current financial pickle. For my first two weeks, I'll work for four days. After that, I return to working two days a week. When I'm back to my routine of working two days a week, I'll be free the other days to continue with my own work on the cottages, as well as pay for the bathroom and kitchen refurbishments. I'll be doing my best to impress Paddy,' Olivia added with a smile, pouring the tea.

'That's the attitude. Now for my news. Mick's hoping to be discharged from the Nursing Home next Friday morning.

Maggie, the Public Health nurse, will arrange to drop off a walker and wheelchair in advance. The Occupational Therapist is calling to see me first thing on Monday morning to do a home assessment. Luckily, we live in a cottage and the bedrooms are all on the ground floor so there are no major changes required there. She doesn't think it'll need much. Just a few adjustments in the bathroom. We already have the shower, so it's probably just a few grab rails and a shower seat. I've done a bit of a tidy up.' Pausing to drink her tea, Sheila carried on.

'Mick will have a clear walkway when using the walker or his stick, but he's determined to get rid of the stick as soon as possible when he gets home. It's amazing his improvement in the last two weeks. Once he heard the promise of getting home, his whole attitude towards his exercise programme changed. He can be a stubborn, old mule of a man when he wants to. But now, he's doing everything for the physiotherapist. The staff tell me he's even walking extra laps up and down the corridor morning and evening as well. There's no stopping him,' Sheila laughed happily.

'Good news all around, Sheila. I'm going to have to buy some clothes as I'm starting work on Monday. As soon as I tidy up here, I'm off to Penneys in Sligo,' Olivia said, munching appreciatively on Sheila's slice of freshly baked, treacle bread smothered in butter.

Sheila tapped her mug for another top up and cut another generous slice of the freshly baked bread, pushing it towards Olivia.

'God, Sheila. I shouldn't eat another slice. It's gorgeous, but so filling.'

'Eat up. You've probably dropped two dress sizes since you came here. All that healthy eating and exercise will be the death of you! You don't need to watch the calories now. Anyway, you'll need the extra sustenance when you're working for Paddy next week. Trust me, he'll be getting his value for money from you. By the time you've cleaned, hoovered and put a bit of order in that office, any calories you've eaten today will be well burnt off,' Sheila winked, finishing her second mug of tea and standing. 'I'm off. Oh, just so you know. I phoned Conor's mother to tell her he's now mixing a bit more and is out and about. I filled her in on all your news about the renovations. She's so relieved and grateful to you for inviting him round for dinner and including him in things,' Sheila confided, making her way to the front door.

'He's a regular visitor now. He and Mark drop in a few times a week for dinner. They're both very good to me. Next week, Conor hopes to start on the woodwork that needs finishing. It's a perfect arrangement all around. Conor wouldn't kill me with a conversation, but I like to think we're good neighbours. I feed and water him and he quietly works away on my carpentry. A perfect arrangement,' Olivia smiled in return.

'I noticed they drop round a good bit, alright. Mark even more so. He's a very handsome young man, isn't he, Olivia,' Sheila remarked coyly, opening the door.

'Goodbye, Sheila. See you tomorrow,' Olivia smiled, ignoring Sheila's pointed conversation.

Patting her neighbour companionably on the back, she closed the door firmly. Olivia did a tidy-up, placing the used mugs in the sink. The rain splashed down incessantly on the windowpane. It was not a great day for driving or shopping, she mused, but she had to buy new clothes for work. Her thoughts were interrupted by another knock on the door. Hastily opening it revealed her neighbour, Suzanne, on the doorstep, struggling with a bulging black sack.

'Hi, Olivia. Sorry for bursting in on you on such a wet day. I nabbed Gerry this morning. He loaded up his van with all the furniture and things I mentioned. He's offloading them with Mark who kindly offered to help. He saw us struggling to load up and stepped in to do the lifting for me. If the truth be told, he probably heard the beginnings of a good row between myself and Gerry. You know what men are like with their daft instructions for lifting and moving things. They're putting everything into your shed until you sort through it. By the way, I heard your great news on the job front. Congratulations,' her neighbour declared, giving Olivia a congratulatory hug.

Olivia stepped aside to let Suzanne enter as she wrestled two more bulging, black sacks. Relieved of her load, Suzanne moved over to the comfort of the stove. Taking off her jacket she shook the droplets of rain from her hair.

'Thank you, Suzanne, for dropping off the furniture on such a horrible morning. I'm delighted with the job. Finances are a bit tight so it couldn't have come at a better time. I'm heading to Sligo to buy clothes for work. I think it's well time to pack away my summer dresses.'

'Now that you mention it, while I was in the clearing out mode, I did a good rummage through my wardrobe last night. I've put some dresses and blouses in this bag for you. Some even have the labels still on them. They were a snug fit when I bought them two-and-a-half years ago, but I bought them as a treat after the birth of my youngest. She's now three!'

Suzanne began opening the bag containing clothes and Olivia peeked inside.

'They were meant to be my goal to lose a few pounds,' Suzanne grimaced. 'The weight loss never happened. Every time I see them in the wardrobe, I feel they're there to torment me. They're mostly sizes 10 and 12. If I'm honest with myself, I'm edging rapidly towards a size 14. I finally realise it's time I accept my weight is not going to change soon. Right now, I don't seem to have ten minutes to myself.'

Suzanne sighed as she reached into the sack, retrieving pretty blouses, trousers and dresses.

'What do you think? Please feel free to be honest. Anything you don't want, just chuck it to one side. I'll drop it off at the charity shop. Some of the dresses are probably too wide for you, but with a good belt and your handy work with the sewing machine, you'll have them up to scratch in no time,' Suzanne encouraged, kneeling and sorting her stash into piles.

'They're lovely and mostly from Zara. I love their cut and fit. You can't give them away. They're in perfect condition,' Olivia gasped, gazing appreciatively at the garments, many sporting shop tags.

Her eyes were drawn instantly to a beautiful cream, long sleeved skater-style dress, adorned with a subtle pattern of brown and dusky-pink splotches. She'd be a perfect complement to her new boss's brown attire, Olivia thought wickedly.

'I'm being realistic. My youngest will be going to kindergarten next year. I'm hoping then to have more time to exercise and shed a few pounds. Unfortunately, these clothes are taking up valuable space so now they have a good home. I'd love it if you would wear them and enjoy them. I'll be delighted they're being recycled and put to good use,' Suzanne replied earnestly, happy she could help her new friend who she found completely refreshing.

Suzanne didn't know the ins and outs of Olivia's situation, but it was obvious there was some sort of domestic dilemma going on at home. Her new friend had turned up unexpectedly, seemingly with the minimum amount of clothes and money. The old-fashioned cottage she moved into hadn't been lived in for years. It was still a project in the making. The other two cottages needed a lot of work to make them anyway habitable. Yet despite all this, Olivia's indomitable spirit shone through. Everyone knew she had done a trojan amount of work in weeks. She was forever cleaning, painting and patching. The light never seemed to go out before midnight in her cottage. She had a regular flow of visitors and a friendly word for everyone, and was like a magnet, drawing neighbours together like never before with her weekly card games.

Her cottages were home to all the casts-offs, or so-called rubbish from her other neighbours or charity shops. But under Olivia's magic spell, the old Fair Isle and Aran jumpers were transformed and recycled into trendy cushion covers. The old furniture was sanded, cleaned and painted and old sheets, duvet covers, and curtains were all remodelled into curtains, bed throws, and sofa covers. The icing on the cake for Suzanne was seeing the transformation to the big old, ugly pine wardrobe she had stored in the shed. It was a cumbersome object, a triple sized wardrobe about six-foot wide and stacked to the brim over the years with paint cans, fabric rolls, and old rolls of wallpaper, and had taken up a huge chunk of space.

Suzanne had suggested using it for firewood, but Olivia was horrified at her idea and would hear none of it. Olivia had assured Suzanne she needed to think about it and would eventually find the perfect home. True to her word, a few weeks later when she called to her enterprising neighbour, she was completely in awe at the transformation. Olivia had manhandled the wardrobe into the last cottage and it was rehomed in the dining-living room. Olivia sanded it down and it was painted a mellow, country cream, blending in perfectly with the background colour scheme.

After rearranging the interior, the single section of the wardrobe housed the fridge freezer. Another section acted as a larder and had shelves installed, containing Olivia's delph and cutlery. The remaining two shelves were left for foodstuff. The third section was now a storage cupboard for the hoover, mop, sweeping brush and all the usual associated bric-a-brac. As with all cottages of that era, the lack of space was always a huge problem. Olivia had figured out the perfect storage solution.

Olivia's reinvention with the horrendous wardrobe was so impressive, it made Suzanne reassess the layout and storage possibilities in her own house. If her neighbour had the vision and energy to transform three pokey old, decrepit cottages into cosy, comfortable homes, she should be able to do a miracle on her own spacious modern house. Olivia didn't seem to be overwhelmed by the enormity of her work with the cottages. Instead, she embraced it with energy and enthusiasm. In turn, Suzanne felt she had inspired all her neighbours with her ideas. It certainly gave them all food for thought about how to remodel and reimagine their existing furniture and made them think twice about purchases in the future.

'Is there anything I can do for you in return?' Olivia pleaded, putting the clothes carefully to one side, overcome by her neighbour's generosity.

'Nothing at all. You're already obliging me by taking my stroppy teenager for work placement. Unless you fancy taking on a very energetic three-year-old as well,' Suzanne laughed.

'I already have two thirteen-year-olds in Boarding School and miss their noise and carry on. I don't mind taking her off your hands now and then. If only to give you a chance to go for a walk once or twice a week and give yourself some head space. Let me know what suits you.'

'I was joking, Olivia,' Suzanne laughed, flabbergasted at the generous offer.

'I wasn't. I enjoy kids. It'll give you a bit of time for yourself,' Olivia insisted.

'I just might hold you to that. Thank you very much, Olivia. I appreciate your kindness. Don't worry, I won't abuse your generous offer,' Suzanne smiled appreciatively.

The doorbell sounded again and Olivia let Gerry and Mark out of the rain.

'Congratulations on getting the job. I believe you're off to Sligo to celebrate,' Mark grinned.

'I'm on a week's trial at the auctioneers. I'm not celebrating just yet. I'm off to Sligo to pick up a few things before I start work next Monday. Thank you all for all your help today. The furniture, the clothes, everything,' Olivia raised her mug to salute her neighbours who cheered in return.

'I'd like to celebrate your job, so I can run you into Sligo to do your shopping, then bring you out for lunch,' Mark offered.

'No, you don't have to do that, Mark. You've already done so much for me. I don't want to impose on your time anymore,' Olivia replied, taken aback at his unexpected offer.

'Don't look a gift horse in the mouth, Olivia. From what I've heard, Mark has had more than his fair share of free lunches and dinners with you since you arrived,' Gerry joked.

'You're right, Gerry. Let me return the favour,' Mark insisted, smiling at Olivia encouragingly.

'How can I say no? Give me five minutes and I'll be ready to go,' Olivia laughed in appreciation.

'We'll be on our way, Olivia and leave you to it. Have a lovely afternoon,' Suzanne smiled, tapping Gerry companionably on his shoulder.

Taking his cue, he got up and they made their way to the front door.

'Thanks, for everything. You're both so good and thoughtful. I'll see you soon and fill you in on how the job is going,' Olivia called, waving goodbye as they dashed to their van in the lashing rain. 'Mark, sorry for holding you up. I promise I'll be changed in just a few minutes,' Olivia shouted, rushing to her bedroom.

'Take your time. I'm in no hurry. It's only early and the shops are open until six. I'll make us another cuppa and we can have a chat before taking off.'

'You're a star, Mark. Thanks for that. It was a manic morning. I'd love to sit and catch my breath.'

'Well, you're a fast worker,' Mark remarked as Olivia returned ten minutes later, dressed in jeans and a sweatshirt.

'That's me. Interview done and a job secured. All I have to do now is try and convince Paddy I'm worth keeping,' Olivia chortled, taking the proffered mug of tea and settling on the couch.

'You'll have no problem there. I've seen you in action. He'll be delighted with you. Just another suggestion. I know you're hoping to rent out the cottages as holiday rentals. You mentioned you're going to do a tourist information guide for your visitors. If that's the plan, you need to get out and about and see what the county has to offer. Call it a bit of market research. Tomorrow's meant to be a good day. A cool, but sunny October day. I could bring you out on my dad's boat on Lough Key. We could see the local sights,' Mark suggested casually, gulping his tea.

'I have been awfully busy. You're right. I probably do need to see exactly what's around. I will have to aim at the tourist market because I don't see much demand locally for living in old fashioned, two-bedroomed cottages. Seeing the local attractions is all part of the plan. Sheila gave me the timetable for the Local Link bus. It travels from Boyle to Elphin, Strokestown, Tulsk, Fourmile House and Roscommon town. I took a spin on the bus last week and visited Rathcroghan Visitor Centre. It's located in Tulsk village. It was fascinating.
Rathcroghan or *Cruachan Ai* is known as the ancient capital of Connaught and was the home of the great warrior, Queen Medbh, who ruled all of Connaught.'

Olivia dipped a biscuit into her tea as Mark waited to hear about the rest of her research.

'That is the site where the festival of *Samhain,* or Halloween, was said to originate, together with the stories of *Cu Chulainn* and the Cattle Raid of Cooley. They have a museum holding local artefacts dating back to the Bronze Age. There are even tours to the caves. One of them is called *Oweynagat* or Cave of the Cats, also known as the Gateway to Hell and the Other World. Slightly scary stuff, but very interesting. There are two hundred archaeological sites there covering 5,500 years of history, with burial mounds from the Bronze and Iron Age, Ringforts and Settlement Sites.'

Mark smiled, enjoying watching Olivia's eyes sparkle as she recounted her findings.

'I popped into Elphin on the way back and visited the Windmill there. It's an 18th-century fully restored, working windmill. It took years of work to get there, but the result is impressive. It was amazing to watch it in action, grinding a bag of oats into flour. There's an agricultural museum on site also showing the machinery used from years before. I'm putting it all in my visitor guidebook. I'm hoping to visit Strokestown House and Gardens and Roscommon town in the next couple of weeks. I spent a day there a few weeks ago doing the whole tour of Boyle with Sheila. It's a very interesting place for such a small town. I visited the Market at King House and loved it. There were different homemade breads, cheese, chutneys and jams. I dropped into the little coffee shop afterwards for lunch with Sheila. It is quaint and has a lovely atmosphere. I've even done a tour of King House as well. There is fantastic history there. We finished the day off with an informative walking tour of the town. I'd love a break from the never-ending painting and cleaning. You can give me the grand tour of the lake and the Forest Park. Show me all its charms,' Olivia said, toasting Mark in agreement with her mug raised.

'Okay, you've sold the county's charms to me. Jeez, you should be the head of the tourism board,' Mark quipped, raising his hands jokingly to stop the tour guide in her tracks.

'Hint taken. Perfect! That's a deal for tomorrow. I'll enjoy the break before Paddy starts working me to the bone,' Olivia laughed companionably.

'The Local Link bus is a great way to get around, but I think you'll need to revise your plan. There's a lot to see in Strokestown and Roscommon, so there's not a chance of packing it all in in a couple of hours,' Mark said, getting out of his chair.

'I know. I'm going to give myself a full day to enjoy them. But I'll get my first few weeks in my new job out of the way first. Then I can focus on local research. That's another job done. The place will be as snug as a bug when I get back,' Olivia replied.

She topped up her stove with a couple more sods of turf and closed the dampers to keep the fire alight until she returned later that evening.

'Right, so. We can hit the road and head to Sligo whenever you're ready,' Mark said, finishing his tea and making his way to the sink.

'I'll just grab my coat and we'll be off,' Olivia jumped off the couch and into action.

# Chapter 15

Sunday morning was ablaze with sunshine, true to the weather forecast predictions. Olivia was up and about by ten, expecting Mark at twelve and looking forward to her day out. She had been to Forest Park a few times since her arrival in Boyle and had every intention of going out in her dad's rowing boat to explore the lake. Unfortunately, the never-ending list of DIY chores had swallowed every minute of the day. Conscious of her dwindling budget, Olivia knew she had to get rental income in rapidly, so while plans of strolling around the county were idyllic, she had to get her priorities right.

Olivia prepared her weekly Sunday treat of a grilled breakfast, brought the tray into the living room and sat at her table. The autumn sunshine blazed through the patio door and she basked in the morning's ray. The stove was banked up with a few damp sods of turf before bed last night and still radiated a gentle hum of heat, taking away the morning chill. Under Mick's instruction, Olivia had mastered getting maximum efficiency from her stove with its essential back boiler for hot water and heating throughout the cottage. Three bags of turf kept her going all week.

Every morning she topped up the stove with more turf and clods, closed off the vents and dampers and could work in comfort. Around six in the evening when the chill set in, she'd open the vents and dampers, top it up with a few more sods and have a blazing fire and snug house in no time. It was a bonus having oil as a backup if she was gone all day and needed an instant hit of heat. The combination of the two heating systems proved cost-effective and worked out perfectly.

Content and snug, relishing her breakfast, Olivia sat back looking at her surroundings. She smiled at the makeover achieved in her humble little cottage on a shoestring in such a short time. Her latest addition had been the window shutters. Despite thermal blinds being good, they weren't good enough to keep out the draughts that sneaked between the sashes of her old teak windows. The budget didn't extend to replacing windows. Instead, she attached a draught seal and new putty to any visible gaps, but not enough to stall those stealthy westerly, winds getting through every nook and cranny.

She had bought a job-lot of kitchen doors on Done Deal to replace the existing ones in her scullery and had quite a few left over. One evening, while wrestling a couple of woollen socks into the window gaps, she was struck with inspiration for a solution to her problem. She admired the sleek window shutters

Conor had crafted out of her spare kitchen door. Due to the wide country cottage walls, the shutters fitted perfectly into the recesses of the window. Olivia had painted them in a flattering Cornish cream colour. They blended in perfectly with the colour scheme, adding French chic to her décor and were fabulous insulators, her sneaky draughts finally banished. The off-white recycled Aran jumpers were now unique cushion covers since removing the sleeves and tweaking them with her darning needle.

The luxurious, crochet throw was reinvented from knitted jumpers Liz got in the charity shop. Liz had rediscovered her love of crotchet from a colleague who inspired her with weekly crafty creations. Motivated, Liz brought home abandoned jumpers, carefully unravelled the lot and reworked them into a beautiful crochet throw she gifted to Olivia, who loved it. Liz said she found the process of unravelling one garment and creating another one therapeutic, insisting it gave her a new love for crochet and knitting.

Even the painted walls gave her pleasure. The plaster wasn't great, but the colour wash disguised any irregularities. Olivia was flattered by the compliments received. It was a few euros for a tester pot of paint she mixed with white to create the perfect colour wash. It only took a few hours to colour-wash the living room. She looked with pleasure at her latest purchase, a fold-up gate-leg table, bleached-ash, accompanied by four folding chairs that were stored away discreetly underneath, freeing up valuable floor space. The previous large solid oak table was beautiful, but its cumbersome dimensions didn't work in her little cottage. Her latest acquisition was just the job in the main room that served as a living-dining room, another great bargain at forty euros from the charity shop. The icing on the cake was getting two hundred euros for the old table on Done Deal. Olivia's thoughts were interrupted by the knock on the door at a quarter to twelve.

'How are you this morning? You're looking well. We've got a perfect morning for our trip, sunshine and calm,' Mark said, glancing appreciatively at Olivia, who was dressed in blue and pink, her hair swinging jauntily in a high ponytail.

'Thanks. You're right. It looks glorious. I'm looking forward to it. I'll just grab the house keys and lock up,' Olivia replied happily.

Fifteen minutes later, Olivia was on a small rowing boat with an outboard engine attached to the back. They had started to move along gently, the surrounding beauty smothering any need for conversation. The vast lake glistened in the autumn sunshine; its mirrored surface was flawless in the stillest of air.

Olivia watched in awe, the unspoiled beauty leaving her speechless. It was just after midday and the last of the morning dew was beginning to disappear, the promise of a sunny day breaking through.

The enchanting castle magically began to emerge, the soft morning pastel light bathing it in shades of mauve and pink, its image reflected perfectly in the surrounding waters. Moving slowly in the water, she noticed there wasn't another boat to be seen. The only sound came from the gentle lapping of the oars and occasional quacking of ducks skimming the water's surface, as they took flight and rose into the air. Their swan companions glided along in their usual dignified, superior manner. The sight of a mere rowing boat was never going to get them in a flap.

The proximity to the water made the whole experience with nature so much more intimate, Olivia thought, reaching out to allow water to ripple through her fingers, with ducks, moorhens and swans, all within touching distance.

'What do you think?' Mark enquired, taking in Olivia's rapt expression.

'I look out at the lake every day and thought I'd seen it all. This experience on the boat gives you a fantastic perspective surrounded by water and whichever way you look, you're blown away with the most amazing views. The castle, the lake, the scenery in the park and the myriad of autumn colours are ever changing throughout the seasons. It's magical,' Olivia replied, her face lit with pleasure.

'I aim to please. You're right. I think it's pretty amazing myself. Without another boat in sight, it's like our own private lake,' Mark laughed.

He was enjoying the boat trip much more with Olivia's company.

'I'll make our way to the island. We can pull this boat in and moor it beside the castle and explore. Afterwards, we can eat. I packed a picnic and a bottle of wine. I thought we should celebrate your new job, your work on the cottages and everything. Make the most of a great day.'

'That was nice of you. Thank you very much,' Olivia stumbled, overwhelmed at his kind gesture, unsure if this was a date or if Mark was just being neighbourly. She was seventeen years out of practice!

Half an hour later, after visiting the enchanting castle, Mark rowed back to the shore and moored his boat at the forest's edge. Following a brisk walk to warm up after the chill of the lake, they found a lovely park bench overlooking the lake where Mark eagerly unpacked his picnic fare. Feasting on crispy brown rolls smothered in egg, onion and mayonnaise, followed with a wedge of warm homemade apple tart, its clove aroma filling the autumn air, Mark refilled Olivia's mug from the flask of tea and topped up his own. The heat of the mug was welcome as the chill nipped his fingers.

'That was good. I'm impressed with your picnic. I'd worked up an appetite. We've practically eaten everything,' Olivia laughed, as Mark produced wine and glasses from his wicker basket.

'I'll confess, my mother helped a bit. She said egg and onion sandwiches are always a hit with everyone and she was right. I made the egg and onion mix myself, but she made the apple tart this morning. I've got a feeling she's trying to offload me,' Mark smirked, glancing mischievously at Olivia.

'She's trained you well. Just work on your pastry skills. I'm sure you'll be snapped up in no time,' Olivia quipped, taking the proffered glass.

'Thanks, I'll work on that,' Mark grinned, as they clinked glasses companionably.

Stretching his legs, he sipped his wine, enjoying the easy silence as they relaxed in the company of their tranquil surroundings.

# Chapter 16

Olivia's mobile phone alarm pinged at seven-thirty. Rolling over, she turned it off, already awake for ten minutes and bubbling with excitement to start her new job. She had been running plans through her head for the day and was pleased she had taken a good mental picture of the shabby state of the office during her interview, so she knew there wouldn't be any big shocks! She had packed a bag containing cleaning products and most importantly her old painting overalls. On a successful shopping trip to Penney's, she bought two pairs of shoes, two dresses, tights and underwear and two bags of clothes for under €50, followed by a lovely lunch with Mark. Work clothes were sorted and Olivia jumped out of bed for her shower.

Twenty minutes later, with hair blow-dried, wearing her dress and fifteen euros shoes, she smiled appreciatively in the mirror. Her mousey, blonde hair had grown past her shoulders and needed styling, so she put it in a sloppy bun. The up-style flattered the wrap dress tied neatly at the side, teamed with her beige shoes. Happy with her bargain style, Olivia applied mascara and lipstick and went to the kitchen for breakfast. Packing her homemade salad and cleaning equipment, she set on her way for the five-minute drive, hoping next week to cycle into work.

'Good morning, Olivia. You're very eager. It's only ten to nine,' Paddy remarked, opening the door to greet his new employee.

'Morning, Paddy. I like to be on time and I'm eager to get started,' Olivia beamed.

'Good! That's what I like to hear. You look very well. That's a lovely outfit. A lovely colour scheme,' Paddy gushed, ushering Olivia into the office. 'Here we are. That's your desk. My office is over there. There's a canteen where you can make tea before we settle down to things. Two decent sugars for me! I'll start the computer and we can get going,' Paddy said, pointing behind the office.

Olivia followed the directions and glanced around the cubby-hole kitchen. She put the kettle on and rescued two tea stained mugs from the grimy sink. The washing-up bottle lay empty. Running boiling water over the mugs, she made tea and returned to Paddy.

'That's a good start. You make a fine mug of tea, Olivia,' Paddy nodded, gulping appreciatively before laying the cup to one side, bringing her attention to the screen before him. 'Now, down to the business of the day. As you see, I have my company website here and use Daft and My Home sites as well. I'm not up to date with the computer side of things. Some photos for properties haven't been uploaded yet. I'm a little flimsy with property descriptions, but not to worry. I have it all in a folder. Sit here and I'll give you a rundown.'

Olivia swapped seats and took the bulging folder from him. Paddy gave a quick summary of the sale and rental sections of the websites. He opened eighteen live current sales and another eight property sales on the market for a year. Noting login details and the contact number of the IT support company, she felt confident as past auctioneering experience came rushing back. There were small IT variations, but overall, the systems were pretty much the same. As Paddy scrolled through various properties, Olivia noticed some had hardly any photos or information on them.

'You can see for yourself, I have a few gaps here and there. Nothing too major. I keep rental payment records in that jotter, but the accountant said I must comply with some newfangled data protection legislation and put it up on the computer. I'll leave that to you,' Paddy said proudly.

He handed her another over-stuffed folder.

'The window display needs tidying up. I've three new properties for you to get started on. I took photos last Friday and have the address, keys, sellers' details and the lot here for you,' Paddy added.

Rummaging in his brown corduroy jacket pocket, he retrieved a camera and notebook and placed them on the desk.

'This jacket is worth its weight in gold. I got it ten years ago and there's not a brack in it. It's got deep pockets too,' Paddy smiled smugly, nodding his head and withdrawing sandwiches and his phone from the other cavernous pocket.

'Lovely,' Olivia replied, unsure of what her response should be.

'You've got the gist of things now. I'll let you get started. Here's a set of keys. I'll be in my office if you get stuck. I'm here for the morning, but I'll be gone after lunch. I'll have another mug of tea. Don't forget the sugar,' Paddy continued, clapping his hands contentedly and sauntering into his office.

Three hours later, Oliva leaned back and stretched her arms satisfactorily. She had trawled through Paddy's folder containing scribbled handwritten property details, uploaded the relevant photos, created descriptions for the three new sales properties and had begun updating other current sales properties.

'Paddy, do you mind having a look and checking things over for me?' Olivia asked, knocking on Paddy's door.

Paddy munched on the remains of his lunch, screwed up his sandwich wrapper and then aimed it perfectly into the overflowing bin.

'My mother makes the best ham sandwiches in the world,'

Paddy grinned, patting his well-rounded middle appreciatively. After a scuffle with the wheels on his chair, he rose and made his way to Olivia's desk.

'You've been busy! I'm going to change this one from, 'Promising potential' to 'Good decorative order'. The owners have tidied since I took the photos, so I'll drop out next week and take a few new ones. They've agreed to drop the asking price by five grand. I'm hoping it might drum up a bit of interest as it's slow to get moving. Other than that, everything's looking good.'

Shrugging on his trusted brown jacket, Paddy continued with his instructions.

'Just print off what we need for the window display. The window might need tidying first. You'll know yourself when you have a look. I think ladies are better at that kind of thing. You can lock up after me at lunch. It'll give you a chance to work without any callers dropping in. I have forwarded calls to my mobile phone, so there should be no one disturbing you. Don't forget to lock the front and back doors at half five. You've done a good job today. I'm off now. See you tomorrow,' Paddy added.

As soon as he left, Olivia turned on the kettle, changed into her painting gear and went through her stash of cleaning supplies to assess what she'd need. Picking out rubber gloves, JCloths, bleach and cleaning spray from her bag, she put on gloves and an apron and sprayed every visible surface, including the kitchen counter and cupboards, leaving them to soak. She then moved to the window display and swept up dead spiders, paint peelings, dust and yellowed curled-up property brochures. She cleaned the smeared windowpane and surrounding woodwork. Noticing some of the brochures were years old, Olivia binned them before wiping the grubby Perspex poster display.

Ten minutes later with the Perspex now shining and smear free, she installed the newly printed brochures. Digging out her white-gloss paint and paintbrush, she gave the woodwork a sanding and rubbed with the white spirits. With a few deft strokes of her paintbrush, Olivia restored the tired woodwork to its former glory.

An hour later, she stood outside the sparkling office window admiring her handiwork. The brochures were vivid in their colours against the gleaming Perspex display and white woodwork. Everything looked professional with not a spider or cobweb in sight. Inside, she wiped the pre-soaked kitchen cupboards and countertop, finishing by cleaning the chipped mugs and sink area with a generous wipe of Milton. Finally, she re-boiled the kettle and sat down to have her well-deserved lunch while mulling over where to tackle next.

Half an hour later, Olivia took her notebook and did an inventory of the office, waiting area, Paddy's office, kitchen and bathroom. After disposing of outdated newspapers, half-filled cardboard teacups and lunch wrappers, she cleaned Paddy's crumb-covered office desk, mindful not to disturb his paperwork and hoovered the entire area. Carrying the bin throughout the premises, she filled it with old newspapers and outdated brochures, noting the reception chairs were tatty and slightly threadbare.

The reception flooring had also seen better days. There wasn't an unchipped cup or plate in the kitchen, the skirting boards and door frames had lost their white shine, instead sporting an unflattering shade of dusty yellow.

Noting everything, Olivia returned to her desk, adding the remaining new properties to the company website. Taking the tired rental folder in hand, she put them in order before setting up a spreadsheet recording all property, tenant and lease details, payments and deposits in one document. An hour and a half later, with the rental folder finally sorted, Olivia leaned back in her chair and viewed her handiwork with pleasure. Satisfied, she closed the property folder and returned to DIY duties.

With renewed vigour, she turned her attention to sanding the skirting boards and door frames in the reception and Paddy's office. Scuffed and dingy didn't attract customers, Olivia thought, launching into her final DIY task of the day. With dust sheets covering all the essentials, she brandished her emulsion roller and set to work on the walls in the reception and Paddy's office.

A few hours later with the last of the white emulsion applied, Olivia tackled the skirting and door frames. With the yellowed woodwork sanded and rubbed over with white spirits, she brandished her gloss paintbrush again. In no time, she had the woodwork gleaming white again. Admiring the results while rubbing her aching knees, she decided this was the only office job she ever had where she spent half the day on her knees cleaning, sanding and painting.

She needed this job. If it meant doing a bit of DIY to keep it, so be it!

Olivia tidied and put away her cleaning products and DIY things, shocked to realize it was almost seven.

Time flies when you're having fun, but the satisfaction gained from such a transformation in one day made it worthwhile. It was almost eight when she let herself out, locked up and contentedly made her way home.

# Chapter 17

The following morning, Olivia found Paddy already in the office with the kettle boiled. Before she had removed her coat, he presented her with a cup of tea.

'You're a topper! I didn't recognise the place this morning. That window display looks great and you even tidied my office,' Paddy gushed, pacing the reception and waiting room area, closely examining the paintwork.

'Thank you. I didn't remove any paperwork on your desk, just binned old newspapers and wrappers,' Olivia rushed, mindful bosses can be protective of their desks. After all, this was only her second day on the job.

'Don't worry. I've checked my desk. Everything is there that should be. I meant to tidy, but I'm run off my feet. You ladies do a much better cleaning job than us fellas,' Paddy complimented, continuing his tour into the kitchen area.

'Thank you, Paddy,' Olivia smiled. 'The two reception chairs are past it and the reception floor is very scratched. Would you consider replacing them?' Olivia ventured, maximising Paddy's current mood of appreciation.

'Huh! I'm not made of money, you know. I'm only a very small auctioneering business. I've taken you on for two days a week, already leaving things tight for me,' Paddy blustered, swinging around quickly and stomping back to the reception desk, armed with his refilled mug and glaring suspiciously at Olivia.

'Again, thank you for my job. I appreciate you're only a small business, but first impressions count in any profession, as an experienced businessman like yourself knows. As you said, the place already looks great. That's only with tidying and a lick of paint here and there. Imagine the difference with new chairs and flooring. I could enquire about getting office chairs secondhand and a price for linoleum flooring,' Olivia appeased, anxious to smooth Paddy's ruffled feathers.

'I suppose you could check out the price of the linoleum, but I don't want any old rubbish chairs from charity shops,' Paddy sulked.

'That's an old-fashioned image people have about charity shops. They stock the best of items for sale and the bonus is you'd be supporting a local charity as well as recycling, so it would be a win-win situation. What do you think? Can I look in the charity shops here in Boyle for chairs?' Olivia wheedled, as Paddy continued to scowl.

'I am a community businessman and all for supporting a local charity. Go ahead, but don't go buying anything until you've run the prices by me first,' he grunted, smoothing his jacket lapels before stomping back to the office.

'Of course. I'll get prices today,' Olivia answered placatingly, as Paddy closed his office door. The resounding thud rang through the office.

Olivia turned on her computer. Paddy needed impressing today to restore his good mood, so she decided to put some order on the For Sale properties. She had been mulling it over the previous night in bed and decided to capture all the property details on a single computerised table. Exactly as it was done when she worked in the multi-million property business in London. It would make life easier for Paddy and herself to be able to glance at the phone or office computer and instantly see the up-to-date position on properties in seconds.

With this brainwave in mind, Olivia emptied the folder with the dog-eared brochures onto her desk, putting them in order. She attached the scribbled Post-its to the relevant property brochure. When she had it all in order, input property details, seller names and numbers, sale commencement date, sale agreed date, solicitors details, asking price, sale agreed price, numbers of viewings and viewings dates, and viewers' feedback all onto the computer; she colour-coded them into yellow, orange and red, yellow for sales up to six months, orange for six to twelve months and red for twelve months and over.

Immediately, she spotted the figures weren't as good as Paddy thought. According to him, he had eighteen current sales for less than a year and eight properties for sale over a year. The table instantly displayed he had thirteen for sale just over the year and the remaining thirteen under a year. Printing the document, Olivia put it aside for Paddy's attention. It was just coming up to eleven. Time for Paddy's morning tea break.

'Just in time,' Paddy smiled, as Olivia laid his mug and chocolate digestives on his desk. 'Chocolate biscuits and all! You're worth your weight in gold,' Paddy exclaimed, his earlier truculent mood forgotten.

'I know you've got a sweet tooth!' Olivia replied, recounting all the chocolate wrappers she had removed from his desk the day before. That packet of chocolate digestives she bought was proving to be a godsend!

'You're aiming high and hitting the target!' he chuckled, clapping his hands with the excitement of a five-year-old in a sweet shop.

Men were so easy sometimes, Olivia mused. Leaving Paddy with his tea, she returned to her desk for a tea break. Paddy mentioned he was going out for the afternoon and she wanted to have costs for the furniture and linoleum for him before he left. If she gave him the costs this morning while his mood was good, he was more likely to be agreeable. She wanted the floor covering and furniture in as soon as possible.

Phoning Liz, Olivia explained what she was looking for and the urgency. Liz reassured her if they didn't have suitable office chairs in their shop, she would chase up the other charity shops in the area and get back to Olivia as quickly as possible. Liz obliged Olivia with the name of the local DIY shop that sold linoleum. Olivia explained she didn't want to chat for too long but would update Liz on the news at their get-together on Thursday night.

Ringing the DIY, Olivia gave floor measurements and asked them for a quote. They had three colours in stock in woodgrain effect, walnut, cherry, or a bleached-ash style. For €180 they could supply and fit it and drop around that afternoon. Olivia quickly took note of the details, saying she'd get back to them shortly. She hung up and only had the phone put down before Liz rang back. They secured two black leather and chrome office chairs in good condition for €60. She'd send Olivia a photo and agreed not to sell them until hearing back from her. Olivia got up from her desk and knocked hesitantly on Paddy's door.

'I've made the calls and got good news all round. My friend in the charity shop has two good quality office chairs for €60. I've got photos of them for you. Also, the DIY store will not only supply the lino but will come around and fit it for you this afternoon for €180. So, for €240 you will have a refurbished office,' Olivia beamed, conscious of needing the hard sell with Paddy.

'Mm...' grunted Paddy, peering reluctantly on Olivia's phone at the chairs. 'That's another €240 on top of your wages. I don't know. It's a lot of money to pay out in one week. Maybe I'll do it in a couple of weeks,' Paddy muttered, scratching his head with irritation.

'I've already glossed the woodwork. You agreed it looks great. I have the paint and paint rollers in the office and can give the reception area a coat of white emulsion this afternoon to complete the look. For €240 you will be getting a completely revamped office, reception and kitchen area. You may as well bite the bullet now and get all the work done in one day. The place badly needs an overhaul. Your customers will love the new look!' Olivia urged, holding Paddy's gaze. 'I suppose you're right. You drive a hard bargain. Okay, deal done. Give the reception a lick of paint. If there's paint left over, you could put a drop on my office door and skirting boards too. Sort out the lino and collect the chairs today. I'll leave the payment. Now that's sorted, we'll have a look at how you're getting on with the two folders,' Paddy grinned, knowing he had struck a good deal and followed Olivia triumphantly to her desk.

'I've put the rental and sales folders in order. They're both now in Excel format, so you'll see at a glance exactly how much rent is outstanding, as well as other details such as contact numbers for owners and tenants alike.'

Olivia clicked on the rental spreadsheet, showing Paddy how to open it and explaining how simple it was. She followed with the property spreadsheet, highlighting the number of properties in the twelve months plus section.

'This looks all a bit fancy for me, Olivia. I don't know much about computers. I scribble notes on Post-its and stick them in the customer's files. It's what I've always done and it's worked just fine. I'm a bit long in the tooth for learning about computerised systems,' Paddy grumbled, tutting as he shifted uncomfortably from one foot to another.

'You're overthinking it all. I'll update the spreadsheet and you'll have an instant update on every property. It'll make life easier for you. I'll log out of the document and then we can start from the beginning,' Olivia offered, mindful it was all bound to be a big change for her new boss, especially for a man who didn't like change.

Pulling a chair forward, she urged Paddy to sit while she got him to start the computer and insert his password. Two minutes later, Olivia pointed out the spreadsheet and encouraged Paddy to open it. As he moved through the headings, he became more confident in accessing documents and understanding the benefits of it.

'I think you've mastered it! I'll update it as needed and email a copy to you when you're out and about so you can have instant access on your phone. It'll save lots of time and look much more professional. What do you think?' Olivia asked, glancing at Paddy's puzzled expression.

'It looks like a great job. I've gotten a few surprises looking at these figures today. Are you sure they're right? I didn't know there were so many rent arrears outstanding from Liam McKeown. I'll be on his case today and there are several properties on my books for over a year. I'll have to put a push on them before the sellers pull the plug on me,' Paddy muttered, slowly standing and scratching his chin while contemplating what he had seen on the screen.

'Those figures are right. I've taken them all from your folders and double-checked. Don't worry, I'll type a step-by-step procedure to make things as easy as possible. I'll print it off and stick a copy on the side of your computer,' Olivia encouraged, as Paddy reached for his coat on the back of his office door, wrestling it on.

'It's a lot for me to take in but has given me food for thought. I'm sure with a few stabs at it I'll manage it though,' Paddy said confidently.

After a few skirmishes with the sleeves, he finally buttoned up his favourite coat.

'I'm going out. We've gone through a lot already and this is only your second day. I've got your bank details and passed them on to the accountant. Your wages should be set up tomorrow and in your account by Thursday. I'm in Dublin this evening and won't return until Thursday. Any problems, give me a call. Thanks for a great start. I'll see you then,' Paddy acknowledged gratefully, shuffling towards the door.

'No problem. See you then,' Olivia waved.

It wasn't yet one o'clock. Olivia exhaled contentedly. Paddy's computer lessons had gone surprisingly well. He agreed to buy the linoleum and chairs. A miracle, as he was a bit of a skin flint. She chuckled in pleasure. Her past experiences of negotiating with Tom and Betty had stood to her today.

# Chapter 18

Liz hummed happily as she tidied the breakfast table. She was in a good mood and looking forward to the Thursday night get together at Olivia's that evening. She was a lovely girl. For someone new to the area, she was the glue that bonded everyone together. Liz smiled, recalling how often Mark mentioned the girl's name in conversation. There was no doubt about it, he was smitten and Liz hoped Olivia might feel the same for him in time. She wouldn't get involved and agreed with her husband to leave their personal lives to themselves. Working in the charity shop proved an excellent distraction from obsessing over her dilemma.

Reluctance to approach her daughter directly was causing tension between herself and John. He didn't understand why she couldn't barge into her daughter's house and introduce herself as her mother. Loading the dishwasher, she turned it on. The kitchen sorted, she went to the hall, plugged in the hoover, picking up her husband's and son's stray clothes and shoes along the way. She couldn't believe she was enjoying housework and smiling she thanked God. It was good to feel content. After spending months on end at home, dwelling incessantly on her problems, she had decided to get out of the house for a few hours every week.

Having casually mentioned her boredom to Sheila, she was told the charity shop in the town was desperate for volunteers. The following day, Liz rang and agreed on a trial for a day or two. That was over a fortnight ago and she now worked half days on Monday, Tuesday and Wednesday mornings, loving every bit of it. She was a natural organiser and the manager in the shop gave her free rein to sort it out and present it as she thought fit. She enjoyed sorting and putting things in order.

Because stock changed daily, she encouraged customers to let her know if they were looking for something specific. As soon as it arrived in the shop or the other branch in Carrick, she phoned them. Customers quickly spread news of this arrangement and the shop manager told Liz sales had increased since she began working there. So yes, she was much happier in herself. The bonus this week had been getting Olivia sorted with chairs and two pictures for the office.

Liz paused and leaned on the hoover considering Olivia's recent purchases. Come to think of it, Olivia had been one of their best customers last month buying curtains, cushions, a table and chairs, two dressers, a couple of wardrobes, three headboards, and numerous other things. Liz smiled, thinking of the magic Olivia had bestowed on the furniture when she saw it afterwards in its glory. All of it was given a makeover with paint primer, finished off with a coat of the palest shade of grey and sealed with a wax coating. She had performed a miracle on those moss-green, dralon-covered headboards. They were transformed and modernised in their contemporary off-white leatherette.

The shop manager couldn't believe her luck seeing Olivia buy the old headboards. She'd been trying to offload them for two years and was thrilled to be finally rid of them. Their departure had created valuable floor space in the shop. Olivia was a wizard with a paintbrush and staple gun. She certainly gave Liz and the neighbours food for thought when it came to redecorating and updating and was certainly the best advertisement for recycling she had ever met. To think Olivia had learned a lot of her revamping skills from YouTube. She had made her neighbours think outside the box regarding reusing household items.

Liz unplugged the hoover, coiling the flex before carrying it upstairs to start on the bedrooms. Her good mood continued as she debated what to prepare for dinner for herself, John and Mark, who would be in around sixish.

Liz smiled contentedly in anticipation of the card game where all the neighbours had such fun. Content and energised, she whizzed through the three bedrooms with the hoover – the usually detested task a distant memory in her newfound harmony.

'Well, you've excelled yourself with that dinner, Liz. It was fantastic,' John purred, rubbing his belly appreciatively after putting away a large portion of homemade lasagne and salad.

'Yeah, Mam. It was good. That bread-and-butter pudding was a bonus and it's only Wednesday. We haven't hit the weekend yet. You're losing the run of yourself,' Mark joked, delighted to see his mother in better spirits over the last few weeks.

'Don't go expecting this treatment every day, Boys. I don't want you piling on the pounds,' Liz retorted, finishing the remains of her desert, topped with creamy custard.

The cinnamon-flavoured raisins, plump and juicy and the crisp topping, had made her dessert perfect. Nice and crunchy on top, just perfect for a change.

Mark and John cleared the delph, stacking the dishwasher while she filled the teapot, their contented banter filling the kitchen. Nursing her cup of tea, Liz wandered happily into the sitting room and made for the couch to watch Fair City.

'Well, you're in a good mood, Liz and looking even better,' John appraised, placing his mug and plate of biscuits on the coffee table before cosying beside Liz on the couch.

'Thank you, John. You're not looking too bad yourself,' Liz teased in reply.

'It's great to see you looking happy again,' John continued, squeezing Liz's hand lovingly.

'I am feeling much happier and content than I've been in a long time. I love working in the shop. It's great to be meeting people. The manager reckons I'm doing wonders for the sales figures,' Liz replied, munching on her favourite chocolate, macaroon cookie.

'I can see it. It seems to be doing wonders for you. So on that note, what do you think about finally tackling our issue? We have met her quite a few times already. The ice is well broken. How do you feel about going for it, tomorrow or the next day?' John coaxed, eager to resolve the issue.

'I know you're anxious to get things sorted, but I want to get the timing right. You can't rush these things,' Liz replied nervously.

'I know. You've told me the same thing numerous times, but we've both got to make the decision and go for it. We're already here over a year. You've felt the timing hasn't been right all that time,' John replied tightly, placing his mug heavily on the table.

'You've been very patient. I promise I'll make a definite plan in the next week, or so,' Liz cajoled, putting her hand on John's hand in a placating manner.

'I know this is hard for you, but it's hard for myself and Mark too. We both want to get it sorted soon,' John said, patting Liz gently on the back.

# Chapter 19

Olivia closed her front door against the dark outside. Turning on the light, she gratefully eased into the armchair. It was just after half past ten. She was exhausted. That morning she had got up early as usual, delighted to have her first week over. Paddy rang her the evening before in an unexpected excitable mood. Calling into the office to pick up a set of keys for viewing, he'd been blown away by the office makeover, stressing again it was money well spent. An exceptional amount of work had been carried out in a few days. He had tested the chairs. They were good and sturdy, and the paint job gave the place a new lease of life.

Thanking her again, he gushed he'd never expected the place to look so well in such a short time. Her gift of prints of Boyle Abbey and Rockingham Castle added the final touch. Ending the conversation, he added her trial period was over and he was mighty pleased with her. Wages had been lodged to her account and he'd added an extra hundred for a job well done.

Olivia touched by Paddy's phone call couldn't help but laugh, picturing him testing the chairs for value. Confident she was now financially solvent until her next pay cheque, she made the snap decision to visit her boys the following day. Following a conversation with the boarding school, she agreed to pick them up after lessons at four.

Making the journey to the school in under an hour and a half, Olivia paid a visit to Tesco to top up the boy's supplies of toiletries and essential Lynx body sprays, including their favourite Haribo sweets. Shopping complete, she excitedly drove to the school. In the car, she heard the school bell ring at four, signalling the end of the day. After announcing herself at the office, within five minutes her sons were standing before her. She resisted the urge to rush forward and hug them in front of the office staff. Instead, she gave them both a big smile. She had a chat with the Office Administrator, confirming to have the boys back by six thirty.

En route to the car, the boys maintained their enforced dignified walk, conscious they were in full view of staff and students. Finally, settled in the car as Olivia drove out the school driveway, they immediately reverted to type.

'Thanks, Mam, for not letting us down and making a holy show of yourself!' Jonathon exclaimed, planting a kiss on Olivia's cheek.

'Yeah, Mam. Smart move there. If you made a show of us in front of an audience of six hundred, we'd never have lasted the first year,' Andrew laughed from the back seat, stretching forward and patting Olivia's shoulder affectionately.

'I'm not that old to have forgotten the rules in life. I still remember my school days and the dos and don'ts,' Olivia grinned in reply. 'Let's get down to the important stuff. How are you settling in and where do you want to eat?' Olivia enquired, driving out the gates.

'It's alright, I suppose. Plenty of learning, but the good thing is there's plenty of sport too. Sure, you know how we're getting on, we FaceTime you every Saturday,' Andrew replied vehemently.

'Yeah, it's not bad at all. The food is great and plenty of it,' Jonathon added.

'Anyway, never mind all that. We're starving. There's a good Eddie Rocket's ten minute drive away,' Jonathon suggested, food ever present on his mind.

Olivia took directions from Google Maps and within minutes, they were outside the iconic red and white restaurant.

'Come on, you two! There's no audience, so I want a proper hug,' Olivia requested, her outstretched arms towards her sons.

'Okay, but make it fast,' Andrew laughed, as he and Jonathon eagerly embraced their waiting mother after doing a quick scan of the area, ensuring there was no audience around.

'I've missed you both, but I'm happy to see you're as handsome and happy as ever,' Olivia chuckled, playfully ruffling their gelled hair, knowing it would spark an immediate reaction.

'Hey, hands off the hair, Mam!' Andrew cautioned, exiting from Olivia's embrace.

'Yeah, come on Mam, enough of the soppy craic! Let's get some food,' Jonathon added, heading for the restaurant.

Inside, they eased into the red and white candy-striped booth. After perusing the menu for all of two minutes, the boys decided on the largest burger in the house, accompanied by cheesy fries, onion rings and a bucket-sized Coca-Cola each. Olivia smiled at their antics, mindful as ever patience was not a big trait with her twins.

'So, all is going well boys? Is there anything bothering you in school?' Olivia enquired, aware the transition from home to boarding school must be daunting.

'Of course! Everything is fine. Didn't we already fill you in? Anyway, what about you and this new job in Roscommon?' Andrew enquired, calmer now food was ordered.

'The same as you. I've already filled you in. I told you I was offered the job at the auctioneers for two days a week. For the first two weeks, I'm working four days to get the place organised. I finished my first week yesterday and really like it,' Olivia told them as the waitress laid generous lunches on the table.

'Yeah, but what about finishing the renovations in the cottages now?' Jonathon asked, tucking into the first bite of his enormous burger.

'That's just it. Now I have a job, I can afford to continue fixing them and finish off the project,' Olivia answered, tucking into her salad.

'So, you're going to stay down there then?' Andrew blinked, fork midway to his mouth.

'That's the plan. Now you're in Boarding School, I'm delighted to have something to fill my empty days because as you know your dad is very busy, days and evenings on the farm. You can imagine it would have been a boring day at home for me,' Olivia replied, forking her salad into her mouth, careful how she worded her decision to escape their father.

'What does Dad make of all this?' Jonathon queried, shrewdly assessing the conversation.

'I'll be honest, he was annoyed the first week or two. But now he gets his dinner in the pub and a cleaner drops in twice a week to do the housework. And, of course, Betty calls in every morning and evening to keep him company. He seems quite happy.' Olivia smiled, issuing the child-friendly version of their parent's marital arrangements.

'You know he went to the GAA dance last week with Margie Dunne? That auld one up the road! The pictures were on Facebook,' Jonathon stated vehemently.

'I heard. Margie's not old. She went to school with your dad. She's only two years older than him,' Olivia replied calmly.

'Jeez, you're joking! She looks about sixty! Are you not bothered about him going with her to the dance?' Jonathon asked, amazed.

'Not at all. She saved me the bother of going. I was never a fan of the GAA dances,' Olivia laughed over-enthusiastically, eager to dismiss any concerns the boys had about Olivia's feelings regarding advances on their father.

Jesus, Olivia thought swallowing hard in shock. Margie going to the GAA dance with Tom was big news, but she had to pretend otherwise to the boys.

'Right. If you're happy working away there and he's happy too, I suppose that's okay then?' Andrew said calmly, searching Olivia's face intently for a reaction.

'Exactly, Andrew! Everything's fine. We're just a phone call away from each other if we need anything. Enough about that. You're abroad next week for the midterm break, you lucky pair?' Olivia said, anxious to close the domestic arrangements conversation.

'Yeah, Mam. We can't wait. We'll visit Germany, France and Belgium for the week. It'll be deadly,' Andrew cried excitedly, rubbing his hands together in anticipation.

'I'm jealous, but delighted for you as well,' Olivia smiled, reaching across and clapping them on the shoulder.

Reaching into her handbag, she passed two fifty euro notes to the boys.

'There's no need to give us money, Mam. Everything is covered for in the trip. Dad has already given us spending money and we've got some of our own pocket money,' Andrew confirmed, grabbing Jonathon's money and returning both fifty notes to their mother.

'Take it back. I have a regular wage and can afford it. Please, take it and enjoy. It's a one-time offer only,' Olivia cajoled, pushing the notes back.

'Thanks, Mam. If you're not leaving yourself short? You've only started working this week and should be treating yourself with your first week's wages, instead of spending it on us,' Andrew replied anxiously.

'Don't worry, Andrew. It's a one-off payment, so enjoy it! My new boss is fairly pleased with me, so I'll be getting paid again next week and the week after. Anyway, I hope to have one, maybe two, of the cottages fixed up by early spring and rent them out. Hopefully, I'll have a steady income coming from the cottages,' Olivia said, eager to reassure them.

'And what about Christmas? You are coming home then, aren't you?' Andrew blurted, finishing off his burger, tomato sauce dripping onto the plate.

'Of course, she's coming home for Christmas. What kind of question is that?' Jonathan cried, rounding on his brother.

'Yes, I'll be home for Christmas. You'll probably be off school for two weeks. I'll be working two days a week, but you can stay with me for a week after Christmas and give me a hand if you fancy that. Anyway, I'll visit you beforehand and we'll sort it all out then.'

Olivia had to think quickly. She hadn't planned for Christmas. It wasn't even Halloween yet.

'Yeah, you're right, Mam. C'mon Andrew, let's enjoy Halloween first and put your bloody yearly planner away. You're as bad as the teachers back there.'

Jonathon punched Andrew's shoulder, eager to finish his meal in comfort.

'Well, Lads, get in your last orders now. It's almost half past five. Do you want any more drinks?' Olivia asked, eager to get back to a safer conversation.

'Yeah, I'll have another Coke. We don't get it in the school, only healthy nonsense,' Jonathon snorted derisively.

'One for me too, please. I need to wash down the last of my chips,' Andrew added, expertly hoovering the last one into his mouth.

Two hours later, Olivia was heading home to Boyle. On the way back to school, Olivia's sweets and Lynx supplies were divvied out after much haggling and bartering between the boys. Their mood was good and conversation was easy among them. The tricky business of their mother escaping to the West of Ireland didn't seem to be the major drama Olivia expected. No doubt the fact she had reassured them she'd be home for Christmas set them at ease.

Undoubtedly, the fifty euros each sealed the deal. Who says kids can't be bought Olivia laughed to herself, singing along with the radio on her trip home.

# Chapter 20

Sheila glanced at her watch and smiled at hearing knocking on her door. Nine o'clock on the dot, reliable as ever. She rushed to the door, letting her neighbour in.

'Morning, Sheila. How are you and Mick today?' Olivia enquired, making her way in, and unbuttoning her coat.

'Great, Olivia. I've just brought his breakfast in. He had a great night's sleep. He was tired yesterday because the physiotherapist visited and gave him a good going-over. She had him on his feet for ages pushing him a little, but he was great. She has a great way of getting through to him and they are making great progress, even with just two visits a week,' Sheila replied enthusiastically, taking Olivia's coat.

'That's brilliant, Sheila, he's doing so well. He's only been out of the Nursing Home a fortnight. You're doing a great job with him,' Olivia encouraged.

'He's doing well thanks to you and the neighbours, and Home Help. You call in a few times a week to give me a hand getting him up and dressed. Liz and John drop over every night to get him to bed. If they can't manage it, Mark obliges. He's a lovely lad, you know. He even had Conor with him a few times.

I can't believe how that lad is coming out of his shell. He still wouldn't kill me with conversation mind, but Mick and himself chat away now,' Sheila added, matter-of-factly.

'I told you people don't mind helping. It's like the old days when people rambled to their neighbours. It's only half an hour from a person's day and no big hardship. Is the Home Help working out alright?' Olivia enquired, following Sheila into her kitchen.

'She only started last week and she's great. Caroline is her name. Doesn't Mick know her father well, her family are from just outside the town. Caroline calls in for two hours every day, an hour in the morning and another around eight at night when she helps prepare him for bed. Her help takes the pressure off the neighbours. She helps get him dressed in the morning and gives me a hand when I do his exercises with him. It's amazing how a young pretty face motivates him to try harder. He likes to show off to her,' Sheila winked mischievously.

'Whatever works. You're not bothered are you?'

'Not at all. As you say, whatever works. He's making great strides. The sooner he's up and about, the better. I'll be delighted. He's had such a hard time. How about a cup of tea while Mick's watching the news? You can fill me in about the new job,' Sheila continued, turning the kettle on again.

Sheila made tea and laid the mugs on the table before sitting beside Olivia.

'I finished my first week on Thursday evening, so week one is over. I'm getting on well with Paddy. I took your advice on board about how he likes to watch the pennies. He agreed to replace the worn out chairs and flooring in the reception area. There was enough left, so the flooring in the kitchen and toilet area got revamped too. With elbow grease and some sprucing up with the paintbrush I was busy for four days, but the effort was worth it. The place looks great and to give Paddy his due, he phoned me Thursday night to thank me again, even giving me a generous bonus. I saw the boys yesterday and was delighted to see them so settled in. All round, it's been a busy but successful week so far,' Olivia smiled, tucking into Sheila's homemade fruitcake with her tea.

'You've had a busy week and it's only Saturday morning. That's great the boys are doing well. It sounds as though Paddy got great value for money with you! A cleaner, painter and decorator, and office girl all thrown in,' Sheila said indignantly.

'It's like this, Sheila. Beggars can't be choosers. I was rapidly running out of funds and needed to finish off the work on the cottages before renting them. The job with Paddy is a godsend and it's only five minutes up the road. I'll have a regular income coming in, as well as five days a week to myself to continue working on the cottages. Just so you know! Paddy said I've passed my week's trial with flying colours. It didn't feel like hard work because I love painting and decorating. I'd say it's a win win situation for both of us. I propose a toast to thank you and Mick again for arranging the interview for me,' Olivia grinned, clinking her mug with Sheila's.

'I'm delighted it's going so well with Paddy. He's still a mammy's boy at sixty-two and a bit old-fashioned in his ways. You can obviously work him! '

'Absolutely! There's no need to worry about me,' Olivia affirmed, putting the empty mugs in the dishwasher and following Sheila to Mick's bedroom.

'Good morning, Mick. Sheila tells me you had a busy day yesterday with the physio?'

'Morning, Olivia. Indeed I had. It was tough going, but she's good at her job. It's only two weeks since she started working on me, but I can notice a definite improvement in strength in my left arm and leg in that short time.'

'That's right! You're coming on great. We'll get you standing. Ease yourself forward to the side and then lean on me and Olivia to get on your feet,' Sheila coaxed, placing an encouraging arm around her husband's waist.

Mick slowly shuffled to the edge, maximising the strength on his right side to drag his weakened left side to the edge of the bed.

'That's it! Lean on our arms and we'll lift you so you can lean forward onto your Zimmer fame,' Olivia encouraged, placing Mick's good arm on hers.

With a final struggle, Mick heaved himself onto the Zimmer frame, steadying himself as he gripped it tightly.

Sheila slowly guided him to the hall.

'That's it! You're up and ready to start motoring. We'll do the usual walk along the catwalk,' Sheila joked, as Mick started his daily walk along the twenty-foot length of the hallway.

Sheila and Olivia resumed position on either side of Mick as he commenced his daily morning walk with a slow steady gait, his left foot dragging along. Aware that Mick found these walks a strain mentally and physically, Sheila knew she needed to distract him before he became disheartened and gave up too easily.

'Mick, did you know Olivia has finished her first week's work with Paddy? He got his money's worth out of her. He had her cleaning, sanding and painting, as well as sorting out his computer and dragging him out of the stone age.'

'That's our Paddy. He's one of the old stock. If he can get value for money, he'll take it. Fill me in on the full story, Olivia,' Mick asked, anxious to get all the news.

'We covered a lot in four days. We trawled through Paddy's rental and sales folders and put everything on the computer. I gave Paddy a few computer lessons and gave the place a makeover, thanks to some paint I had in addition to some Paddy bought a few years before, but never actually made it to the walls. Oh, and I bought some office chairs from the charity shop. So, the final transformation, thanks to some serious scrubbing, a bit of paint and a new lino was quite amazing,' Olivia informed him.

'And you did all that work yourself?' Mick asked her with amazement.

'The local DIY shop arranged to lay the lino. I did the other bits and bobs. I enjoy that kind of thing. I've plenty of practice at recycling with the three cottages,' Olivia replied.

'You must have performed a miracle on that place. It hasn't seen a lick of paint since it opened twenty years ago. He's not a man open to suggestions, Sure, myself and some of the other fellas have been onto him for years that his office has no curb-side appeal. People take one glance at the state of the window display and keep walking. As for cleaning the place and keeping it tidy, it wouldn't be a priority for Paddy. He still lives at home with his eighty-year-old mother who runs around after him.'

Mick puffed deeply as he started on his third lap of the hallway, oblivious to the distraction tactics his wife was using on him with Olivia's news.

'I don't know whether it was the cheap labour or that I caught Paddy when his defences were low. Either way, he was agreeable and gave me the okay to go ahead. I was happy to do the work. He phoned me Thursday night when he saw the results and was very appreciative altogether. So yes, we've got off to a flying start,' Olivia enthused, as Sheila and herself helped turn Mick's Zimmer frame for his fourth and final lap.

'That's great news it's working out so well. But remember, Paddy's a shrewd businessman. He got a great bargain when you agreed to take the job, but he's a decent, sound man at the back of it all,' Mick gasped, as he finally trudged to the end of his walk. 'Sheila, you have me killed out walking this hall! Will you let me sit down to catch my breath,' Mick wheezed, finally steering his walking frame towards the sitting room.

'No problem. You've done fantastic today. Four laps instead of your usual three,' Sheila said encouragingly, while covertly winking at Olivia as they led Mick to his favourite recliner armchair.

Holding an arm each, Olivia and Sheila helped Mick as he eased himself down and Sheila adjusted the recliner to stretch out his legs.

'I'll let you rest for a while. Here's your exercise squeeze balls to build up strength in your hands and arms while you watch the telly,' Sheila said, kissing him on the cheek as she fussed contentedly, wrapping a blanket over his lap.

'I'll just top up the stove and bring in a bag of turf from the shed before I head off,' Olivia called, putting on her coat.

Olivia emptied the filled turf bag into the fuel box beside the stove and filled it, conscious Mick felt the chill much faster since his stroke as his mobility was greatly limited since.

'Okay, folks. I'm off now. Mick, it's great to see you doing so well. If you need anything give me a call,' Olivia smiled, as Mick waved her off and she made her way out.

'Thanks again for all your help, Olivia. I'll walk you to the door,' Sheila offered, hurrying to Olivia's side and stepping out with her. 'Thanks for filling Mick in on the new job. It was a perfect distraction. If you weren't here, he'd have given up after the first lap. Men need an awful lot of coaxing through life you know,' Sheila whispered conspiratorially.

'I didn't know I was just being used as a distraction tactic, but if it helps Mick, I am more than happy to oblige,' Olivia joked back.

'You know exactly what I mean,' Sheila laughed, giving Olivia a playful nudge with her elbow.

'I'm only joking with you! Listen, I'm off. I'll see you both on Thursday night at half eight. Remember, if you need anything, give me a call. I'll be around all day to finish painting the woodwork in the second cottage.'

'Perfect. No doubt I'll drop up to see you later,' Sheila waved as she closed the front door.

'Would you believe it's ten o'clock already? Time to wrap up things for the night,' Sheila suggested, gathering the cards from the group seated around the table.

'I'd say that was a good night, all around,' Mick declared, counting his takings from the game.

'You're definitely on a winning streak at the moment, Mick. You cleaned up at the card game tonight. You're turning into a real smooth mover with that walking frame,' John joked, helping Mick out of the chair.

'You'd better watch out! There'll be no stopping me now,' Mick boomed, expertly positioning himself onto his frame.

Sheila gathered the coats and passed them to the group.

Liz and John rinsed and dried the mugs, passing them to Conor who placed them on the dresser.

'Well, Olivia. I'll have Jack over to you tomorrow morning at half past nine. Are you sure that suits you?' Suzanne enquired.

'Perfect. I'll be back from Sheila's by then so the timing will be fine. I'll have the paint and everything ready. I'll be glad to get the ceilings painted,' Olivia replied, helping Mick into his coat.

'I'll drop in tomorrow around three to finish off the skirting in the sitting room. I'll give Jack a quick lesson in carpentry while I'm at it,' Conor said on his way to the door, accompanied by Mark.

'I'll drop in tomorrow too, Olivia. I'll finish connecting the stove next door and start installing the last electric shower. Another two or three days of work should finish it,' Mark said, hugging Olivia as she called goodnight to the group parting company at the door.

'Thanks, guys, for the company. We had a great night again. See you tomorrow.'

Olivia waved her neighbour's goodnight before closing the door firmly against the cold. She pushed the deadbolt securely on the cottage door and happily made her way to her bedroom, eagerly looking forward to another busy but content day tomorrow.

# Chapter 21

'Okay, Jack. You're all ready to get started. As you can see, it's uncomplicated really. I have the bedroom and bathroom cleared out, so it should make it easier for you to use the roller on the ceiling. The two drums of paint are over there with the paint trays and dust sheets. I'll leave you to it. If you fancy a cuppa or something to eat, feel free to help yourself. I'm heading out shopping. I should be back around midday or so,' Olivia said after doing a demo with Jack, showing him how to use the roller and set up the dust sheets.

'Right, so,' Jack grunted absently, studying his mobile phone intently.

'Are you sure you're okay with this painting? I can stay if you like,' Olivia enquired, observing Jack's obvious indifference to her conversation.

'Huh? Nah! It's only a quarter to ten now. That'll give me plenty of time to sort out the two ceilings. When I'm finished with those, what do you want done next?'

Jack perked up and put his phone away, finally aware he better show some interest.

'It's been years since those ceilings got a lick of paint. I would say they will both probably need two coats. If you have any energy left after that, the skirting boards in both rooms need a second coat of gloss too. I've left the paint and white spirits with the other stuff. But don't bother about that for today. If you manage the two ceilings, I'll be more than happy with that,' Olivia said, remembering the conversation she had with Suzanne the night before.

Suzanne confided that Jack wasn't handy around the house and to show him down to the last detail what was involved in the painting work. In her opinion, modern teenagers weren't big on basic domestic or maintenance skills of any sort.

Olivia got her coat and backpack and made her way to the door, reassured that Jack finally seemed eager and interested in getting started.

'I'm off. Any problems, give me a call on my mobile. I've left the number on a notepad on the table. See you later.'

Olivia waved goodbye at the doorway, made her way to her car and headed into town.

'Hi, Olivia. Great to see you,' Liz welcomed, as Olivia arrived at the charity shop.

'Hi, Liz. Just dropping in to have a rummage around. Anything interesting come in this week?' Olivia enquired, putting her backpack on the counter.

'Nothing too exciting so far, but I put something aside for you. I thought they'd look good on that chest of drawers Suzanne gave you last week,' Liz replied winking, rushing from the counter.

Liz went out to the back of the shop and emerged minutes later with her hands laden. She placed six rose-petal, pink-tinted glass doorknobs on the counter. The vintage knobs glittered brilliantly in the morning sunlight. Olivia picked up one to examine it closely.

'Liz, they're exquisite. You're spot on. They would look fabulous on the chest of drawers. I have already given it a coat of eggshell paint and it's transformed it. These knobs will be fabulous on it,' Olivia trilled, examining each one in detail, delighted to see all six were in good condition.

'That's good. I'm delighted you like them. I know you love recycling, so I enjoy keeping an eye out for you,' Liz said, carefully wrapping the knobs in layers of newspaper.

'I love recycling and hate waste. Fortunately, I also love a good bargain. It's just as well I don't have expensive tastes as my current budget doesn't extend very far. When I think of the huge, expensive kitchen I left behind filled to the brim with every modern gadget, it's a pleasure to downsize and use only what you need. It certainly makes life easier in so many ways,'

Olivia ascertained, placing the six packages carefully into the bottom of her rucksack.

'Your recycling hobby has served you well, so far. You've made great headway on the three cottages already,' Liz confirmed, thrilled to help her neighbour.

'I certainly have. Between the stuff you have found for me and the other local charity shops, the furniture and stuff from the neighbours and free paint and wood from the recycling centres; not to mind the help Mark and Conor gave with the plumbing and carpentry has been an absolute godsend. I have probably three or four more weeks of work left. I hope to have the bulk of work on the three cottages pretty much finished by then. After that, I can explore marketing them for rental,' Olivia smiled with pleasure.

'And you're on that sewing machine every night! You must be nearly sorted out with curtains and bedlinen?' Liz quipped, rifling through a box of donated books on the counter, attempting to put some order on them.

'You're right. My mother's sewing machine has been a godsend. She had bales of extra wide cream and grey, pinstriped fabric, so I'm using all that to make duvet and pillow covers. God bless her, she couldn't resist a bargain, so bought the lot. There was even enough left over to make a few Roman blinds. I've altered those two sets of off-white floor-to-ceiling curtains you got me. Country cottage windows are small so that curtain fabric has gone a long way. I've managed to make four sets of curtains and two sets of cushion covers from them. I'm very pleased with the progress of the work. How much do I owe for the glass knobs?' Olivia asked, reaching in the rucksack for her purse.

'Oh, don't bother with that. It's a present from me. A thank you for entertaining us again last night,' Liz protested, flapping her hands at Olivia who continued to rummage in her bag.

'Are you sure, Liz? You know, I can't see my purse. I must have left it at home. I'll have to go back and pick it up as I need to do a big grocery shop, as well as pick up things in the DIY place. I'm pretty much low on everything so I better head back straight away. Thanks again for your very kind gift. Very much appreciated,' Olivia added, hastily zipping her rucksack and making her way to the door.

'It's only just after eleven. You've got the whole day ahead of you. Enjoy it,' Liz grinned, waving goodbye to Olivia.

As the car made its way home on the familiar drive, Olivia slowed down to admire the magenta-pink fuchsia and the last remaining dancing daisies lining the laneway. The golden autumn colours shone in all their tones, from the palest yellow on the few remaining leaves on the ash and oak trees, to the enduring deep, russet, bronze leaf cover on the beech trees. The overall colour scheme exuded a warm glow, adding to Olivia's current state of contentment.

She passed Jack's mother Suzanne and rolled down the window to say hello.

Her kids were happy, a job was sorted, she had wonderful new friends and her renovations were coming along nicely. Life was pretty good.

# Chapter 22

Olivia parked the car and walked to the door she had left on the latch for Jack. Pushing it open, she let herself into her sitting room. The complete silence immediately struck her as she made her way into the spare bedroom, careful not to startle Jack who was obviously engrossed in painting. She opened the bedroom door, but there was no sight of Jack. Calling his name on her way to the bathroom, there was still no sign of him. She checked the scullery at the back, before finally going into her bedroom.

'Jeez, what are you doing in my bed,' Olivia screamed, staring in disbelief at the bare-chested teenager sitting in her bed, accompanied by an equally scantily clad girl.

'You said you weren't due back till later,' Jack cried, equally irate at being interrupted.

'What the hell are you saying? You were never supposed to be in my bed! You're supposed to be painting. Who's this girl?' Olivia gasped in panic.

How could things change so much in seconds, she wondered.

'I'm sorry about this. My name is Ellie McKeown,' mumbled the embarrassed temptress, pulling the sheets further up and covering her poorly concealed breasts.

'McKeown! You're not Liam McKeown's daughter by any chance?' Olivia enquired, recalling the surname of the school principal she spoke with last week, regarding the Work Placement form.

She vaguely remembered him mentioning he had a daughter in Transition Year.

'Yeah, I am,' the girl stuttered, slinking under the covers.

'You're winding me up! So your father is the school principal? The same person I spoke to yesterday to discuss Jack's placement with me. Do you realise the front door was left on the latch? Anybody could have walked in, including your father. I'm going into the sitting room. Get up and dressed straight away. I'll go and lock the front and back doors before someone else walks in on you,' Olivia gasped in absolute horror, knowing she had to think fast as she exited her bedroom.

My God, this is an absolute nightmare, Olivia thought, running out and checking she had locked the doors properly. Confident the doors were bolted, she ran back to the living room to find her two visitors standing awkwardly, anxiously awaiting their fate. Ellie's smeared makeup and long copper-red tresses resembled a very messy bird's nest. Jack's open jeans zip and runners with trailing laces were the most obvious tell-tale signs of dodgy behaviour Olivia had ever witnessed.

'The doors are locked, so there will be no more intruders,' Olivia laughed nervously, conscious further humiliation was not going to help the situation. 'Tell you what! Go into the bathroom and do a quick tidy up,' Olivia suggested, scanning them from top to bottom.

'Okay, will do,' Ellie replied, grabbing Jack and steering him towards the bathroom.

Having them out of the way, Olivia did a quick house tour to make sure there was no other incriminating evidence hanging about. She started with her bedroom, pulling the sheet and duvet back in place, before doing a quick scan between them. Safe enough there! She searched the other rooms, happy to find all okay.

Ellie and Jack returned to the living room, with their hair groomed and not a fashion faux pas in sight. Their manner was more self-assured.

'Good, everything's sorted. Jack, put the kettle on. We'll have lunch before you get started on the painting,' Olivia suggested pointedly.

'Yeah, sure,' Jack replied, rushing to the scullery, delighted to think his earlier misdemeanour was forgotten.

With the kettle boiled, he set the table with mugs, plates and cutlery. Their newfound domestic bliss was interrupted by a loud knocking on the door. Olivia hastily opened it.

'Hi, Olivia. Hi, Jack. I thought I'd call in with some lunch. He's a growing boy with a big appetite you know!' Suzanne laughed, carrying a bulging carrier bag.

'Hi, Suzanne. There was no need to bring up lunch. I've plenty in already,' Olivia answered shakily, taking the bag from her neighbour.

'Oh, but he has such a big appetite. To be honest, I'm being nosey and wanted to see how he's getting on with the painting,' Suzanne whispered to Olivia, making her way to the armchair beside the stove.

God thought Olivia. He's got an even bigger appetite than you'd ever realise.

'Oh, hello, Ellie. I didn't see you there,' Suzanne continued, surprised at spotting Ellie tucked away on a stool in a corner of the living room.

'Hi, Mrs. O'Hara. I just dropped in to say hello to Jack,' Ellie muttered sheepishly.

'Jack has spent the morning sanding and preparing the woodwork. He'll start the painting after lunch,' Olivia cut in quickly, anxious to avoid any more awkward questions.

Jack placed the filled teapot on the table, dividing his mother's generous rolls between the plates, before pouring tea for everybody.

'Olivia, I think you've performed a miracle on my son. You've made a perfect gentleman out of him in one morning. Tell me what the trick is, because in the last seventeen years, he has never laid the table once in his life for me. Never mind making me a cup of tea. I'm very impressed, Jack,' Suzanne gushed, proud as punch with the transformation in her son.

'Okay, Mam. Can you stop now? You're making a show of me!' Jack mumbled, his face coloured a vivid shade of scarlet.

'Okay, I'll say no more. But I'm very pleased with your good manners. Keep up the good work,' Suzanne smiled, taking a mug of tea from her son, her face glowing with pleasure as she gazed at him with newfound admiration. 'Just one more thing. I've put in a packet of your favourite chocolate Kimberley's. Pass me one Jack and I'll have it with my tea. Don't worry, I won't delay and keep you from your work,' Suzanne finished.

'Enjoy your cuppa, Suzanne. We're only sitting down to lunch now anyway, so there's no rush on you,' Olivia appeased, topping up Suzanne's mug.

'No, I'll be quick. I don't want to upset your schedule. And what about you Ellie? What were you up to?'

'I just dropped in to say hello to Jack. I wasn't up to anything,' Ellie stammered, taken aback at Suzanne's question.

'Oh, I know that. I was just wondering what you are up to for your work placement. For Transition Year, I meant?' explained Suzanne quickly.

'Oh, sorry. I'm not sure yet. My dad is trying a few different places, but I'm not too keen on any of them. I hope to do architecture in college,' Ellie added, anxious to clear up any misunderstanding.

'Hopefully, something suitable will turn up. I'll say goodbye and leave you all to your work.'

Suzanne rose abruptly and went to the sink, washed her mug and put it back on the dresser.

'Thanks for your lovely lunch, Suzanne. It was appreciated,' Olivia said at the front door.

'Jack, we'll get down to some work now. Ellie, did you want to head off, or what suits you?' Olivia enquired, aware of the sensitive situation.

'If you don't mind, I'd love to give a hand. If you just show me what to do then I'll get started,' Ellie blurted in a conciliatory tone.

'If you're sure. I'd be delighted with some help with the painting. But first, text your parents and let them know where you are. Secondly, I don't want you to ruin your good clothes. I've got an assortment of old jeans and jumpers you can borrow if you like,' Olivia suggested.

'Why not? I'd love to give the painting a go,' Ellie replied, smiling cheekily at Jack as he waited anxiously for her reply.

'Great. I'll leave you some work jeans and a jumper on my bed,' Olivia said, going to her bedroom.

Half an hour later, after a quick demo on the do's and don'ts of painting, all three were engrossed in their work. Jack had started the ceilings in the living room and Ellie, whose slight figure was dressed in Olivia's way too-big old jeans anchored on by a belt looped nearly twice around her waist, had started glossing the skirting boards and doors. Olivia resumed her work on the sewing machine in her bedroom creating duvet covers. All three were utterly content, listening to Spotify free music in the background. It was a perfectly blissful afternoon and all previous angst was forgotten.

'Look at the time,' Olivia called, horrified to see it was almost a quarter past six.

'Sorry about this, Folks. I didn't realise it was so late. Down the tools fast and get home. Your parents are going to think I'm a right tyrant altogether,' Olivia hollered, jumping from her seat at the sewing machine and joining her workmates. 'Jack, I'm so impressed. I thought you'd only get the ceiling done, but you've already got half the walls painted in the other bedroom without a run of paint in sight. You're a very fast learner,' Olivia said, carefully studying Jack's handiwork. 'And you, Ellie. You've all the skirting board and architrave glossed.'

Olivia examined the woodwork carefully, noticing only one or two dribbles on the floor.

'That gloss paint can be hard to manage, especially the first time around. I'm delighted. Thank you both so much for all your hard work. You need to get home now. I'll drop you off before there's a search party out.'

'That's okay. I think we owe you from earlier on. So, do you want me to come again tomorrow? Jack asked, sheepishly studying the floor, poking his runner along the edge of the terracotta tiles.

'I think it's best if we forget about earlier. Just one word of caution. Be more discreet in the future and don't forget to practise safe sex. And no, I won't say a word to anyone else. I've said my piece and the subject is closed. Of course, I want you back, Jack. If that's okay with you?' Olivia asked, eager to reassure her visitors as she rushed to get their coats.

Olivia returned with the coats and after closing the paint cans, she wrapped the rollers in cling film to keep them from drying out.

'Ellie, you go ahead and get changed in my bedroom, then we'll get going,'

With Jack dropped off, minutes later Olivia was parked outside Ellie's house.

'Ellie, thanks for all your help today. I appreciated it,' Olivia said, as Ellie stepped out of her car.

'No bother. I can come again tomorrow if you like. I've nothing lined up for work placement and your renovation project is probably the nearest thing I'm going to get relating to architecture around this place,' Ellie suggested, swishing her long tresses away from her eyes.

'I don't know if that's such a good idea.' Olivia was caught completely on the hop.

'There won't be a repeat of this morning's incident,' Ellie emphasised, holding Olivia's gaze.

'It's not that, Ellie. I think your parents might have different ideas about your work placement.'

'Another thing, I remembered you mentioned there's no insulation in the attics. What did you plan on doing for insulation?' Ellie asked, deftly ignoring Olivia's concerns.

'Right now, I have no plan regarding insulation. I'll just have to suck up the cold for the next winter. Anyway, my budget doesn't extend to insulation nor the replacement of rattling, wooden windows at the moment,' Olivia replied.

'My dad is big into eco-friendly stuff. He insulated our attic a few years ago with sheeps' wool and he's very happy with it. The house is warmer. He has bag loads left over as he bought it for a song from the local farmers. I could ask him if you like. It would be in keeping with your whole traditional and recycling theme. You'd be doing my mum a favour as it's cluttering up the garage this past year. Would you be interested?' Ellie enquired expectantly.

'I'd be more than interested. Natural wool sounds fantastic. I won't lie, the prospect of a cosy home appeals, but I don't want to impose on your family. I don't even know if they'll be happy about you working up here with me,' Olivia said, overwhelmed at Ellie's knowledge and thoughtfulness.

'Don't worry about that. I'll sort it out with them. Restoring your cottage is the only option remotely related to architecture in this area and I can be very persuasive. I'll see you tomorrow around half nine,' Ellie smiled assuredly, giving a jaunty wave as she turned on her heel.

That was the most impressive example of assertiveness I have seen in a while, Olivia thought. That girl could give lessons on confidence building and self-esteem. Good on you Ellie!

# Chapter 23

'Hi, just catching up with all the news. How's the renovations going,' Angie asked, checking in with her sister on Facetime for their weekly catch-up.

'Everything is going very well. The boys are having a great time on their school tour. I've got two Transition Year students helping me and they're working out great. They're doing wonders with the painting and sanding. Jack has gotten very handy using the drill. Ellie is big into architecture and is a mine of information about natural insulation materials. Would you believe she got bags of sheep's wool for me for the three attics? After a quick sewing tutorial, she's a whizz on the sewing machine. They're two quick learners. This is only their first week with me and they're flying through the work,' Olivia gushed in admiration of her two assistants.

'They certainly don't sound like the usual stroppy, gobby, fairly useless teenagers you usually hear about nowadays,' Angie replied, surprisingly impressed at Olivia's description of her teenage assistants.

'I'd have thought the same, but I must admit they're great. We had a few hiccups at the beginning, but now they're brilliant and everything's working out great. I couldn't ask for better. The carpentry and electrical work is almost finished in the three cottages. Conor and Mark have been brilliant. I've survived the first week in my job and everything's going well. We're having our weekly card game tonight and I'm looking forward to it. That's enough about me. Any news with you?' Olivia asked.

'Not a lot. I'm beginning to think I'm having a very dull life compared to you. Myself and Stefan are heading to Paris on Friday for a few days. He's planning to visit his parents and sister and pushing me to meet them. I'm not that keen about the whole family visit thing as this will be my first time meeting them. Stefan has asked me a few times already, so I'd better bite the bullet and go for it.'

'But you've been going out together for two years and you haven't met his family yet? I certainly don't blame Stefan for pushing the subject?' Olivia exclaimed, surprised at her sister's hesitancy.

'I don't see the need to. I like to keep things uncomplicated and avoid family connections. After all, I'm going out with Stefan. I don't need his family's approval,' Angie huffed. 'And, aren't you suddenly the modern forward-thinking sister? Abandoned the husband only a few weeks ago and you have become a new woman. I can't believe how confident and assertive you've become in such a short time! Maybe I'll take your advice on board, little sister, and see how it goes,' Angie laughed agreeably.

Olivia had really found her voice over the last few weeks. She seemed to be well and truly finding her old self again, Angie thought happily.

'You and Stefan seem to get on great. C'mon, go on and indulge him. Meet his family. You never know, you might have a great time. Remember, you've already introduced me to him, so you've got to have a bit of give and take,' Olivia cajoled, eager to encourage her sister.

Olivia knew Angie liked to strike the persona of a liberated woman with no ties, but when Olivia saw her sister and her boyfriend together, she knew they had a special bond and was determined her sister's stubborn principles wouldn't jeopardise it.

'Okay, I'll give him the good news tonight at dinner and put him out of his misery. I'm going to have to let you go. I have an hour to get showered before my date. Trust me, this beautifying takes so much longer in your mid-forties. Enjoy your card game and I'll let you know how the family meeting goes,' Angie laughed as she said goodbye to Olivia.

Olivia glanced at the clock. It was coming up to a quarter to eight. The gang should be here in the next ten minutes. She looked appreciatively at the transformations that had occurred in the past week. She was thrilled with her two new apprentices. They couldn't have worked out better. It was the beginning of November and Olivia was thrilled with the work progress. The three cottages were almost completely renovated in just over six weeks on a rock-bottom budget. She was overwhelmed with the support from her new friends and included Ellie and Jack in that group.

True to Ellie's word, she returned the next morning having charmed her parents into agreeing to her work placement. Her father dropped her off and after a tour around the cottages and discussing the renovations completed to date, Mr. McKeown reassured Olivia she was welcome to the remaining bags of sheep wool. He was a great advocate for the use of natural materials and suggested using a lime whitewash on the exterior walls. He told her lime was a natural antifungal product traditionally used to whitewash houses in Ireland years ago. The other advantage was it cost a pittance compared to the cost of exterior paint. Another bonus for Olivia's budget.

Having given her instructions on how to lay the insulation and make up the whitewash, he told her the bags of wool were ready for her to collect any evening that suited. Olivia smiled, remembering Ellie's father's enthusiasm about the renovations. He had been engrossed and Olivia told him to feel free to drop in any time to check on their progress.

Back to the present she reminded herself, as the gang would be rambling into her soon. Olivia put two of Sheila's homemade apple tarts on the stovetop. They'd be nicely warmed when the gang arrived. She filled up the kettle and clicked it on. It was a cold evening and she knew a few hot toddies would go down a treat with the group. Olivia set the table with her array of charity shop delph and glassware, setting the bottle of Paddy whiskey amongst them.

Finally, everything was in place. She did a quick once over on her surroundings. The stove door was open, flames burning brightly, the skirting boards and architrave were gleaming in their new coat of white gloss and Olivia beamed as she looked at her new colour-washed walls.

She had painted the whole living/dining room walls in brilliant white a few weeks before, but over the last week, she felt the colour was a little stark for the cottage. Last night on a whim she experimented with the very palest dove-grey, rag-roll on a corner of the room. She'd been bowled over by the instant depth and atmosphere it gave to the previously glaring white walls. Before she realised it, she had the four walls done and dusted within two hours. Even better, she had used less than two tablespoons of paint on the whole job.

This morning, she had been a bit cautious examining it, concerned the look might not be quite so wonderful in daylight. It looked even better with sunshine streaming in. She felt it flattered her cream and grey-painted dresser perfectly. The overall look complimented her understated cream blinds and simple sofas, scattered with comfortable throws accentuated with cushions recycled from discarded woollen jumpers and cardigans in varying Fair Isle patterns and colours.

Olivia couldn't be happier. She loved the look. More than that, she thrived on the pleasure of being able to make every decision without the input of Tom and Betty. Life was good she thought, as knocking on the door signalled the first of her visitors for the evening.

# Chapter 24

Olivia tried again to settle at her desk without success. There was something amiss with Paddy this morning. She had only worked with him for seven weeks but already felt she knew him inside out. He was a creature of habit. First thing every day she made tea which he liked to start the day with, followed by plenty more tea for the rest of the day. He'd have his morning chit-chat for ten minutes, then settle in his office and spend the morning on the phone, until she brought in another mug at eleven o'clock with two digestive chocolate biscuits. Afterwards, he always left the office to do viewings or check on rental properties. But today, there was undoubtedly something wrong.

He was shuffling in and out, anxiously glancing at his phone and mumbling to himself. Despite Olivia asking him if everything was okay, he just grunted in reply, 'Yeah, it is,' but everything about his behaviour suggested otherwise. It was twenty minutes to eleven. Time for a cuppa. The kettle boiled and Olivia made two mugs of tea, heaping two generous spoons of sugar into Paddy's one. He needed extra sweetening today she thought, placing a few extra biscuits on the plate.

'Teatime,' Olivia called, scanning Paddy's desk for a spare corner.

He was hunched over his desk studying dog-eared property brochures. Glancing at his troubled face she carefully pushed aside some paperwork, putting his cup in front of him.

Paddy raised his mug dejectedly, slurped deeply and placed the mug heavily on his paperwork. He was completely indifferent to tea dribbles sliding onto the tired brochures, before rising again to do another march of woe around the desk.

'What's the problem? You've been pacing all morning. Tell me what's on your mind. Should I be worried? Am I getting the sack?' Olivia enquired, anxious to get to the crux of the problem quickly as she stood hesitantly, mug in hand.

'It's nothing like that. You're doing a great job,' Paddy assured her, shaking his head.

'That's a relief. I thought I was in trouble. What's up then?' Olivia enquired, relieved her job was safe, yet eager to see her boss's easy manner restored.

Paddy picked up brochures from his desk, passing them to Olivia.

'It's these two bloody cottages. They've been on the books for over a year. They're both in bad shape and there's been no interest or viewings on them for months. Wasn't I out playing a bit of golf yesterday with Johnny Callan who owns one of the properties. He never stopped going on about the cottage, giving out like hell that it's still not sold. He ruined my day to be sure and then to make things even worse, I was only settled last night after my dinner and Charlie Beirne rang from Dublin.'

Eager to offload his woes after Olivia's encouraging enquiry, Paddy continued.

'He owns the other place. I had to spend another full hour listening to him blathering on. He finished the call by saying he'd phone today to get an update on my 'new marketing strategy' as he put it. Between the two of them, they ruined a good day for me,' Paddy exclaimed.

Olivia pulled a chair and sat down at Paddy's desk to study the two offending brochures, admiring the photos on the front of both. She continued to read the descriptions, turning to Paddy with a puzzled expression.

'I can't see how there's a problem with selling either of these. The photos look good. The cottages are just like my own. According to the descriptions, 'A perfect hideaway, with rustic appeal set in beautiful rural surroundings,' they sound lovely.' Olivia looked at Paddy enquiringly.

'You know by now how these flowery descriptions work. The real description should read, 'A completely dilapidated cottage in the arsehole of nowhere,' but that doesn't get the punters in,' Paddy said dejectedly, scowling over Olivia's shoulder at the offending brochures.

'Your description sounds a bit brutal. Surely they can't be that bad?' Olivia asked, blinking in shock at Paddy's outburst.

'Sorry, I'm just fed up hearing about them. Those pictures were taken months ago. They went on the market around the beginning of September last year. The gardens were tidied so both places looked presentable on the outside. They were both in a rough and ready state inside. I was up there a month ago and think one of them has a leak. When they first went on the market they had a few viewings within the first couple of weeks, with definite interest from three buyers. But by the time they came back for a second viewing six weeks later, the briars and nettles had taken over the gardens again. Once you opened the door, the smell of damp and cold soon wiped out any trace of rustic appeal,' Paddy blurted.

Turning away from Olivia, he plodded back to his desk, slumping despondently in his chair.

'What's your plan if the owner is ringing back today?' Olivia enquired.

'That's just it. There isn't a bloody plan. Unless you can come up with a miracle and transform those cottages into something half decent,' Paddy sighed, drumming his knuckles on the desk.

'Let me think. I could have a look and give my opinion. Sometimes a fresh pair of eyes may spot some hidden potential. In the meantime, you could take the bull by the horns and phone them back this morning. Say you're visiting the properties today and you'll report back with your findings later this week. At least phoning them this morning will put you out of misery and you'll be taking control of the situation. What do you think?' Olivia suggested, hoping to offer some ray of hope.

'That sounds like a good plan we've come up with. I'll be able to get a bit of breathing space and stall the pair of them for a few days. You get up there this morning. You know where the keys are hanging up. Don't forget to bring your wellies! It's probably like a swamp with all the rain the last few days. We're a good team without a doubt,' Paddy cried jumping from his chair, a broad smile of relief lighting up his face as he clapped his hands together.

'Great. I'll get going right away,' Olivia laughed.

Happy Paddy's mood was returning to some normality and eager to keep it that way, Olivia grabbed her coat and wellies, plastic gloves, keys, and brochures and made her way to her car. She entered the property's Eircode and thanks to the wonders of sat nav, arrived at the first property in ten minutes. Donning her plastic gloves, she entered the small, rusty gate noting its peeling yellow paint. Pulling back the reluctant bolt, it eventually screeched back, its metal railings scoring the moss covered footpath on its way.

Olivia studied the property brochure again, comparing it to the house before her. The main brochure photo presented a tidy, freshly painted. white country cottage, with a red front door and windows. The gardens to the front were cut and tidy. The other photo displayed an inviting back garden with apple trees. Olivia repeatedly glanced from the photos to the sight before her now, reassuring herself she was indeed outside the right house because the present view was far removed from the images in the brochure. Having finally wrestled the front gate wide open, she entered under the wildly overgrown, rose archway, pushing an errant branch's tentacles away from her face and cautiously made her way up the short pathway. She dodged overgrown briars snaking treacherously around her ankles, skidding on the spongy moss along the way.

Despite the mildew-streaked exterior, on closer inspection she was glad to see the paintwork still looked good on the walls and windows. Feeling optimistic, she turned the key to the front door. It opened freely and feeling more confident, Olivia let herself in, eager to see the interior. She stopped in her tracks instantly, her senses assaulted by the smell of dampness and dirt, blinking in the unaccustomed dismal lighting. Fumbling around in the hallway, she finally found the light switch and clicked it on, while scanning all before her. Going into the sitting room, she was astounded to find there was hardly a square inch of floor space to move. Despite the additional brightness of the hallway and the sitting room lights, Olivia still struggled to see properly. The curtains were drawn, so she went to the windows to let in the daylight.

Tugging gently on the reluctant fabric, she was startled when the smoke-stained curtains gave way, ripping in her hand. Paddy had warned her a bachelor lived here all his life. His only companions were his two cats and the house probably needed a bit of tidying. Olivia was shocked to see how bad it was. Everything about the property suggested a sad, lonely life. Newspapers covered the floor, with clusters of cats' droppings and books piled up on every surface. The paperbacks were now the sole inhabitants of the crowded three-piece suite. Even the window ledges were stacked with books against the tattered net curtains, completely blocking out any vestige of outside life.

Olivia sighed as she took it all in, the once flowery, 50s curtains and the dusky pink walls suggested an era where time had stood still for this poor man. She carefully made her way into the back of the house where a kitchen and bathroom extension had been added. The soaked bathroom floor was an immediate eyesore. After investigation, it was apparent to Olivia the cylinder in the hot press had sprung a leak accounting for the streaming and mildew-stained walls. Again, the newspaper covered floors and dropping's theme continued. Olivia smiled as she opened the kitchen cupboard and counted fifteen cans of peas and beans. The man obviously felt you could never have enough of them.

She lifted out one rust-crusted can, noting it was ten years out of date. Returning it to the shelf, she closed the mustard melamine door slowly. The kitchen wasn't in too bad of condition. It was dirty and untidy but didn't look as though it had got a lot of use - probably a lot of beans, or peas, on toast over the years. The cabinets were all back in vogue again and might be exactly what a young trendy buyer would love. Taking her notebook and pen from her bag, Olivia began making notes, videoing each room on her phone as she walked through the house. She made her way into the first two bedrooms where the same book and newspaper floors continued until she reached the main bedroom which was kept surprisingly tidy.

The double bed was covered in a perfectly draped pale blue, candlewick bedspread. Instantly recognisable Foxford woollen blue, striped blankets were peeping out underneath. The numerous empty Rennie's packets on the bedside locker suggested they were a regular nighttime companion for the owner. The bedroom walls were painted a soft cream, now freckled in the corners with pervading mildew. The wall facing the bed was completely adorned with family-framed photos. Judging by the frames and yellow speckling on the photos, Olivia guessed they were taken a long time ago, maybe in the 70s and 80s. Many of the frames held the same family group, a couple, with a boy at various stages of growing up.

There was one with a toddler in a Silver Cross pram, grinning at the camera. A First Holy Communion and Confirmation one, together with a scattering of other larger family occasions. Olivia surmised this wall of memories must have represented the man's whole life. Sighing, she studied the collage.

Paddy mentioned the man was an only child and remained single all his life. He had been born, grown up and died in the very same cottage.

She hoped he had a happy childhood and took pleasure in reminiscing over his life as he nodded off to sleep every night. Returning to the front door, mindful to dodge the cat droppings on the way, she finished her notes.

# Chapter 25

After a short drive, Olivia arrived at the second cottage. It was typical in style to the previous one but had the addition of a PVC double-glazed, door and windows. The front gardens were in good condition, not overgrown and no evidence of wild brambles, thank God. The grass was overgrown, but otherwise it looked promising so far. Greatly encouraged, Olivia turned the key and pushed the door open, leading into the front porch. Feeling resistance, she gave it another shove. She pushed harder, finally squeezing through the limited opening, puzzled by the obstruction before letting herself inside.

Instantly, the mystery was solved as she studied the overstuffed bin bags crowding the space that had spilt over, before finally landing in a drunken pile against the front door. Inching her way past them, Olivia turned into the sitting room, the smell of damp clinging in the air. Again, there was evidence of a haphazard attempt at packing. Half-packed black sacks appeared to have been abandoned mid-way through the job. Olivia surveyed the room, immediately struck by the differences between this cottage and the last one, noting the pretty chintz curtains matching the mauve pink, faded velour three-piece.

The willow basket beside the stove was heaving with multicoloured balls of wool, knitting needles and patterns poking out the top.

The shelf over the stove was laden with a motley collection of porcelain cats, black, white and even a ginger one, all sporting varying expressions, smiling and shy. Finally, a black, tall sleek one that looked downright menacing. This owner obviously had a wicked sense of humour. Stepping through the obstacle course of black sacks, she went to the back of the house leading to an extension containing the kitchen area and bathroom. Immediately, Olivia was met with a puddle of water and one streaming wall, displaying varying shades of mottled mildew. Noticing it was the wall adjacent to the original house that had the problem, she took some notes for Paddy's opinion.

Poking around, Olivia noted the cream kitchen cupboards and matching table, and chairs were still in good condition, so this leak was relatively new. The background sound of a humming fridge and ticking clock gave an air of domestic contentment, despite the leak, cold, and general untidiness of the house. The overall impression was the owner had spent many a happy day here. She made her way into the bedrooms and bathroom and again was met by well maintained, cosy rooms that needed major decluttering but were otherwise perfect. After jotting her notes and taking photos and videos, Olivia entered the garden.

The grass was overgrown and had the company of a few snaking, treacherous briars wielding their way around the shrubs and trees, but otherwise, it was a simple lawn framed with some lovely mature fruit trees and flowering shrubs. Nothing too major. A few hours of work with secateurs and cutting the grass should make a world of difference. One of the trees had a couple of broken branches. After investigating, Olivia came upon two broken roof tiles amid the overgrown back garden. The leaking roof mystery was solved and with her notebook updated, Olivia locked up and returned to the office to update Paddy on her findings.

Later, she was about to sit down and have her afternoon cuppa at half past three when the office door was pushed open.

'How did you get on? Tell me the worst. What did you make of them?' Paddy asked, trundling in with his briefcase and a handful of property brochures he offloaded in a messy pile onto her desk.

'Not too bad! I took plenty of notes and recorded the lot on my phone. I've drawn up a plan of works for the cottages because in their present condition, they're neither fit nor safe to show prospective buyers. First things first! Sit down and I'll bring you a cuppa,' Olivia suggested.

'Right, that's the job, A good mug of tea and a chocolate biscuit will sort me. I'm worn out. I got caught twice today in that bloody rain and I'm not the better of it,' Paddy grumbled, flapping the lapels of his brown, well-worn raincoat, spraying droplets in all directions on his way to the office.

Setting a steaming mug of tea and inviting plate of chocolate digestives before him, Paddy tucked in. Olivia discreetly picked his soggy weather-beaten raincoat off the floor, draping it over the radiator. Paddy munched away, oblivious to all around him. Within minutes, the magic in the mug had once again restored Paddy's easy manner.

'Show me your worst,' Paddy asked as Olivia joined him, showing the video on her phone.

'I'll start with the bachelor pad. As you can see, firstly the front garden and pathway will have to be cleared, or you'll never get any potential customers through the front door. There's serious rubbish with newspapers and cat droppings. Finally, we move to the bathroom where the crux of the problem is. There's a leak in the hot water cylinder in the hot press causing water damage and mildew on the walls,' Olivia said, zooming in on the photos.

'You're right. I think the cylinder has acted up. It's made an almighty mess,' Paddy mumbled, rubbing his chin speculatively as he played the video again. 'Give me a look at the other one. It shouldn't be as bad,' he enquired expectantly.

'It's better than the first one and again completely stuffed with black bags of rubbish, with a leak in the kitchen extension. I found roof tiles in the back garden. There might be some problem with the roof flashing, but I don't think it should take too much work.'

'What you're saying is, they're worse than I thought,' Paddy whined, throwing his arms in the air convinced he'd never offload the cursed cottages. They'd prove to be the death of him.

'I wouldn't say that. A few days' work in both places tidying and fixing the leaks should probably do the job. Do you use a local property maintenance company for your clients or how do you sort these problems?' Olivia enquired, glancing at Paddy.

Paddy blinked in confusion, staring at Olivia. 'A property maintenance company! You're joking, aren't you? I'll have a job and a half getting my fee for advertising and covering my costs on those two houses. All the diesel I've wasted showing them two places off, I'll never see a red cent of it back. Never mind asking them to pay thousands for maintenance costs. You're not in London now,' Paddy blustered, annoyed at such foolish suggestions.

'You do want to sell these properties, don't you? They need urgent repair work, or they'll end up completely flooded and worthless. I've been doing up my three cottages. I had to get repairs done to roofs, heating systems, flooring and lot. I do know what I'm talking about. I use a neighbour who is fantastic and very reasonable. I can ask him for a quote this evening for the water leaks for both cottages. The other work is just a matter of cutting the briars and packing up all the rubbish. When both cottages are tidied up, I'm sure we can make them presentable and set up weekend viewings. I'm confident they should get their asking price, if not even a bit more,' Olivia pitched confidently.

'I suppose it's worth a shot. Get a price from your man this evening. I don't want to be up there tidying other people's rubbish. I don't have time for that carry-on,' Paddy moaned petulantly.

'I can sort that out myself. I know two Transition Year students who might be interested in making a few euros, so don't worry about that. Hopefully, in the next few days I'll have the costs for the repairs, together with a price for cleaning and tidying. When you make calls to your clients you'll have facts and figures lined up. Send the videos of their current state of repair, so they can see for themselves how bad a state they're in. I don't think you'll have much trouble convincing them to cough up. You did say they're both eager to sell,' Olivia smiled, confident she had an answer to Paddy's many expected objections.

'I know you're right. If we leave those cottages as they are, they'll be flooded and derelict before the year is out and I'll be the worst in the world for not telling the owners,' Paddy conceded dejectedly, examining the video footage again.

'Good! I'll get the ball rolling and phone my repair man straight away to see if there's any chance he could have a look at the cottages this evening,' Olivia reiterated, gathering Paddy's mug and empty plate on her way out, relieved she finally had a plan.

'Perfect! That's the job. We've made a good start on it. You know what? I think with all my experience I could make a very decent saleswoman out of you. I'll be off. See you in the morning,' Paddy laughed, jumping up and gracing Olivia with a broad grin before rescuing his toasted raincoat from the radiator.

Shrugging his bulk into its snug interior, he swaggered towards the door, banging it firmly shut on his way out.

Now Paddy was on board, Olivia decided there was no time to delay.

'Hi, Mark, Olivia here. Just a quick call. Sorry for bothering you. Can you do me another big favour?' she asked cautiously.

'How's it going? No problem at all. Great to hear from you anytime. What can I do for you?' Mark replied, eager to reassure Olivia. He had gauged by now his new neighbour was very independent and hesitant to ask for help.

Relaxed by Mark's affable manner, Olivia filled him in on the condition of the two cottages, asking if he could have a look at them as soon as possible. She told him she needed a quotation for making them watertight and safe enough for prospective buyers to view, without falling through the floor or exposed to an unwanted shower.

'I think I can manage a price to make them safe and watertight. They're only up the road. I'll make sure to sort them out for you.'

'Thanks a million, Mark. I appreciate it. Hopefully, they won't cost a bomb to fix and Paddy will finally be able to offload them from his books. Those cottages are playing havoc with his blood pressure these days. If they remain on the books another six months I'm sure they'll play havoc with mine too, listening to Paddy's daily ranting,' Olivia laughed companionably with Mark. 'I'll bring the keys home this evening and property brochures. I can show you the interior photos to give you an idea of their current condition. I'll be home around six. Thanks again. I appreciate it,' Olivia expressed.

'No worries at all. To save blood pressure problems all around, I'll have a look at them as quick as I can,' Mark chortled, ending the call. A broad smile spread across his face, delighted to have an unexpected reason to call into his gorgeous neighbour.

Hanging up, Olivia put property brochures and keys into her bag and set off for home. Mark agreed to call at both cottages first thing the next morning and have quotations to her before eleven o'clock. Olivia sighed with pleasure. He was such a lovely lad in every way, easy on the eye too and always so obliging. She'd pick up a bottle of wine on the way home and share a glass with him later.

# Chapter 26

Just after six, Olivia turned the key in her front door, taking her shopping inside. Putting the Chardonnay in the fridge, she unpacked her groceries, hit the heating button and the boiler rushed into action. She had bought fresh pasta and reduced price smoked salmon and prawns, intending to rustle up a quick dinner. Sautéing leeks and garlic, she added white sauce and a dollop of fresh cream. The pasta was simmering gently and Olivia added flaked salmon and prawns to the sauce and finally, linguine to the mix. Ten minutes later, dinner was ready. Just as she was about to tuck in, the doorbell rang.

'Mark, come in. I'm about to have dinner. Nothing fussy - smoked salmon with pasta. There's plenty for two,' Olivia offered, ushering Mark out of the cold.

'Are you sure? I don't want to bother you, but dinner smells great,' Mark answered, delighted to be in her company.

'Of course! I'd be delighted. Sit down and throw your coat over the couch. The heating is on, so it should be warm in a few minutes as I've just stoked up the stove as well,' Olivia said, going to the kitchen to serve dinner.

Minutes later, Olivia placed two pasta bowls on the table. Returning to the kitchen, she retrieved the chilled wine and corkscrew and sat next to Mark.

'You're spoiling me! A fancy dinner and wine on a Tuesday evening. Are you trying to seduce me?' Mark joked, his brown eyes twinkling.

'Sorry, is it a bit much? I wanted to say thank you for obliging me by doing those quotations,' Olivia blustered, a hot flush of embarrassment chasing across her cheeks.

'Not at all! I'm not complaining about being wined and dined. You're more than welcome. You have been feeding me every week since you arrived here. I owe you one, not the other way around,' he added, anxious to ease Olivia's obvious discomfort. He reminded himself flirting didn't come easy to her. She had been married since twenty, so he'd better take things easy.

'Getting back to the cottages, you already know the score. Both owners will only want to spend the minimum on repairs. I have photos and videos,' Olivia said, passing over the brochures and phone.

Mark glanced at the brochures before taking up the phone. Slowly scrutinising the photos, he studied them intently, enlarging ones with the damaged hot press, cylinder and leaking ceiling.

'You have some good photos. I know those cottages well; they're only a few minutes drive up the road. I have a ladder in the back of the van, so I'll be able to check out the roof too. I'll write up a quotation and have it in by half ten tomorrow. I know how much this job means and I know Paddy's ways by now,' Mark reassured, patting her hand.

'Thanks, Mark. I didn't realise I was fussing that much. This job means a lot to me and if I have to keep Paddy sweet, so be it,' Olivia sighed.

'Drink up! You never know, Paddy might be open to giving me a bit of regular maintenance work if this goes well tomorrow. He has quite a few rentals on his books I think?' Mark smiled, raising his glass towards Olivia.

'You're right. He does have a few rentals and a big number he owns himself. So absolutely, if the price is right he may well be open to some ongoing work. Cheers to the future,' Olivia grinned, reaching across and clinking Mark's glass.

'Cheers, to a long and happy future,' Mark murmured, holding Olivia's gaze.

'Now we have that sorted, start your dinner and enjoy before it goes cold,' Olivia stammered, not sure how to peel her eyes away from her neighbour's gorgeous, brown eyes.

She was aware she sounded like a clucking hen but didn't have a clue how to respond in this situation. Jump on him as her instincts told her, or behave in a respectful, neighbourly way by stuffing him with food, stalling any possibility of awkward conversation?

'With pleasure,' Mark replied, grasping his fork eagerly in response to rumbling hunger pangs .

Olivia surreptitiously glanced at her dinner companion, amused at the intensity and speed his fork worked across the plate. Olivia grinned. Her plan had worked. All conversation stopped and his full concentration was focused on the task at hand. Olivia, flattered by his enthusiastic appetite, took up her fork and returned to her meal.

# Chapter 27

Angie's number came up on her phone at eight o'clock on Friday evening. Olivia smiled in anticipation of her weekly Facetime chat with her sister

'Well, how are you? You survived meeting Stefan's family?' Olivia asked.

'They were so nice. His family were very polite. No personal questions. No one asking about our intentions. No mention of weddings or anything dodgy like that,' Angie laughed in relief.

'I was about to ask if a date was set for the big day?' Olivia joked, riling her sister.

'Oh, please! You're too provincial and Irish, Dear. We're living in the $21^{st}$- century now; fortunately, the days of being obliged to marry are well and truly over.'

'Okay, I'm only joking. I'm the last person in the world to preach about marriage with mine being well and truly over,' Olivia added; eager to reassure Angie she wasn't questioning her rigid views on matrimony.

'Sorry, I was getting a bit tetchy. Let me start again. We had a lovely time with his parents and sister. So much so, we hope to make a monthly visit from now on. I'm conscious his parents are in their eighties. Stefan was so grateful to me for going on this trip. I'm sorry I didn't agree to go before. They're lovely people,' Angie acknowledged. 'Enough about me! How's the job going with Paddy? You didn't get sacked yet?' Angie jibed.

'No, I've been there six weeks and I'm a 'topper' according to Paddy. He's right. I'm a painter, cleaner, decorator, interior designer and executive administrator. To top it all, also a daily counsellor to my boss. It took a while to get used to his ways. I'm sure he felt the same about me. I think we've settled into a comfortable working relationship. Probably because sales are moving and he's getting up to date on everything, he's more relaxed now, thank God,' Olivia laughed, thinking back to her first week on the job and Paddy's constant coat-flapping episodes.

'Great! You've made yourself indispensable - a smart move. I like your style,' Angie surmised, delighted to see her little sister's confidence and enthusiasm from her twenties finally restored.

She had been worried Tom's controlling ways during their marriage and final rejection would destroy Olivia, but no, she was stronger and more capable than ever.

'How's the cottages coming on? Have you had any more

jaunts around the place?'

'I'm doing surprisingly well. Mark and Conor have been great. Electric showers have been installed in all three cottages. The attics have been insulated with sheep's wool. I got a great bargain on two second-hand stoves with back boilers and a complete kitchen - cupboards, doors, worktop and appliances. I got the whole lot on Done Deal. There were enough kitchen units for all cottages. Mark and Conor have done all the plumbing and carpentry work. Now I have a job, I can afford to pay them and it feels great. I'll send you some photos. I think you'll be impressed,' Olivia replied.

She was thrilled at regaling Angie with stories of her bargains.

'Before I forget, I had to go to Strokestown last week to get photos for a rental property he's taking on. I had a few hours to spare so visited Strokestown House and Gardens. The sun was shining and it was magical. I did a tour of the house and famine museum. It was riveting, with many interesting facts and details. It even has a collection of original letters from tenants during the famine. There's an audio-visual tour explaining the tenant's experience of hunger, eviction and exile through assisted migration and the landlord's perspective. It's so interesting and transports you back in time.'

Olivia continued detailing her recent visit, her sister listening spellbound from France.

'The house itself is a fabulous 18th-century mansion retaining its original furnishings. The guided tour of the house allows you to experience Georgian Ireland first-hand, the grand rooms of the gentry and servants' quarters, including the workings of the kitchens. After the House and Famine Museum, there are the wonderful six-acre Georgian walled gardens to wander through. When you enter the garden and open that green arched door in the stone wall, it's like entering a gardener's paradise. There is an array of formal pleasure gardens, the summer house, the croquet lawn, Victorian rose gardens, fruit and vegetable gardens, the lily pond, the long flower-filled herbaceous borders and wonderful woodland trails. It was magical, tranquil and so beautiful. I could have happily spent days there.'

'So, you are getting around and visiting the old haunts from years ago?' Angie said, reminiscing fondly on the good times.

'Yes. And before I forget. I visited Roscommon town last week. Sheila needed a pair of shoes and the only place she'd buy them was in a particular shoe shop on Main Street. We had a great day there. It has a lovely main street dotted with a great choice of restaurants, coffee shops and some lovely gift shops. It's a nice compact town with fancy hotels and everything within walking distance. At the entrance of the town is a beautifully landscaped Market Square. Opposite is the old gaol, an impressive stone building dating back to the 18th- century which housed Lady Betty, Ireland's only hangwoman. Scary eh? There's a gorgeous park tucked directly at the rear of the jail, Loughnaneane Park, meaning 'Lake of the birds'. The lake is home to many native species and has lots of interesting sculptures along the trails. There are the ruins of Roscommon Castle in the park also - an Anglo-Norman Castle dating back to the 13th century. It has fabulous, mullioned windows and fireplaces still in place and access to a viewing tower. You'd love the town, Angie. It's small enough to be homely, yet has everything you'll ever need,' Olivia added.

'You seem to be impressed with it!'

'I was! I'll be adding Strokestown, Rathcroghan and Roscommon to my Visitor Information Pack when I'm up and going with my rental accommodation in the spring. They're all accessible from Boyle on the Local Link bus service.'

'I don't think I need to ask if you're missing home. You seem to have carved out a new life for yourself already. I'm slightly jealous, to be honest.'

'I'm shocked at how quickly I've settled in. I'm loving my new life. I think Tom leaving me in the lurch was the best wakeup call I've got in years. It forced me down here on a whim. If I'm being honest, I thought I'd calm down after a few days and be happy to return to the *status quo*. But I've found an energy and drive I thought were long gone. And it's all thanks to the support of a lovely bunch of people around me. The best neighbours and friends you'd ever meet,' Olivia explained.

'I think you're truly an adopted Rossie already. I'm delighted for you. I might surprise you one of these days and go over for a weekend and see this good life for myself,' Angie retorted, delighted to hear Olivia happily tell her stories.

Angie had feared her sister's previous experiences of life with Tom and Betty might have quashed Olivia's spirit forever.

'You're more than welcome any time. I have the spare room all spruced up. It wouldn't get a four-star rating and it's not a patch on Kildare, but it's snug and comfortable,' Olivia babbled, excited at the prospect of a visit.

'I will make a few plans. On that note, I've got to go. I'm meeting Stefan in half an hour. Keep up the good work, Sis. I'll chat to you next week.' Angie smiled and blew her sister a kiss, finishing their Facetime call.

# Chapter 28

'Morning Olivia, your quotations as requested by the boss,' Mark said, entering the office waving his paperwork and placing it with a flourish before Olivia on her desk.

'Thank you. I'm impressed with your super efficiency,' Olivia smiled. 'Paddy will be happy with your eagerness. He's out now, but I'll look to see what the damage will be. I'll get us a cuppa first. Pull up a chair,' Olivia added, clicking the kettle to life. Returning five minutes later, tray laden with mugs and biscuits, she sat beside Mark, passing the mug across the table to him.

'Cheers! I have completed two quotations for the cottage with the leaking cylinder. Firstly, the good news is the water was fortunately turned off at the mains, so even though the cylinder had completely emptied, the water damage wasn't too bad and limited to the bathroom only. I noticed the cylinder had leaked from the seam on the top. The copper had corroded. I could weld it up in situ and it probably would be fine, but I can't guarantee it won't leak again as there's every chance it's between twenty and thirty years old. But it's not in bad condition. I think you could get a few more years out of it.

Sixty euros should cover materials and labour.' Mark placed the quotations on the desk. 'The second quote I've given is for €250. That covers the removal of the old cylinder and replacing it with a new cylinder and fittings. They should cost about €150 with another €100 for labour.' Mark pointed out the various items in the two quotations to Olivia.

'That sounds reasonable. What about the other cottage?' Olivia enquired, studying the figures while passing another biscuit to Mark.

'The problem is the extension roof. It's just where the flashing on the extension roof joins the wall of the main house. The flashing is completely lifted. Some ridge tiles are missing and there's no option but to remove and replace the damaged flashing and put the tiles back on. Some felt may need replacing, but I won't know until I start working on it. Afterwards, when the heat is left on for a few days, it won't take long to dry out and then the ceiling can be replastered and repainted. The roof work should come to about €150 to €200 to cover materials and labour.'

'All the leaking and water damage could have been sorted out easily by fixing a couple of roof tiles?' Olivia asked, shaking her head in dismay.

'Exactly. A bit of early intervention in both houses could have saved a lot of damp and hard work down the road,' Mark agreed, casting a further desultory glance at the house photos.

'Those costs sound reasonable, but most important, when can you start? Paddy needs to have all the answers today when he rings the owners,' Olivia asked, eager to have replies to Paddy's anticipated questions.

'I'm working on an extension outside Boyle for another couple of weeks, but don't worry, I can slot those jobs in as they're small. I'd have them both finished in a couple of days. Just let me know what Paddy decides,' Mark said, raising his mug and draining the tea before standing up.

'I'll pass the good news to Paddy and thanks again. It's all appreciated,' Olivia replied.

'No bother at all. I'm heading out to play pool and have a pint with Conor this evening. I'll drop into you later to get Paddy's instructions,' Mark added on his way out.

'Enjoy your pint with Conor. You're welcome to drop in any time, but I can't guarantee I'll have Paddy's decision by this evening. No doubt he'll have to mull over the figures for a while and wait for a response from the two sellers. But you never know, seeing as he's so anxious to offload the cottages, I could very well be proven wrong this time,' Olivia stated, as Mark lingered at the doorway.

'I might drop into you on my way home, just in case,' Mark grinned, closing the door after him.

Olivia smiled in reply, flattered by Mark's kindness. He was so handsome too. She gave herself a mental shake to stop daydreaming and focus on the job. Clapping her hands, she settled back into her chair and turned her attention to the screen. It would take all her attention to try and decipher another of Paddy's scrawled, flowery descriptions of their latest property on the books.

*Rose Cottage is a rustic three-bed traditional cottage set in a rural idyll amid a meadow of wildflowers and gardens overflowing with bramble roses. It has all the potential to become a rural piece of heaven.*

Olivia wondered if it was more like a briar-covered shack ten miles from civilisation in a field of thistles, dock leaves and flaggers. I really should rein in my cynical thoughts fast, she thought. Such a negative attitude isn't appropriate in the auctioneering business.

A few minutes after two o'clock, Paddy burst in, head down and still sporting his woebegone expression of the last few days. Trudging toward Olivia's desk, he dumped his well worn briefcase heavily on her desk, its leaden thud matching the footfall of its owner.

'Well, Olivia, any news back from that young fella yet? I'll bet he didn't even phone back?' Paddy huffed, shuffling his way to the office without waiting for an answer to his question.

'I'm happy to tell you you're wrong. He's already inspected both cottages and dropped in quotations first thing this morning,' Olivia answered, reaching for the paperwork and passing it to Paddy, who settled himself heavily onto his chair.

'Well, I'll be damned. That's a first with a builder in my lifetime,' he exclaimed, twisting impatiently in his chair, comfort evading him with every manoeuvre.

'I think you have to be a little open-minded in life. This time you might be pleasantly surprised,' Olivia encouraged, pushing the paperwork closer for his inspection.

'I'm trying to be open-minded, but hard experience has taught me to be otherwise. When you're at this game as long as me, you'll have met a quare number of cowboys by then,' Paddy grumbled, a long sigh of resignation escaping him.

Olivia nudged his glasses forward, eager for him to get on with reading the quotations and dispel the fog of despair threatening to smother them both.

Exhaling noisily, Paddy eased the glasses on and pulled the paperwork into view, lips pursed.

Olivia watched his expression change from blatant scepticism to blinding admiration, the transformation in mood bordering on a miracle.

'By God, this is a first for me. A proper detailed quotation and these prices aren't too bad either.'

Paddy lifted the quotation delicately as though handling a masterpiece.

'Yes, a punctual and reasonable price. Mark said he could repair both houses in a few days and to let him know as soon as possible so he can fit the work in with his other jobs.'

'Could he sort out the repairs in the next week or two? Do you think he's reliable? Not just full of fancy paperwork and nothing behind it?' Paddy enquired expectantly, his eyebrows suddenly furrowing as another wave of anxiety washed over his face.

'He's very reliable. He's the builder I've been using to do my work. I'm very pleased. He's got years of experience and is well-established in the area. You don't need to worry. He needs the go-ahead as soon as possible to have supplies ordered in advance. What do you think?' Olivia was baffled at Paddy repeating the same questions.

'I've been stung so many times over the years with builders. Firstly with them not turning up and when they eventually start the job, not sticking to the time frame. When the work is completed, rows over the final price, no written quotations … I could write a book on it. It's bad enough having these problems with my own property. Can you imagine the hassle I'd get from customers if I arrange a builder and these problems arise? At this stage in my life, I can't face any more aggravation. I'm way past all that craic by now.'

Paddy rose to his feet, scratching his head in contemplation. He didn't need any more headaches.

'I get it. You've had some tough experiences, but you must decide. Those cottages will fall eventually if you do nothing with them. The bonus this time is I know the builder well and don't think you'll be disappointed,' Olivia cajoled, eager to get past this stalemate situation.

'You're right! Go ahead with it. You can be the middleman, so to speak. Leave it with me for now and I'll get onto the owners straight away,' Paddy replied, pulling his trusted notebook from his brown sports jacket.

Leafing through its dog-eared pages, Paddy finally landed on the required targets. After rifling in the other inside pocket, he produced his mobile phone, punching in the number of the first owner.

'Johnny, how are you, my good friend? As promised, I have given another thorough inspection to your cottage and have a good proposition for you,' Paddy bellowed, leaning back in his chair, his confident and ebullient auctioneer persona quickly restored.

Olivia took her cue and closing Paddy's office door gently, returned to her desk. Paddy's belly laugh resounded in the background, his 'proposition' obviously going down well.

Ten minutes later, his door thrust open and Paddy made his way to Olivia's desk.

'All sorted! Give that young lad a shout straight away and we'll get the ball rolling. They're both happy enough with the quotes. To be honest with you, I think they're as anxious as me at this stage to get rid of those bloody houses and agreed to a bit of leeway in price. They're happy enough to pay a couple of hundred to cover the garden tidy up and gather the rubbish inside. But don't go mentioning the leeway back to our builder man – I want the best price we can get. I hope he's up to the job. I don't want to go back to the sellers again with another sob story,' Paddy mumbled, performing his daily battle at trying to get his coat on, never quite managing to control the ever escaping sleeves.

Olivia rose to his assistance, guiding his wayward arms to their rightful place before he shrugged the coat with a flourish onto his shoulders, buttoning it firmly in place.

'Mark's been working on property maintenance for nearly twelve years. He did great work for me with very limited materials at an excellent price, so I would say he's highly recommended.'

'Right, so! I'll trust you on this one. Will you sort out the tidying up? Get rid of everything that's in the cottages, clothes, personal belongings, the whole lot. You mentioned you'd be able to line up some help with those students?' Paddy enquired expectantly, a warm glow building at the thought of his tormentors being finally off his back.

'That's right. It's probably going to take a full day on each cottage for the three of us. €90 each per day for the students and €150 for myself. That doesn't cover the cost of disposing of the waste. I'll provide the petrol strimmer, electric branch cutter and cleaning materials. I'll put the old clothes in the recycling depot. We'll stack the waste in the shed for the owner to dispose of. '

'That's an awful price! €330 a house! That's daylight robbery,' Paddy puffed his cheeks in shock.

'That's no problem. I'll leave it with you to sort. You've already seen for yourself the state they're in, so you know exactly how much work is involved,' Olivia replied, firmly holding her ground. It was exactly the response she had expected from
Paddy.

'You know I'm a busy man with not a minute on my hands for that sort of carry-on. I'll give you the go-ahead this time. Go on, try and make them presentable. Don't let me down,' Paddy blustered, thinking Olivia was a force to be reckoned with.

She wasn't budging an inch with the price and not a chance of her backing down, but it was worth a gamble he decided. Paddy approached the door, tucking his mobile into the inside pocket of his treasured corduroy jacket.

'I'm off for the day. Must catch up with a couple up at Priors who are thinking about selling up. I'll have a bite to eat with them and we'll sort things out. I'll leave you to it. I'm on the mobile if there's anything urgent,' Paddy bellowed, opening the door, eager to escape.

'That's perfect. Hopefully, I'll get my helpers organised for this weekend. I'll let Mark know you have given him the go ahead. I'll see you on Monday. If there are any problems I know where to catch up with you,' Olivia answered, mindful that Paddy was bursting out the door

She set to action straight away and messaged Jack and Ellie who were delighted to get the work. She knew the promise of 180 euros and a decent lunch should seal the deal for them. Christmas was only around the corner and teenagers loved spending. With Mark in Dublin for the day, she decided to catch up with him tomorrow evening on returning from her dreaded trip to Kildare to finally sort out things with Tom.

'Stop thinking about it now,' she chastised herself loudly.

There was a stack of paperwork to get through before five o'clock.

# Chapter 29

Tossing and turning again for what felt like the hundredth time, Olivia leaned over to glance at her phone - only ten past six in the morning. I may as well get up she mused, if I can't go back to sleep.

Trudging into the kitchen Olivia clicked the kettle on, its soothing hum soon filling the air. She had finally built up the courage to phone Tom a few days ago. Again, he didn't answer her call, so she left a voicemail saying she needed to pick up some clothes and car insurance paperwork, suggesting Saturday around one. She knew he'd be off work and hopefully, they could have a proper chat and clear the air. Up until now, he had ignored her calls. It was typical of Tom to bury his head in the sand when there was an awkward conversation to be had. For the first few weeks she had tried calling once or twice a week. After a month of him ignoring her calls, she had given up.

Finally, late last night he responded to her message by text saying, *Okay, you have your keys to let yourself in*. She always knew he wasn't a man for many words, but that short text message certainly wasn't giving away much. Was that a friendly text to tell her to go ahead, let herself in and he'd be ready and waiting excitedly to see her? Or did it mean he didn't give a damn about her?

Olivia shook her head in frustration. She had been married to this man for years and should have known him inside out at this stage. Yet, here she was nearly eight hours later still trying in vain to interpret his short and vague message. Last night, feeling frustrated with her futile analysing, she replied with an equally short text response, *Perfect. See you then.*

Mentally giving herself a quick shake, she decided to get a good breakfast and make herself presentable. With her breakfast of sausages, pudding and rashers sizzling on the grill, Olivia boiled the kettle, filling the teapot to the brim. Turning off the grill, she heard the knocking on her door. Cautiously she went over, noting it was only ten to seven in the morning.

'Hello. Who is it?' Olivia asked warily, as she peered through the spyhole.

'It's Mark. I saw the light on. I'm checking you're okay?'

'Come in,' Olivia urged, unlocking the door, always pleased to see her handsome neighbour.

'I don't want to bother you, but is everything alright?' Mark enquired walking into her living room, pulling his beanie off, his dark curls bursting free.

'Yes, all fine. I have to go to Kildare to meet my husband this morning to collect some stuff and didn't have a great night's sleep. To be honest, I'm anxious about it. I don't know what sort of reaction I'm going to get from Tom. I might have mentioned before that the communication between us hasn't been good since I came down here in September. But never mind all that. Have breakfast with me. Your calling has been a lovely surprise and I'd love the company. I've plenty for the two of us and the kettle's just boiled,' Olivia babbled as Mark followed her into the little kitchen, immediately aware of the bubble of warmth and comfort surrounding him.

'If you're sure?' Mark asked concerned at Olivia's anxious state, completely out of character.

Sitting at the table, within minutes Olivia had a steaming mug of tea and breakfast placed in front of him. After his second generous mug of tea and a chunky rasher and sausage sandwich, he noticed Olivia reverting to her usual calm and relaxed self.

'What's the plan today?' Mark asked, hoping to encourage Olivia to unburden her woes before going on the difficult journey.

'Firstly, I need to collect my belongings. Hopefully, he'll have calmed down and we can have a civil conversation and sort out an arrangement regarding the boys for Christmas. The usual stuff.'

'I'm sure he has by now. You've been here nearly three months. I'm sure he's resigned to the fact you're not going back for good. You're not planning to stay up there, are you?' asked Mark uneasily, standing to finish his tea.

'No, I don't think so. I don't plan to,' Olivia replied absently, beginning to gather the empty breakfast delph and cutlery, placing them in the sink.

'You are coming back, aren't you? You know, you'd be missed by everyone here and you have the three cottages almost sorted now. You love your new job. It'd be a shame to pack it all in. I thought you were happy here?' Mark trailed off, looking expectantly at Olivia for reassurance.

'Thank you. That means so much to me. I am happy here. Happier than I've been in a long time. I've been putting my showdown with Tom on the long finger for too long. I have to get things sorted once and for all,' Olivia explained, encouraged by Mark's kind words. 'I almost forgot to tell you. Paddy gave the okay for you to start the work. As soon as you have those supplies sorted, you can get started,' Olivia rushed, clearing the remaining items from the table and wiping the oilcloth.

'Great news. Have your showdown with Tom, but don't forget to come back. We'll be missing you. Maybe some of us more than others,' Mark added, wrapping her in a hug.

With one hand cradling the back of her head, he gently planted a tender kiss on her cheek before reluctantly breaking his embrace. Turning, he made his way hastily to the door.

'I'm off to work. Thanks for the unexpected breakfast. Don't worry too much. Have a safe journey and I'm sure everything will work out just fine,' he winked, closing the door on his way out.

Olivia stared at the door dumbstruck, still reeling from Mark's speech and hug, and what a sexy hug it was. She had been feeling so miserable earlier, but being smothered into Mark, feeling his strong, muscular body pressed against her chased every bit of anxiety away. Her heart was still fluttering excitedly. It hadn't tingled like this in years, never mind months. It felt so good to feel a strong male body. She hadn't realized how much she missed it, especially with someone as gorgeous as Mark.

Buoyed up with the dizzying combination of excitement and attraction, and bowled over by Mark's touching speech, Olivia suddenly felt confident, energised, and decisive. She reminded herself it was completely normal to be worried about meeting up with Tom. Anybody in the same situation would be feeling the same, if not worse. She reminded herself no matter what outburst she got, she'd get over it. She had made a new life for herself despite challenging financial means. After ten years of relying on her weekly housekeeping money doled out by Tom, she was now a financially independent woman with a job and she had a further potential business with her revamped cottage rentals.

You never know, someday she might find romance again. The prospect of gorgeous Mark on her return was a wonderful boost to a girl's confidence and another good reason to come back to Boyle. Wearing her new Penneys jeans and crisp white shirt, Olivia knew she looked good. Losing that stone and a half had done wonders for her figure and self-esteem. Her hair was past her shoulders and Liz had put her past hairdressing skills to work and done some deft touches with her scissors, adding a few highlights that flattered her. Her skin still retained a glow from her holiday and her hair, subtly layered and multi-toned in shades of gold and caramel tones was her new crowning glory. Gone were her dowdy days of a chin-length bob and suburban Arnott's outfits, relying on her husband for her housekeeping money. She had left her old life as a lamb in the past and was returning as a lion.

# Chapter 30

Edging onto the main Dublin road, Olivia accelerated into fifth gear feeling liberated and confident, ready to tackle the world. Selecting a Leonard Cohen track, she turned the volume on high, the passion and intensity of, 'Halleluiah' driving her on.

Just before one o'clock, she rolled into the driveway of her former home and slowly got out of the car. She walked to the door, keys in hand, knocked and waited patiently, waited some more, but there was still no answer. Olivia checked the message on her mobile again to ensure she had the agreed time right. Yes, one o'clock. She phoned Tom and again it went to voicemail. She left a message to say she was at the house.

At twenty-past-one, Olivia gave up. Hesitantly turning the key in the lock, she went inside. On the hall table, Tom had stacked her post. Looking around, she was impressed to see the house looked tidy and everything was in its place. Tom had a cleaner every week which accounted for that, because of course Tom and Betty always had high standards. Ambling into the kitchen, her eyes were drawn immediately to a woman's pink raincoat draped casually over the kitchen chair. In the back hallway, a pair of floral wellies stood in company beside Tom's green ones.

Tom obviously has a partner and didn't mind her knowing about it. Olivia considered this information as she went upstairs to her bedroom to collect winter coats and boots. Opening the bedroom door, she was immediately aware her bedroom had been out of use for some time. It smelled musty and tired as dust motes danced in the weak winter sunshine rays. Tom's half of the wardrobe was cleared out without a stray sock in sight. On opening her half, she noted everything looked exactly as it was the day she had left. Even down to the discarded outfit she'd slung over the bed the day she rushed off on holiday. The same duvet cover still remained on the bed since August.

The room confirmed closure for Tom on this part of his life Olivia realized, slowly walking onto the landing. Strolling to the guest room across the hallway she pushed the door handle to find it securely locked. Tom had obviously relocated here. Continuing along the landing she glanced into Jonathon's bedroom. The cleaner had paid a visit as everything was back in his wardrobe. No stray runners or wandering socks in sight. Everything was in order as Tom would like it. Andrew's bedroom was a mirror of his brothers, ship-shape and ready for their arrival at Christmas.

'Is that you, Olivia?' Tom boomed, climbing the stairs.

Startled, Olivia left Andrew's room, suddenly feeling like an intruder in her own house.

'Yes. I'm in Andrew's room. I'm getting some of my stuff now. I have to get a bag from the car,' Olivia stuttered, uncomfortable and self-conscious, not wanting to appear as though snooping around.

Tom strode into the room. Stopping in his tracks, he almost bumped into Olivia leaving Andrew's room.

'I let myself in as you weren't here at one. Hope that's okay?' Olivia muttered, as her husband appeared in the room.

'Of course. How are you?' Tom asked, his eyes doing a double take as he stared at his wife from head to toe, pointedly taking in the entire picture.

The silence stretched awkwardly between them and he shifted clumsily from side to side.

'I'm good and you? Are you okay? I see you've settled into your new room,' Olivia mumbled, wondering how in God's name things could be this awkward with a man you were with for nearly fifteen years.

Tom's eyes blinked repeatedly and his face immediately hardened as he clenched his fists in his habitual manner.

'What exactly do you mean by that comment? Yes, I've moved into the other bedroom and yes, I do have a new partner.

What else was I supposed to do? You never bothered coming home,' Tom barked, his initial conciliatory manner instantly disappearing.

'Tom, calm down. I merely said you've moved into the other bedroom. I didn't come up here to have a row with you. Nor am I going to listen to you shouting at me. I've come to collect my stuff. We can go downstairs and have a civil conversation, or not. You decide,' Olivia said calmly and assertively, holding his gaze.

Tom stared, taken aback at her response, suddenly unsure of this new version of his wife.

'Right, so! I'll put the kettle on. We need to have a conversation, anyway,' Tom huffed, turning on his heel and stomping downstairs.

Olivia gave him a few minutes to calm down, thinking time hadn't mellowed him much. His quick-tempered moods hadn't changed one jot. Taking a deep breath, she made her way into her old kitchen. Pulling out a chair, she removed a jewel coloured, silky scarf from the seat, before draping it on the back of another chair.

Tom bristled as his gaze fell on the scarf, anger clouding his features.

'Sorry about that. I didn't realise it was there. It's Marie's. I didn't get a chance to put things away,' Tom fussed, tidying away Marie's scarf, gloves and raincoat.

'Don't worry about it. I'm glad you've got company and are content,' Olivia soothed.

'I didn't have much choice since you went on holiday and didn't bother coming back,' Tom hissed, his voice getting louder by the second.

He roughly placed a mug of tea in front of Olivia, its contents spilling gently onto the tablecloth.

'Tom, I thought we were over this. I'll say it again for the final time. I went on holiday and you didn't come as agreed. I expected you to join me, but again you didn't come. I came home from holidays and after being married fifteen years, thought you'd miss me and be waiting at the airport. But no, again you didn't come. So, I went to Boyle to clear my head. I waited and you never bothered coming to see me. Not even for an hour,' Olivia stated matter-of-factly.

'I explained I'm a busy man and you know that. When you didn't bother coming home, I was left on my own to fend for myself with no company. Marie started knocking in to see if I was okay. She'd even tidy up and drop dinners in for me. She took an interest in farming and was delighted to come to the

GAA dance. She gets on great with Mam and makes time for me. Olivia, don't you see that? How could you not see that's what every man wants? Was that too much to ask?' Tom pleaded with a martyred expression.

Leaning forward, his hands were steepled on the kitchen table as he searched Olivia's face.

'Well, I'm glad you're happy now. I really am. You're right. Everybody wants to feel special. Even me. So please forgive me for wanting you to spend ten days holidays with me. I had all the plans made, but you just couldn't give me that time. Oh, and just so you know - I'm glad Marie has all this time to spend on you. Being a single woman she hasn't quite the same demands on her time as me. I spent my time cooking, feeding, cleaning up, shopping and bringing your two sons to and from school, football matches, Karate and whatever else might be going on. Because you didn't have time to do any of that, ever. As well as feeding and doing the washing and ironing for your mother every day for years. But we've both moved on so we'll leave all that in the past, shall we?' Olivia added boldly, raising her mug and watching a baffled Tom digest her rant.

God, she thought to herself. It felt good offloading onto him for a change.

Tom stared at the woman in front of him, his fingertips making an impatient rapping on the kitchen counter. He could hardly believe how she had changed in a few months. There was no doubt she looked great and could pass for twenty-five in those jeans. That was the longest speech he ever heard from her and was glad he wouldn't have to listen to more of them. The woman didn't know when she had it good. In comparison, Marie was such easy company. She always had a smile for him, loved watching a GAA match and knew how to make a man feel wanted.

After a few minutes of awkward silence, Olivia decided the stalemate wasn't getting her anywhere. She'd have to offer him an olive branch or he could sulk for days on end and nothing would be resolved.

'I wish you well. I'm glad you're happy with Marie. I'm happy in Boyle and plan to stay there. Maybe that holiday was the tipping point for us. It made us realise we were just plodding along without enjoying life. What about the arrangements for Christmas? What'll we do?' Olivia asked with a weak smile, reminding herself Tom was not a man for taking any criticism, constructive or otherwise!

'Christmas is around the corner. The boys will be off for two weeks. Of course, they'll be here for Christmas Day. Could you come up for the day, stay over that night and go back on St. Stephen's Day?' Tom enquired in a more conciliatory tone.

'I could do that. They could have Christmas with you and spend the New Year with me. What do you think?'

'Stay with you? That cottage isn't fit for them to stay in,' Tom bristled.

'The cottage is perfect. I live there, so there's no need for you to worry about that. It's all sorted then. I'll come for Christmas and head back on St. Stephen's Day. They can come on the train to me for New Year. Right, I'll get my bags, do my packing and be on my way. I'm glad we've had this conversation and cleared the air,' Olivia gave Tom a conciliatory smile as she got up, pushing her chair under the table.

'I suppose so,' Tom replied, thinking the arrangements were too rushed for his liking.

He liked to consider and weigh things up. This new woman was not going to stand around waiting for him. She seemed to drive all the suggestions and decisions now. It wasn't an approach he was used to, but he was relieved the air was cleared and everything said that needed to be.

The sound of the front door opening, followed by a bustling noise in the hallway distracted them both. Olivia turned around to see her mother-in-law rush into the kitchen.

'Well, Madam, you finally made your way back. My Tom is a patient man. I always thought him too good for you. I never like to interfere, but it must be said,' Betty glared at Olivia.

'Mum, just leave it,' Tom raised his voice, eager to nip his mother's speech rapidly in the bud.

However, Betty was in full stride, oblivious to any of his entreaties. 'You've finally come to your senses, skedaddling all over the place. Bad enough going off on holiday without your husband, instead of coming home and apologising like any decent wife would - what did you do? Off you went again to Boyle of all places. What's in a God-forsaken place like that and you kept in the lap of luxury here? Tom pays you good housekeeping every week. There's no pleasing some people in this world,' tutted Betty, her eyes scanning Olivia from top to bottom.

She placed her handbag on the table and dropped her shopping bag onto the floor.

'Mother, can you just stop,' Tom shouted.

'No! Betty, please go on. Is there anything else you'd like to add? You seem to have an awful lot to get off your chest,' Olivia replied shocked.

In her heart, she wasn't really surprised at her mother-in-law's venom.

'I'm just saying it as it is. I hope you've finished your gallivanting and finally appreciate how good you have it,' Betty sniffed, worn out from her outburst. This girl had humiliated her son to no end.

'Now it's my turn, Betty. Firstly, surprise, surprise. This is a free country. Women don't have to get their husband's permission to go anywhere. Boyle or France, or anywhere. This 'lap of luxury' you refer to was built by a large part of my earnings, as was all the land Tom bought over the years. The housekeeping money you refer to wouldn't pay a fraction of the cost of the cleaning, cooking and housekeeping I've done for you and this house. But never mind all that! No amount of money would pay for the bullshit and nonsense I've listened to from you over the years. Oh, and as you're such a good catholic mother, just to remind you, it's your Tom who has taken up with a new partner. Not me. And finally, Betty. No, I'm not coming back here and never plan to. I've made a new life in Roscommon. I have a job. I have a life with lovely genuine, decent neighbours. Tom and I have had our private conversation and sorted our business without your input. It's possibly the first decision we've ever made in our marriage without your unwanted opinion. That's both of us offloaded. We know where we stand with each other.'

Olivia calmly assessed her mother-in-law's thunderstruck reaction as she gobbled for air, looking at her son in askance.

'How dare you speak to me like that! Tom, this is not good enough. Tell her now this minute. Tom!' Betty screeched, as she waited for her son's support.

'Betty, may I remind you, you are in my house. Yes, my house. You're the one who started this vicious attack on me. I'm very much aware there is no love lost between us. We will have minimal future contact, but when we do I'd appreciate it if you try to be civil,' Olivia suggested, eager to finally set boundaries for Tom's mother.

She wanted to be sure Betty got the message loud and clear, not wanting further episodes at Christmas with the boys around.

'I've never been so insulted in all my days and all I've done for you and your kids over the years. Isn't that right, Tom?' Betty cried, looking expectantly again at Tom for backup.

Her Tom had always understood and appreciated his mother's wisdom and guidance all his life. Well, good riddance to this harpy, she thought. A right jumped up and thankless upstart if ever there was one. If the truth be told, Betty didn't miss her one jot. Marie was a lovely woman, more mature and sophisticated and much more suited to Tom. She had a great interest in farming and Betty and herself had loads in common. The sooner this one packed her bags and left permanently the better. Good riddance to her.

'Mother, maybe it would be better if you called back another day. Olivia is here to collect some stuff. I'll talk to you later,' Tom hissed through gritted teeth, anxious to diffuse this toxic situation.

'Indeed, I will not let you down now, Tom. I've come to have our usual lunch with you and Marie as arranged. She's such a lovely girl,' Betty smiled pointedly, placing her grocery bag territorially beside Marie's scarf and cardigan on the countertop.

'Look, Mother. It's not a good time. Olivia has to finish off a few things and I'm going out directly afterward. I'll call you this evening.'

Tom's voice rattled with irritation as he quickly moved to the counter gathering up his mother's shopping bag and handbag on the way before bundling them at her.

'But, I...' Betty grumbled, embarrassed and humiliated in front of Olivia.

Typical, Betty thought. That woman wasn't back in the house for five minutes and was causing friction between herself and her lovely son. The sooner she was gone the better.

Tom held her by her free arm and steered her out of the kitchen, bumping off furniture on the way in his haste to the front door.

Olivia sat at the kitchen table. The muffled, but heated exchanges between Betty and Tom in the hall came to a sudden end with a firm bang on the front door. Tom stalked back into the kitchen, irritation etched across his features.

'That was unpleasant and unnecessary. I didn't know you and mother didn't get along.'

Tom gritted his teeth as he sat down at the counter, raking his hand through his hair.

'Yes. Betty was very unpleasant. We got along once I agreed with Betty's plans in life,' Olivia replied calmly.

'I'm also referring to you being unpleasant. You do realise Mother is getting on. She's in her seventies and is very upset with this business,' Tom retorted, glaring at his wife.

'Let's get the facts correct. She strode into my house, immediately insulting me without any provocation. She has been rude and unpleasant for years. I always chose to ignore it, but not anymore. She spoke her mind today. For the first time, I finally spoke mine in return and seventy-two is not particularly elderly. She is blessed with good health, so I wouldn't worry too much about her if I were you. I'm sure she'll bounce back in no time. I'm getting my bags from the car to pack my things,' Olivia stated bluntly, rising from the chair.

She was disappointed for Tom it had all turned so unpleasant with Betty. She'd had no option but to respond to her as she did, or she wouldn't have a shred of self-respect left after such an attack.

'Whatever,' Tom mumbled, bewildered at Olivia's reply.

He had lived with his wife for years in this house. His mother had been here every day during that time. He could honestly say today was a complete eye-opener for him. Unaware of any issue between them, they'd revealed their true feelings for each other. He had a headache and would be glad when this day was over. It was proving to be a pure nightmare.

'I'm sorry about this argument. Everyone's had their say, and the air is cleared for better or worse. On the good side, Betty is obviously fond of Marie. I'm happy you have found a new partner, and she has Betty's seal of approval. We've made our arrangements regarding the boys. Let's not spoil our future get togethers because of today's outburst,' Olivia coaxed in an appeasing tone as she fixed her eyes on Tom's defeated pose.

His head was bent into his cradled hands. She knew Tom was in shock and was eager to coax a smile from him. They had come so far today before Betty's outburst. She didn't want to return to Boyle with a lingering atmosphere of anger and recriminations between them. He never liked confrontation and much preferred to pretend it wasn't there. Olivia had made many subtle and not-so-subtle hints concerning Betty's intrusions in their early years of marriage but to no avail. He either completely ignored them or laughed them off. After a while, she accepted Tom was on Betty's side, so played the game of marriage, bearing those rules uppermost in her mind.

Tom sighed heavily and dragged his hand wearily across his temple.

'I suppose you're right. Everyone's had their say. Betty and Marie do get on well. They're probably more suited to each other. More in common I guess,' Tom agreed truculently. 'Betty seems very fond of her, so it's a win-win situation all around, don't you think? So, we're good?' Olivia asked amicably, turning to leave the kitchen.

Tom stared intently at Olivia, unsure whether her response was sarcastic or genuine. He was unsure about this new Olivia on many fronts.

'I suppose so. Do you want a hand packing?' Tom responded as Olivia bustled her way to the hall, eager to get started. He was unsure what to say or do in this completely unfamiliar situation.

'Not at all. I'll be sorted in no time and be on my way. I'll just grab my paperwork and bundle my winter clothes and boots into a couple of bags. I can sort out the remaining stuff at Christmas,' she replied, placing her hand decisively on the front door handle.

Tom strode over to her side, placing his hand firmly on the door. 'Olivia, I'm sorry it's all come to this sad ending,' he blurted, putting his other hand heavily on her shoulder. His voice broke as he dragged the words out.

'It's been uncomfortable and unpleasant for both of us, but I think it was possibly inevitable we were going to part sooner or later. If I was still living here, the children going away to Boarding School was going to become a bit of a crossroads in life for me anyway. What would I have done all day without them? We probably should have had some meaningful conversations early in our marriage. All the dos and don'ts should have been ironed out early on. Boundaries on privacy should have been set for Betty. But we didn't have any of those conversations and for whatever number of reasons, we have got to where we are now. We still have two great sons. All the difficult conversations are over and we're still on talking terms. All things considered, I think it was a productive morning,' Olivia smiled encouragingly.

'I suppose you're right. Are you happy in Boyle? Are you managing alright? Tom enquired, scanning her face.

'Yes. I'm happy with my job and doing up the cottages. All is good with me. Nothing for you to worry about,' Olivia replied firmly.

'Right! You have my mobile number if there is anything at all. This time I mean it. If you can't get me the first time, leave a message and I'll get back to you. I'd never leave you stuck,' Tom stressed.

'Good to know. Thank you, for that. I better start packing,' Olivia replied grateful for his kind, if unexpected thoughtful offer as she gently pulled the door open.

Twenty minutes later, she zipped her bags shut, packed with essentials and a few favourite family photos from her dressing table. After putting her ransacked wardrobe back in order, she closed the doors and speculatively gazed around the bedroom that once meant so much to her. This room that she had decorated, dusted and hoovered so many times. It contained all the private conversations between herself and Tom over the years. There were many happy memories of the boys bouncing around the bed at six in the morning when she wished they were better sleepers. All their dreams and hopes, rows and special moments had been contained within these four walls. But already the room assumed the forlorn air of abandonment, all hints of a previous life and happiness completely gone forever. Its only company were the dust specks dancing in the morning sunshine.

'Let me give you a hand,' Tom offered, rushing from the kitchen as Olivia descended the stairs to the front door.

'Thanks. I've left the other bag on the landing. The only things I've taken are picture frames with family photos of the four of us from my dressing table. If that's okay with you?' Olivia met Tom's anxious gaze as he passed her on the stairs.

'Of course! Take them. You have loads more all over the house. They're yours. You took the photos and bought the frames. You always looked after that kind of thing. I never bothered.' Looking away uncomfortably, he rushed to the landing.

Olivia sighed in response and made her way to the car.

'Here you go. I'll put it in the boot for you. I'm sorry I messed things up. If only I'd gone on that holiday,' Tom stammered in anguish, pushing the bag alongside the other one into the boot.

'Stop upsetting yourself. Everything will work out just fine. Don't worry. I'm not bitter or annoyed with you anymore. I've gotten over all that. I'm happy you've Marie in your life. Let's part on good terms,' Olivia wheedled, anxious to chase away Tom's guilt-ridden mood.

Tom blinked defeatedly at Olivia, various emotions chasing across his face.

'Thanks. Maybe you're right. We are, where we are. Just so you know, I am sorry for many things ...' Tom affirmed, reaching across and pulling Olivia momentarily into a tight embrace, before quickly releasing her and hastily stepping away from the car.

'Thanks, Tom,' Olivia sighed, appreciative of how difficult that speech must have been for him.

'Take care and drive carefully. Give me a call anytime,' said Tom, before turning on his heel. Marching to the front door, he made his way inside, closing the door.

Olivia hopped in the driver's seat and turned the ignition, eager not to prolong the uncomfortable situation. Putting the car into gear, she drove out of the driveway as quickly as possible. Heading for Boyle, her head swam with mixed emotions.

Sadness for Tom, regret their marriage didn't pan out as she had thought, but most importantly she treasured the frank conversations she had with Tom. They had both learned more about each other in the last few hours than in fifteen years.

# Chapter 31

It was just after four o'clock when Olivia drove into her driveway, parking in the usual spot. Unloading her boot and gathering up her bag of groceries, she trundled to the front door, letting herself in with a sigh, and locked the front door. She'd had an early start, wakening at six. It was only late afternoon, but she felt exhausted. Laying her bags heavily on the living room floor, she plodded to the kitchenette, clicking the electric kettle into life. Making a mug of tea and grabbing the chocolate Hobnobs from the counter, she cradled her mug in her other hand, traipsed into her bedroom and stretched out on her bed.

The comforting firmness instantly soothed her aching muscles from head to toe. Gosh, it had been one busy day, she thought, recounting its events, snatches of conversation between herself, Tom and Betty flitting through her mind. Slurping from her mug and savouring the crumbly chocolate coated biscuits, Olivia eased her head onto her pillow while resting the mug on her bedside table. Crumbs strayed down her top and wandered onto the duvet cover before trailing their way onto the wooden floor. Smiling, she leisurely took another biscuit, savouring the simple but intense pleasure of lobbing in your own bed, in your own house, doing pretty much anything you wanted. She turned over on her side setting the alarm for an hour's rest and a well deserved snooze, laughing aloud. Betty and Tom would have a stroke if they could see her now. The idea of catnapping during the day! Witnessing such slovenly behaviour would have sent them to an early grave.

An hour and a half later, feeling refreshed and recharged, and having the bedroom floor set right, Olivia felt the rumble of hunger, reminding her she hadn't had a proper meal since morning. Opening the kitchen cupboards she looked for inspiration for a quick and tasty dinner. She had worked up an appetite but wasn't in the mood to put much effort into cooking. The knocking on the door broke her thoughts and she made her way to answer it to find Sheila on the doorstep.

'Am I disturbing you? I heard you unlocking the door. You're settled down early for the night, aren't you? It's only half six. Was today terrible for you, you poor thing?' Sheila was surprised to hear the key unlocking the door, the wicker basket in her hands.

'Come in, Sheila. I had a very early start and a busy day, so had a snooze for an hour. I'm just up and about to start some dinner. You're more than welcome to join me.'

'Don't bother making any dinner. Didn't I know well you were gone for the day? A very difficult day it must have been. I knew you'd be shattered by the time you got back, so I made a hearty shepherd's pie earlier. Mick's already fed and watered and is stuck into a game of poker for the night with Paddy Murphy, so he's sorted. I can share my dinner, if shepherd's pie is okay? I've apple crumble for dessert. They're both piping hot and ready to go if you fancy them?' Sheila offered earnestly.

'Sheila, you're a godsend. I'm howling with hunger. Put your casserole on the table. I'll grab the cutlery and a bottle of wine and we're ready to go. I'll fill you in on all the news,' Olivia said, clapping her hands in anticipation of a wonderful meal as the hearty waft of dinner filled the air.

The bottle of wine was a gift from a grateful customer at work and a welcome addition to this impromptu dinner.

'Good! You know I love a bit of news. I've got some very interesting news of my own too. Let's get started on this dinner while it's nice and hot.'

Sheila took the proffered plates from Olivia, ladling generous portions of pie onto them, the rich sauce dripping invitingly over the golden-crusted, potato topping.

'Thanks, Sheila. That looks amazing as usual,' Olivia approved, eagerly receiving her heaving plate, her stomach growling in readiness.

For the first few minutes, the conversation ceased as they both gave full attention to their rumbling appetites. The only sound was the rhythmic scraping of cutlery as they took pleasure in savouring the rich aroma and taste of wholesome home cooking.

'Sheila, this is fabulous. I was famished. Now that I've more than half of it eaten, I can finally start a conversation and put you out of your misery,' Olivia said, patting her tummy in appreciation.

'Conversation never flows well on an empty stomach. Dinner tastes all the better because the spuds and veg all come from our own back garden. Fill me in. How did it go today? Was it awful?' Sheila enquired anxiously.

'It was a strange experience. In part awful and sad, but in other ways it was the most open and honest conversation I have ever had with Tom. We were both brutally honest with each other. Of course, Betty appeared to support her son. She too had some strong opinions to express, so everybody including myself said exactly what was on our minds. In the end, Tom sent Betty on her way and in private we finally aired all the unsaid grievances buried over the years. It all came out. Warts and all. Not pretty at times, but at the end of it all I think we both have a better understanding of each other thanks to our very frank chat. We parted with a new understanding of each other and made plans to have Christmas Day together. I think all things considered it was a good meeting and good to finally have a proper and honest chat. I really think we'll work it out together.'

'I can't believe it. That must have been a hard day for you, but you did the right thing. You had to sort it out head on with Tom and I'm glad you did. I'm delighted to see you're not bitter or upset because carrying around anger never leads to a happy ending. It must be such a relief to have all that aggro behind you,' Sheila murmured sympathetically, listening attentively to her neighbour.

'You're right! I'm so relieved the difficult conversations are over. I'm happy to see Tom content with his new partner. I thought I'd be jealous, but not a bit. If I'm completely honest, I think the fact Tom already has a new partner made things easier really, so no, I've no regrets at all. I'm happy to move on with my new life here. I'm finished with my news. I know you're itching to tell me all yours, so I'm going to continue eating this scrumptious dinner while you fill me in,' Olivia insisted, helping herself to another portion.

'Enjoy and don't forget to leave a corner for dessert. I bumped into Elaine the other day and we had a great chat altogether,' Sheila began, eager to relay all her news.

'Elaine, that's Conor's girlfriend you know! I didn't know you knew Elaine,' Olivia asked, looking up momentarily from her plate.

'I've known Elaine for years. A lovely Polish girl. I didn't know she was Conor's girlfriend. She makes and sells home cooking. Lovely stuff. Pickled vegetables, chutneys, jams and cheeses, bread. A bit of everything and sells it with her organic veg at the market in King House in Boyle on Saturday mornings. She has a little girl, Jessica. She must be seven or eight by now. Over the years I've gotten to know her and Jessica well. She always had Jessica at the market with her from when she was a few months old. To give her a break when she was working, I'd take the little one for a walk around the town, or the playground. I've babysat for her a few times as well. Anyway, I'm just saying Elaine's such a great catch, very well grounded. She's only about twenty-seven or twenty-eight, but she's fabulous with her little one. She has bought her own cottage out the road a bit, nothing fancy mind, but ever so snug and homely. She's so independent and self-sufficient, happy and content, as well as being a looker.'

'She's stunning, isn't she? I've seen her going to Conor's a few times lately. You know her well then?' Olivia enquired, wondering if there was anyone within a twenty-mile radius Sheila didn't know.

'Indeed I do. Her mum and dad too. They're the same kind of people. Very self-sufficient who do their own thing and keep to themselves. Not gossipy kind of people. Lovely people,' Sheila nodded.

'Really? Not gossipy kind of people who keep to themselves and you know them well?' Olivia teased, failing to suppress her laughter at her neighbour's *faux pas*.

'Okay, I get the joke! Stop messing around. You're distracting me from my story because there's much more to it than that,' Sheila scolded, furrowing her brow in concentration, eager to impart the details in full.

'She's a very open and straightforward kind of girl. She told me she and Conor were getting on great and understood the situation with him and his previous girlfriend. She even coaxed him into getting counselling in Boyle for his depression and saw a big improvement in a few weeks. Of course, I'd never pry into the details, but I mentioned to Elaine his mother was in regular contact by phone to check he was okay. His mum told me he had finally phoned her back to say he was doing all right and not to worry about him. He was months here before he made that first phone call. Naturally, his mother worries about him all the time. Probably because he's an only child and Elaine understands, being a mother herself. We thought we should do something about it before it goes on too long,' Sheila carried on, scanning Olivia's expression for feedback.

'That was a long conversation with Elaine. She's right! Conor has come on leaps and bounds. It's easier to talk to him now. Whether it's Elaine's magical presence or his counselling that did the trick, doesn't matter. I didn't know relations were still awkward between him and his mum though. That's such a pity. But you know, Conor is probably like most fellas and wouldn't have great insight into things like that. He phoned his mum and told her he was all right. In his mind, she knew he was okay, so the matter was sorted and closed. We all know he likes to keep conversations short and sweet at the best of times. I can imagine the conversation with his mum was probably very brief and to the point,' Olivia said, mulling over the news.

'Exactly! Elaine summed him up pretty much the same way. She told me she'd have a word in his ear as soon as possible because she's not happy with the idea of ongoing tension with his mum. In Elaine's mind, it's not acceptable. She's a very family focused kind of girl,' Sheila added.

'That was fast work between the two of you. I think Elaine is right. If the situation goes on much longer without thrashing it out, it will probably get to a point of no return for Conor and his mum,' Olivia cautioned, listening intently as she finished the last of her dinner.

'I think so myself. I felt so bad for Maeve, Conor's mother. She usually gives me a phone call every fortnight or so. She plays it down as though it's just an idle catch-up, but I know she's hoping for news about Conor, so I always bring her up to date to reassure her,' Sheila said earnestly.

'I see! All that spying on Conor was for a good cause,' Olivia joked, enjoying the crumbly texture of the dessert and the cinnamon-flavoured, apple filling.

'Absolutely! That lad is only twenty-six. Lads need a lot of watching at any age. I knew he was struggling on his own and not mixing with anyone. When you came along you certainly brought him out of his shell. Now Elaine has taken him on, he's like a new man. I'm relieved because men, young and old, need a woman to steer them in the right direction. They can get odd living on their own,' Sheila stated.

'That's a pretty harsh synopsis of the male species. I get what you're saying though. While I wouldn't always agree with your opinions, I know your heart is in the right place,' Olivia acknowledged, aware Sheila was trying to be as tactful as she could manage.

'You might think I'm harsh, but I'm talking from experience,' Sheila sighed, her face crestfallen. 'We were very close to Mick's nephew, Simon. He and his two brothers stayed with us regularly for weekends when they were young lads and two weeks every Summer. They went fishing with Mick and camping in the Forest Park and had days out with them, simple, easy stuff, but we had great craic with them. They were the family we never had. As they became teenagers they didn't visit quite as much and that's normal, isn't it? They still came two or three times a year. We thought Simon had become less chatty and withdrawn. We mentioned it to his mum, but she reassured us he was the same at home with her, moody and withdrawn. She said it was just a rite of passage for teenage lads, morose and monosyllabic for months on end. We accepted his mum knew best. Sure, she lived with him day in and day out. We were happy with the idea we'd have the old Simon back in a few years.'

Sheila twisted her wedding ring absently mindedly around her finger as she spoke and Olivia noticed a deep sadness in her friend's eyes.

'That never happened though because a few weeks after that same conversation with his mother, Simon took his own life. We were all devastated. His parents and brothers only found out weeks after his death that he'd been having a hard time in school. Everyone took his withdrawn and sullen ways, buried in his bedroom, for normal teenage hormone moods. But we were wrong.'

Olivia's heart went out to her friend.

'We've had long family conversations about it since and following bereavement counselling, the family agreed we should have pushed the conversation on him, no matter how difficult and awkward it seemed at the time. If Simon had talked and offloaded his problems, it would most likely have saved his life,' Sheila whispered, staring into space, grief casting a shadow on her face.

'My God, Sheila. I'm so sorry. I didn't mean to write you off as a nosey neighbour. I'm sorry to hear about Mick's nephew. It's all fitting into place. Conor didn't know he had a guardian angel all along,' Olivia gushed, wrapping her arms around Sheila, tears of sorrow in her eyes.

'I probably am a nosey neighbour. Sometimes, it is quiet around here with just myself and Mick sat opposite each other. I like to go looking for a bit of chat. I'm hoping Conor is sorted now. He's helpful and kind. He's been a great support to me the last few weeks with Mick and chats away to him about football and the like. Mind you, he still hasn't much to say to me.' Sheila perked up as she drained the last of her tea.

'The upshot is we had this chat a few days ago and didn't Elaine call to see me earlier, saying she'd had the big talk with Conor? I told you she's not the sort of girl to hang around or avoid awkward situations. She said it started a bit awkward, but she got around him. The good news is Conor's mother is visiting tomorrow and hopefully they'll finally sort things out. '

Sheila had raced through her story as always and finally caught her breath to finish off her dinner, relieved to have offloaded her news.

'She doesn't hang around does she? Beauty, brains and decisive. I agree with her plan. Nothing worse than doing nothing about a problem. I'm sure it'll all work out. You're going to be bored now without Conor to spy on anymore,' Olivia teased, a glint in her eye.

'I don't know about that. I have noticed that young Mark is making regular trips up this direction at all hours of the day and night. I'll have to start keeping an eye on him instead. I'll just make us both another cuppa,' Sheila smirked, rising from the chair and going to the kitchen.

# Chapter 32

Conor paced the floor again, indignation boiling over. Why did things have to turn out like this he wondered. Just when everything had been going so well. Resignedly he threw himself onto the couch, kicked off his battered Adidas runners and planted his feet on the nearby table, exhaling a slow, deflated sigh of despair. Casting a desultory glance around his sitting room, he pondered on what his next step should be. Everything had been going okay, even better the last couple of months. Meeting Elaine had been great for him. What had started as a favour to Olivia, giving her a hand with the carpentry and giving a few pointers to the work experience lad, had given him a love for carpentry again. It had led him to giving Mark a hand two or three days a week and he'd even taken on a few jobs on his own.

Mark wasn't taxing company and after a hard day's graft, he enjoyed the get-togethers in Olivia's place with the odd dinner thrown in. With the bonus of Elaine's company after work, his days were filled and he felt better than he had in months. Physically tired every evening, he slept through most nights. The nightmares of waking up at two in the morning and rehashing all that had gone wrong in the past were becoming a distant memory. He knew Mark and Olivia had helped him along the way, but it had been Elaine who put him back together again. Never a guy for cliches and baloney, in this case, he had felt broken until she came along.

Throwing back his head, Conor smiled at the memory of the first night he had chatted to her. He still couldn't believe they had clicked so easily. He had seen her a few times in the pub chatting away to everyone. On that evening she had drifted into their company as everyone was hogging a spot near the blazing fire because it was a freezing, windy night outside. It was a Friday evening and he and Mark had finished off the week with a couple of pints and a game of pool, having fallen into the habit over a few weeks. When Elaine joined their company Mark was full of easy chat as usual and the conversation flowed comfortably, despite his usual reluctance to make conversation with strangers.

Elaine had made every effort to engage him in her conversation, her smiling and laughing manner impossible to resist. She had worn a dark green mini dress with black, suede knee-length boots. With her sea-green eyes and long blonde, curly hair she looked stunning. Any man would need to be made of stone not to notice her. After ten minutes in her company, he quickly overcame his shyness and fell into easy conversation. Mark had drifted off talking to the local auctioneer and an hour later had said his goodbyes, leaving him and Elaine to themselves. She chatted openly about herself and her daughter, and her work as a local food market producer.

While Conor's instinct was to withdraw from disclosing any personal information about himself, he couldn't resist Elaine's easy and relaxed manner, soon forgetting his usual shyness. He filled her in that he was living locally, was a teacher but currently taking time out and had recently taken up carpentry work. He smiled, recalling closing time had come around far too fast for his liking that night. Sighing with pleasure, he reminisced about their first meeting. They had said their goodbyes and Elaine must have found him to be half alright because before they parted company, insisted they exchange phone numbers. She had a friend who had bought a bargain kitchen on Done Deal three months before but had no luck locating a carpenter to install it.

True to her word, she phoned him the following day with her friend's details. Conor had arranged to sort out the kitchen predicament and he and Elaine met the following Thursday night and as they say, the rest was history. Falling into an easy pattern, they usually went out for a drink, or she would call up and they would have dinner together, mostly prepared and cooked by Elaine, he mused. Stretching back on the couch, he cast a speculative glance around the room, taking note of Elaine's touches everywhere. She had replaced the dark curtains with white Venetian blinds, encouraging him to give the sitting room walls a coat of fresh paint. With her additions of sofa throws and bright cushions, she had transformed the sitting room from a drab room to a cosy, bright, and homely room. He'd been amazed at the transformation, ashamed he hadn't noticed how dull the place had looked.

Before her first visit, he fortunately had the sense to remove photos of his ex. Bloody hell, he never realised he had so many around the place. The kitchen, sitting room and bedroom were all a shrine to smiling photos of himself and Ashling. He had gathered them all, stuffing them in the bottom drawers, proud of his quick thinking at the time. However, his quick thinking wasn't that quick because a few weeks later when Elaine was looking for some placemats she discovered his stash of photography. He squeezed his eyes tight thinking about it now.

They were just about to sit down to dinner and in great form, and she whirled around with a large photo bearing the over cheesy smiles of himself and his ex. He was floored and froze on the spot, but Elaine wasn't fazed. Breaking the ice, she explained jokingly she didn't have a cupboard full of ex boyfriend pictures but did explain she had photos of herself and Senan, her daughter's dad and her ex-partner. She understood his ex girlfriend had meant a lot to him. Despite every instinct in his body to clam up and disappear on the spot, he shocked himself by explaining the whole sorry story of his past to her. He included his tale of woe for the past year and his long-term plans to buy a house, settle down, and start a family.

He shared the humiliating story of Ashling's wish to run away from him as far as possible. Finally, he whispered his slow descent into depression and isolation leading him to pack in his teaching job and escape to Boyle, away from everything and everyone. What had started as a light-hearted evening, ended up with him offloading all his woes. Elaine had been great, just fantastic.

She had come over and put her arm around his shoulder, encouraging him to talk and share his sorrow. Despite the initial embarrassment, the more he talked about his past the more relieved he felt sharing his story. She told him she understood his pain and said anybody else who had been through as much as he had would have reacted the same. It was only natural his confidence took a battering. His plans in life had been shattered. She then reached across and hugged and kissed him. In that instant, he'd felt ten years younger and more carefree and at ease than he had in a long time. By the time the evening was over he was overwhelmed at her compassion and understanding, relieved she hadn't thought him a complete loser, bolting for the door when she heard his sorry tale.

Now, he was bracing for another difficult conversation about his parents, or more to the point his mother. Elaine had casually brought up the subject of family and how important it was to her. She had one sister, Jane, who lived in London and she was very close to her, and her parents. They in turn were very supportive to her and her daughter. She was passionate about the subject and went on to say maintaining strong family ties was essential throughout life, as family was the strongest and most loyal bond we could ever have as human beings. This of course had led her to ask about his siblings and parents, and his relationship with them. Conor brushed it off by saying he was an only child and his parents were grand, and lived in Dublin. This prompted her to ask when he had last visited them.

She was completely shocked to hear it was when he left Dublin for Boyle, nine months before. This in her opinion was a completely unacceptable length of time. He tried to brush it over by saying his mother tended to be very interfering and get too involved in his personal life. He didn't appreciate her interference, especially during the break-up with his ex girlfriend. He thought Elaine would understand his need for space. However, her look of shock and disbelief rattled him.

They had never disagreed before and she left early with the parting comment that as an only child, he should be flattered and downright grateful he had parents who cared so much about him. He was hurt by her parting comment and spent a restless night tossing and turning, going over their conversation.

The following morning he had rung to explain his side of things and apologise if she misunderstood him. Elaine being the good listener she is, heard him out and casually mentioned she had bumped into Sheila that morning and his parents were making a visit to her and Mick the following day. Elaine decided it couldn't be a more perfect opportunity for Conor to have a proper catch-up with them and sort out his issues with his mother without delay. Elaine had it all sorted. His parents would be calling to visit him shortly and to ensure all was okay, Elaine called earlier to give the place the 'once over' as only a woman can do.

All he could do was wait for the inevitable nightmare to unfold. Ten minutes later, there was a brisk knock at the door, opened by Elaine letting herself in.

'Hi, Conor. Your visitor is here at last. Go ahead, Maeve. Conor is dying to see you,' Elaine said to his mother who hovered anxiously on the doorstep, eying her enthusiastic chaperone cautiously.

Maeve blinked uneasily, unsure of what her next move should be. She wasn't comfortable barging in on top of Conor, but Elaine was impressively encouraging.

'That's it. He's itching to catch up on all the news, aren't you Conor?' Elaine confirmed, herding Conor's reluctant visitor over the threshold.

'Of course, I am,' Conor spluttered, jumping to his feet.

Scratching his lowered head awkwardly, he glanced surreptitiously at his mother, trying to gauge her mood and reaction to the whole situation.

'Great, Conor,' Maeve whispered, covertly drinking in the sight of her only child while standing awkwardly inside the living room door, unsure how to react in this situation.

God bless this poor girl, she hasn't a clue about my son Maeve thought. The very idea of Conor making the most basic small talk after nine months of total silence would be a big shock. Never mind the suggestion of him 'itching to catch up on all the news'. That would be nothing short of a miracle.

'Sit down and make yourself comfortable by the stove. Conor is going to make a pot of tea,' Elaine suggested, leading Maeve to the nearby couch.

Maeve happily made her way to the couch, glad of the warmth of her childhood black enamelled stove. Its gentle warmth filled the cottage with the old familiar, sweet smell of peat. Peeling off her grey winter coat, she relaxed a little.

'I'll sort out the tea,' Conor stammered, going to the back kitchen, glad of the respite to catch his breath in comfort.

Elaine was a right whirlwind today, he thought. She could teach the Irish Diplomatic Corps a thing or two. She was some wheeler and dealer when she set her mind on something. He boiled the kettle and filled the teapot before placing it on Elaine's preset tray, laden with cups, plates, milk, sugar and Elaine's sliced and buttered homemade brack. God, he loved that girl. She had an amazing knack for making everything look so easy. Hopefully, he prayed, she could do miracles on his mother too, returning to the living room.

'That's great, Conor. You can just put it here on the table between yourself and your mum.'

Elaine patted the small side table between the couch and armchair, bestowing an encouraging smile. Dutifully following her instructions, Conor filled out three cups of tea, conscious of his mother intently studying his every move.

'Maeve, it must be nice to be back in your home place again. Conor told me you grew up here with your family before moving to Dublin.'

Elaine being the perfect host, mustered up easy conversation to break the ice and encourage her companions to relax and engage with each other.

'That's right. When my parents passed away twenty years ago the cottage was left to me and my two sisters. They lived in England and had no interest in it, so Joe and I gave my sisters their share and we kept it as a holiday home. We had some great times here all through the years,' Maeve smiled, her eyes wandering nostalgically around the living room, taking note of the fresh paint and pops of colour throughout.

'That's lovely. So, the cottage is even more special because it's your family home, and full of treasured memories. You're so good to let Conor borrow it, especially when you used it so much. Isn't she, Conor?'

Elaine smiled, refilling Maeve's teacup and passing her another slice of brack, delighted to see Conor and his mum finally relax a little.

'That's right. Thanks, Mam. I love living here. I've really settled in.'

Conor mulled over Elaine's comments. He never gave much thought to the fact this was his parent's holiday home before, or that he might be putting them out for the last year and depriving them of the use of it.

'Not at all. I'm glad to see you're happy here, Conor. You've done a great job on the place. It's looking lovely and fresh with the new paint and blinds. It looks so much better.'

Maeve complimented him enthusiastically as she turned in her seat to get a proper eyeful of the place. Yes, she thought, lovely female touches everywhere. A nice crochet throw on the couch, new cushion covers and healthy houseplants all suggested Elaine was a regular visitor, without a doubt.

'Thanks. It does look better. Elaine was the drive behind a lot of it and gave me loads of help,' Conor smiled appreciatively at Elaine, for having the magic touch to allow him to finally break the ice in his mother's company.

'You just needed a little encouragement to get started. You've made the place look great. Now, folks, I'm going to head off for a couple of hours. I'm sure you have loads to catch up on. I'll call back around six and we can have dinner together,' Elaine suggested, finishing her tea and putting her cup back on the tray.

Buttoning up her black, mid-length army coat to the chin in preparation for the outside November chill, she rose to her feet, making her way to the door.

'You're off already? I thought you'd stay another while?' Conor jumped to his feet, panic registering in his eyes as he followed her outside.

'You need this time with your Mum. It's been months since you saw her. It is time to talk it all out and finally clear the air. Remember, you're her only child and she loves you to bits,' Elaine whispered in reply, wrapping her arms around him and planting a kiss on his cheek. 'Go in and be kind and grateful that she loves you so much! I'll talk to you in a while,' Elaine grinned, resolutely walking up the lane.

Conor dutifully returned to the living room to find his mother sitting on the edge of her chair, looking equally anxious. The relaxed atmosphere had disappeared with Elaine's exit.

'I'll make us another cup of tea,' Conor blustered, anxious for a reprieve from his mother's intense stare.

'Never mind the tea, Conor. Tell me how you are. Is everything okay with you?' Maeve asked, jumping to her feet.
'I'm fine, Mam. You've been talking to me for half an hour, so you can see I'm fine.'

'I see you're looking well. I don't know that you're fine. I've had no contact with you in nine months, so no, I don't know how you are, at all. That lovely girl did all the talking so far, but now we're on our own I want to know how you really are,' Maeve pleaded, trying to make eye contact with Conor who walked aimlessly around the room, clearly intent on escaping at the first opportunity.

'Mam, can you stop the cross-questioning? It's what drove me down here in the first place,' Conor hissed through clenched teeth, his irritation boiling to the surface.

'When your relationship broke down with Ashling you spent three months buried in your bedroom, progressively getting worse. You didn't leave the room once to go out and meet friends during that time. I brought your meals up to you every day. Your anxiety went through the roof. You spent the nights pacing your bedroom floor. You didn't speak to me or your father, absolutely nobody. The doctor called to see you six or seven times, had you on Valium and described you as high risk for suicide. Then out of the blue, you decided one morning to go to Boyle. I got one text from you in all those months. So, please forgive me for asking how you are?' Maeve wrung her hands in despair.

'Sorry. I needed to get away. I thought a change of scenery and new people would do me good. The medication on its own just wasn't doing it for me,' Conor mumbled despondently, slowly doing a lap around the living room, focusing intently on the floor.

'I'm not angry with you for coming here. When you didn't bother replying to all our calls, your Dad and I felt you were blaming us for driving you away.'

'I didn't mean it that way. I didn't think how it might affect you. I probably did blame you to a degree. You were forever knocking on my door offering me my favourite dinner or trying to round up some local girls to visit, trying to find me a replacement girlfriend. Jesus, you even suggested calling old Fr. Clarke to have a word with me at one stage, so, I had enough. I thought I'd get some peace in Boyle.'

Conor slumped into the armchair beside his mum, relieved to offload his grievances at last.

'We were at our wit's end, Conor, willing to try everything and anything. We saw you change from a happy, contented lad, into a broken one in a matter of weeks. Can't you see we were out of our minds with worry, Son?' Maeve pleaded. 'Sorry, Mam. I never thought how this affected you and Dad. I just needed to get away from everything and everyone and try and sort things out in my head. I'm embarrassed remembering how bad I was,' Conor muttered, as his thoughts flitted back to those dark, haunted days.

'Conor, your life changed overnight. When Ashling ended your relationship, naturally it had a huge effect on you. You'd been going out together since you were seventeen. You holidayed together. Socialised together. Shared the same friends. You had started house hunting. No doubt you had plans to marry. Eight years together is a long time. It's completely normal to be devastated when a long relationship like that ends. Your life map is torn up before your eyes and you're left abandoned, and alone. You start questioning everything about yourself and blaming yourself for situations you have no control over. Without talking it out with friends or counsellors, your mental health suffers and depression sets in,' Maeve stated, looking compassionately at Conor's earnest expression as he held her gaze.

'Thanks, Mam. That's exactly how I felt. I didn't think you'd understand. I was embarrassed, ashamed and felt stupid for not seeing the split coming. I thought we knew each other inside out. It just shows how wrong I was. I felt like a complete failure,' Conor whispered.

'We have no control over someone else's feelings changing towards us at any stage of a relationship. Whether we are in a short or long-term relationship or even fifty years married. Ashling wanted to leave and everyone has a right to leave a relationship when they're no longer happy in it. She was a lovely girl and probably struggled for months wondering how to tackle the subject, trying to figure out the gentlest way of telling you. But the crux of it is, we can't make anyone love or commit to us forever if they don't want to. All our lives we will experience rejection in some form or another - at school, work, friendships, and family. It's very important to be aware of that and learn coping skills to deal with it.'

Maeve reached forward and pat Conor lovingly on the shoulder. Conor looked up, eyes moist at his mother's words.

'I know what you're saying is true. I spent endless days and nights wondering what I could have said or done differently to make her stay but came up with nothing. I attended a counsellor in Boyle. She was great. Elaine was behind that too, encouraging me to attend. I was sceptical of the counselling at the beginning, but she was pretty good. She mentioned all the stuff you just said about developing coping skills in different situations and managing stress. I'm surprised you're a wealth of information on the subject.'

Conor smiled, with a newfound respect and admiration for his mother.

'When you became a recluse at home, myself and your dad were devastated. I googled and got informed about the cycle of depression, the triggers causing it and various coping skills for managing it. I did try to get you to listen to me, but you were too low at that stage to ever hear me. I won't upset you anymore by rehashing the whole thing. Are you honestly better now?' Maeve repeated.

Conor looked in awe at his mam, embarrassed to think how much stress and aggravation he put her through by shutting her out. Reaching forward he placed his hands on her shoulders.

'Mam, I'm genuinely in a much better place now. I did fester here for a while licking my wounds and keeping away from everyone. That nosey auld biddy, Sheila, tormented me, constantly knocking on the door and peeping in windows. She dragged me back into civilisation. When Olivia moved in, Sheila insisted I give her a hand, which I did very reluctantly. With poor grace at the beginning, I'll admit. But, I got better at it. I started to mix more, took up a bit of carpentry work with

Mark and met Elaine and the rest is history,' Conor laughed, watching relief and joy wash over his mum's face as she broke into a smile.

'You might think Sheila's an auld biddy, but you know, she's been your lifeline here. Despite your total lack of charm towards her initially, she never gave up on you,' Maeve smiled at her son.

'I do, Mam. But she's still a nosey biddy,' Conor chuckled. 'Enough of all that. Where's the quiet man? Waiting in the car for the aggro to be over?' he joked, aware of his father's habitual absence at the slightest hint of aggravation.

Joe was notoriously known as the 'quiet man' both within the home and outside it. He never engaged in confrontation or rows. He said his piece and wouldn't waste two words when one would suffice. When matters got heated, he simply got up and walked away.

'He probably is. He was going for a walk first, but most likely be back in the car by now. Pop that kettle on again and I'll go out and rescue him,' Maeve winked, pulling her coat on and going to the door, the blast of winter hitting her as she opened it.

As her eyes adjusted to the November darkness, she walked over to Joe who had his seat reclined, waiting patiently.

Maeve gave a little knock on the driver's window to alert him and opened the door.

'Well, how's the negotiations going?' Joe asked calmly, searching his wife's face.

'Come in. We have our old Conor back. We've had a good talk and cleared the air. You'll be glad to hear the shouting match is over. He's made a new life for himself here and you know what, I think he's emerged a much stronger and more mature character,' Maeve whispered earnestly to her husband who was hanging on every word.

'By God, you've performed a miracle. And he's alright now?' Joe enquired, recounting all the slamming of doors, shouting matches and the long silences for months before Conor's departure.

'I know it's hard to believe, but it's true. We've had a great chat. C'mon, he's putting the kettle on,' Maeve reassured him as they approached the cottage door.

Opening it, Conor stood in the halo of the sitting room light and led his parents to the couch in front of the stove.

'Well, Son. You're looking well,' Joe said, looking him up and down carefully.

'Yeah, Dad. You'll be glad to know I'm sound again. I'm back on track. There's nothing for you to worry about,' Conor replied, rubbing his father's back reassuringly.

'Good! It's all in the past. Learn from the experience, Son, and focus on the future. Where's that mug of tea I heard about?' Joe asked, sitting comfortably on the couch, glad of its comfort after the chill of the car for the last hour.

'Don't overdo the cake. Elaine has dinner ready to go in an hour and a half,' Conor shouted on his way to the kitchen, relief washing over him that everything had gone so well.

Elaine had planned everything today and he had reluctantly fallen in with her scheme. She had reassured him not to overthink things. While his instinct was to avoid or at best defer meeting up with his parents, he was grateful he'd gone along with her plans. Hearing his Mum and Dad chuckling in the background filled him with pleasure at a sound he hadn't heard for a long time. He boiled the kettle again and refilled the teapot, taking them into the sitting room.

'My God, Lad, I think you might well have rightly landed on your feet with your new girlfriend. I met her earlier at Sheila's and thought she had it all, brains and beauty. Hang on to her tight. I was blessed with your mother, and may you have the same good fortune,' Joe said, ready to settle in for a pleasant evening.

'Thanks, Dad. I'll do my very best. Oh, why don't you stay the night? Elaine has the bed made up. By the time we have dinner, it'll be too late to drive to Dublin,' Mark suggested, passing a mug of strong tea to Joe.

Conor didn't mention he had just received a text from Elaine suggesting an overnight stay. He'd never have thought of that idea himself. Maeve and Joe exchanged glances; the excitement barely concealed on Maeve's face.

'Well, Joe. What do you think? You're the driver?' asked Maeve, her face gleaming.

'We don't have an overnight bag, but I think we'll manage without it. We'd both love to stay for the night, Conor. It'll give us a chance to have a proper get-together as a family and chat with Elaine,' his Dad replied, as Maeve nodded agreeably beside him.

'Good! That's settled and thanks. I'm looking forward to us all being together,' Mark answered, subtly texting his reply to Elaine.

# Chapter 33

Betty shifted again uncomfortably in the car seat. She was aching from head to toe, totally exhausted and in desperate need of a good cup of tea and wholesome dinner. She hadn't driven her car in nearly seven years and the stress of this trip today from Kildare to Roscommon nearly killed her. Mind you, she had nearly killed half the other motorists too but didn't want to think about that. Between the honking of other drivers and her jumping between lanes of traffic, her nerves were shattered. Early this morning after another sleepless night, she had decided on a whim to finally sort things out. Following a hasty breakfast, she rushed to her car and after a few spluttering attempts to start it, finally coaxed it back to life and was on the road just after half-seven this morning.

Considering she had never travelled this route in her life, she felt she had done amazingly well. She was not leaving now. She was going to get to the bottom of things, having endured enough stress and carry-on over the last couple of weeks. If she suffered any more, she would put herself in an early grave. To make herself more comfortable, she stretched her cramped legs and eased her hand down the side of the car seat to adjust the seat angle. With a sudden lurch, her neck and shoulders jerked back unexpectedly. To finish it off, she thumped her head off the driver's window.

'Ah,' she moaned, today seemed to get worse by the minute.

Wolfing the remains of a half-eaten bar of chocolate found in the glove compartment, she ignored the mouldy colour it had developed. Still, her stomach rumbled on, it's gurgling sounds adding to her ongoing misery. Arriving early this morning, she had knocked on the door but got no answer. Seven hours later she was still waiting impatiently and wasn't going to give up now. Wherever Olivia had wandered off to, she was sure she would be back soon. Betty felt her whole life had been turned upside down the last few months. She needed to have a frank talk with Olivia and get everything back on track again. With years of experience of marriage behind her, she'd soon iron out the blips between Olivia and Tom. Harmony would be restored and she'd finally have her old life back.

Rubbing her aching head and massaging feeling back into her numb legs, Betty sighed as she pondered events over the last couple of weeks. Where had it all gone wrong, she wondered.

Things had been going so well, then gradually she could feel the coolness set in between herself, Tom and Marie. She could nearly pinpoint exactly when it started. Subtle changes to her daily arrangements were made. Tom wouldn't be able to make lunch, or when she called up in the evening for dinner he'd have planned to have dinner out with Marie. Just the two of them mind, no invitation offered to her. To top it all off, Betty's washing was left sitting in bags in the utility room. She didn't mention it the first or second week. After all, she wanted Marie to settle in and get comfortable with the household arrangements. By the third week, she was practically down to wearing the same jumper and trousers for days. She felt mortified at the state of her.

She had dropped several hints to Tom, subtle and not so subtle, but to no avail. There were even two weekends in a row she didn't see her son at all. This strange behaviour started within a week or two of Olivia's very unpleasant visit. Marie, while still being pleasant enough, was now keeping a discreet distance and was a cute mover all around. Betty felt duped by her. After all the welcome and kindness she had shown Tom's new partner, there was no doubt she was completely monopolising her son and destroying the wonderful bond she and Tom had. Betty would soon sort out her daughter-in-law.

She'd have a firm conversation with Olivia. She'd forgive her gallivanting off to France and get her to see the madness of moving to the sticks and have her back with her husband and proper home in no time at all. Betty's thoughts were interrupted by the approach of headlights winding their way in her direction. Finally, her ordeal was over. Olivia's car pulled up in front of the cottage with the yellow door. Betty watched as Olivia opened her front door and went inside.

Olivia was bone tired. Every muscle in her body ached. Sighing, she leaned against the closed front door for support, stretched her arms over her head and groaned as she listened to the gentle bone-cracking sounds emanating from her body. She was physically exhausted and only fit for a very early night.

It was only Tuesday, but she was doing an extra day's work tomorrow in the office. Paddy was eager to get the two renovated cottages back on the market as soon as possible. That meant redoing the marketing blurb and uploading the new photos she had taken over the weekend. She was tired after working all weekend, putting in over ten hours both days on Paddy's two patched-up cottages, preparing them for viewings by potential buyers. True to his word, Mark had the essential repairs to both roofs done in a few days and finished with a lick of paint to the ceilings. Within a week both houses dried out.

Olivia and her transition year students had taken on the mammoth task of wading through all the rubbish and trying to put some order in its place. After filling about thirty rubbish bags and sorting out reusable items from rubbish, sweeping and washing away years of grime and dust, reattaching a few stray curtain poles, and adding screws to wayward cupboard and wardrobe doors, it was amazing the difference in a weekend. Jack and Ellie had done trojan work. Jack worked in both gardens, sawing the most overgrown tree branches and clearing away the briar-ridden gardens. There was now ease of access to view the wonderful potential in both gardens.

Olivia had already picked up a medley of curtains and throws from the charity shop purposely to dress the cottages. When the existing furniture was spruced up and rearranged, curtains put on clean sparkling windows, throws strategically covering bulging settees and a snug fire in the stoves, all three of them were in shock at the wonderful transformation achieved. While the cottages were never going to compete with the beautiful interiors of modern homes and all their hi-spec conveniences, even the teenagers commented how snug and homely both cottages looked. Olivia had kept a lot of the personal items of the previous owners, left books on the shelves, unfinished knitting on a table by the stove and the selection of bird books, and binoculars on the same window she had found them.

She knew the type of people interested in this type of property, down-to-earth, straightforward people, looking for peace and tranquillity. The cottages were homely, easily heated, within proximity to town and the train station and set in the most idyllic location. She felt confident they'd be snapped up in no time at all. Having taken a video tour and plenty of photos for the website, she was dying to bowl Paddy over with the revamped cottages. While she loved the job, every week was a busy week. Business was booming due to their much-increased online profile and the office facelift certainly helped as well. Local people visiting the office openly told her they wouldn't have set foot inside the door before because of the unkempt state of the brochure window. Spiders, dust and yellowing brochures didn't appeal to the public to venture inside.

Being diplomatic and eager to keep her job, Olivia didn't divulge this information to her boss who certainly wouldn't regard the comments as constructive criticism. She was happy with Paddy these days and couldn't help smiling in remembering the business relaunch two weeks ago. Following a lot of very persuasive conversation Paddy finally came around to Olivia's idea of having a publicity launch to celebrate the revamped look. It would be a waste not to show off the smart new office, together with the slick professional window displays. After quite a few mugs of tea, he agreed to the launch party—just a small affair, inviting about thirty influential business people in the town.

He dithered over the idea of a press blog Olivia had suggested but finally came around when he read Olivia's primed script. Even he was impressed with the range of services they were now providing, sales, purchases and rental arrangements. Thanks to Mark's impressive work on the cottages, Paddy was more than willing to offer maintenance services to interested clients. As he was a regular advertiser with the local newspapers, they did him a great deal on the publicity blog for his relaunch and that sealed the deal. The newspapers ran his article a week before the launch and the phone hadn't stopped ringing since. The launch started at two on Friday afternoon and was planned to be over by four. Paddy was anxious nobody would turn up. By ten past two. he had resumed his usual pacing and handwringing of former times. Wine and nibbles were prepared well in advance. The more uptight Paddy became, the fewer nibbles were left on the plates.

Discreetly, Olivia did her best to distract him. Fortunately, at around a quarter past two, the crowd slowly trickled in. Paddy quickly reverted into auctioneer mode warmly welcoming his guests. Soon the office was filling, the conversation was buzzing with good humour and business cards and details were exchanged. Olivia had discreetly taken opportune shots throughout the evening for the local newspaper. Paddy even made a little speech, thanking all his local business supporters for their attendance and most importantly his new staff member who made all this transformation happen. Olivia had been speechless and humbled, especially when Paddy presented her with a stunning bouquet to thank her. The crowd cheered and clapped, wishing Paddy and Olivia all the success in the world.

The crowds continued to come, well more than his thirty invitations, because good news travels fast. The laughter and conversation attracted passers-by who wandered in to say hello. Finally at six o'clock, after emptying numerous wine bottles, Olivia locked up the office and the group made their way to the local pub to continue the celebrations. The following day, Paddy was still beaming and told Olivia it was the best party he ever had. He confided he wasn't comfortable with the idea of the launch at first because he didn't think he was particularly popular. He was still a single man and didn't mix much in social circles anymore as in the last few years most of his former friends were married off and had families. He felt very much out of the loop.

He confided he was worried in case nobody turned up. He was delighted to tell Olivia that following the launch, he'd been invited to join one fella for a game of golf and agreed to join another group heading to a comedy show the following week. He was a changed man. He came into work on the odd occasion even bearing a packet or two of the expensive chocolate digestive biscuits for their regular tea breaks. Paddy was a successful and established auctioneer again and felt he truly belonged. He had more rentals and sales on his books than ever before, and these days sported the confident stride of success.

So, while she was working tomorrow, Olivia told Paddy she wouldn't be in till eleven and was looking forward to a lie in! Life was good all round. Clicking on her oil heating for twenty minutes, she stoked the embers in her stove, adding wooden kindling to give it a kick start. Within a few minutes, orange and yellow flames leaped to life. She carefully mounted a few sods of turf on top, content in the knowledge her stove would have the cottage snug in about a half hour.

In the kitchen, she clicked the kettle into life. With a large shepherd's pie already made from yesterday, she put a portion on a plate and popped it in the microwave for dinner.

# Chapter 34

Lost in her thoughts, Olivia jumped to attention when her daydreaming was brought to a sudden end by a loud knocking on the front door. Olivia left the kitchen, the persistent banging filling the cottage and hastily opened the door. Peering in the darkness, she blinked in confusion at her visitor, her brain not quite registering what she was seeing.

'Well, Olivia. I've been waiting here all day for you. Aren't you going to ask me in?' Betty snapped in annoyance, pushing past Olivia as she made her way in.

Still in shock, Olivia remained speechless as she watched Betty dash to the stove and heave herself with a resounding thud into the armchair beside it. Her trusted brown, leather handbag was thrown from her lap and abandoned on the floor as she reached forward to warm her hands at the fire.

'I'm exhausted and worn out, Olivia. I've spent the whole day waiting for you,' Betty hissed through clamped teeth, her eyes darting accusingly at Olivia.

'Well, Betty, excuse me for holding you up. I've been working all day and wasn't exactly expecting you.'

'Well, no, I suppose not. This was a rather impromptu visit I agree, but things must be sorted,' Betty fidgeted in the chair.

Olivia looked closely again at Betty trying to gauge exactly what was going on because there was something seriously amiss here. Betty's usually well-groomed 'lady of the manor' look was nowhere to be seen. Her hair was practically standing on end, her one-inch, grey roots on full display. Her usual twin-set matched look was now replaced with a shabby, slightly dirty mismatched jumper and trousers. She was wearing purple trousers and a very knobbly-looking, dark green jumper. This whole look was completely out of character for Betty, quite manic looking really. Olivia guessed it was better to tread carefully.

'Look, Betty, I'm just about to have some shepherd's pie. Would you like a portion and a cup of tea?' Olivia offered placatingly.

'I haven't eaten since before eight this morning, Olivia. I'd love some dinner and a cuppa,' Betty croaked, anger slowly deflating from her like a balloon.

'Give me two minutes and we'll be sorted,' Olivia replied, returning to her kitchenette.

Betty sat back in her armchair and exhaled a sigh of relief. The comforting heat of the stove warming her bones at last and the prospect of being served a wholesome dinner by her daughter-in-law would help a little in thawing her animosity towards her. But Betty reminded herself not to be getting too soft with Olivia. It would take quite a few hot dinners before Betty would forgive the stress and upset she caused her over the last few months.

Opening out the gate leg table and setting her heavy tray on it, Olivia placed the two plates down with the cutlery.

'Come on, Betty. Tuck in and I'll make us a mug of tea afterwards,' Olivia coaxed, noticing Betty was looking downright worn out.

Without further coaxing, Betty got to her feet, making herself comfortable at the table. Within seconds she started into her steaming shepherd's pie, washing it down with her customary glass of milk.

Olivia was relieved to see the old Betty restored, her appetite as good as ever.

'Thank you, Olivia. That was good. I'll have that tea now if you don't mind. I've had such a long day, you know,' Betty sniffed, ignoring the fact Olivia hadn't finished her own dinner yet.

'No problem, Betty,' Olivia smiled, rising to her feet, relieved the old Betty was truly back in usual form again, despite her appearances.

Returning with her tray, bearing teapot, jug, mugs, biscuits and two generous slices of apple tart, Olivia poured the tea and handed Betty her mug and apple tart. She watched in amazement as they disappeared within seconds. After drinking the second mug at a more leisurely pace, Olivia felt it was time to get to the bottom of this visit and gauge when Betty was planning to leave.

'Betty, it was good of you to visit me. Such a long journey for you in this cold weather. Did you come on the train?' Olivia enquired pleasantly, finishing her now cold dinner.

'Didn't I already tell you, Olivia? I drove down. I've been waiting here for you since before ten this morning,' Betty blinked indignantly at her host. Olivia never did listen properly.

'But you don't drive! You stopped driving when you were sixty-five. You haven't driven in years. When did you take it up again?' Olivia asked, amazed Betty had driven all the way.

'You know I haven't driven in years, but matters need to be put to rights Olivia, between you and Tom. So, I thought I needed to visit,' Betty replied, returning to her armchair beside the fire.

'Okay. I think everything is sorted. Tom and I had a long conversation when I visited. There's nothing for you to be worried about.' Olivia was acutely aware this was not a casual visit by her mother-in-law. Past experiences of Betty's behaviour confirmed Betty was on a mission.

'Well, Olivia, here you are, away from your home, not knowing what's going on with your husband. The house is not a home anymore. Tom often eats out. I hardly ever see him. He sees far more of that Marie one than his own mother. She's just not good for him. A bad influence all around,' Betty spat, unable to contain her frustration and anger any longer.

Olivia gazed in amazement at Betty. Oh my God, she thought, the enormity of Betty's crazy journey finally sinking in. Her mother-in-law had taken the longest journey of her life in a car she hadn't driven in years. Today would have been the first time for Betty to drive on a motorway, never mind driving over a hundred miles to come here to vent about Tom and Marie. Communications in Kildare must be very bad between them for Betty to make this hike.

'I think you are upsetting yourself over nothing, Betty. I spoke to Tom only last week to discuss the boys and he seemed very content. Don't worry. Everything is fine between us. Sit down and relax,' Olivia coaxed.

'Don't be upsetting myself over anything, you say. I've every reason to be upset. I'm completely deserted up there now. I don't see a face from one end of the week to the next. I could collapse in my own house, be there for weeks on end and wouldn't be missed. I'm an elderly lady and practically abandoned, trying to cook, clean and look after myself. I'm completely left on my own to fend for myself.' Betty jumped up with indignation, her face puffed with annoyance and frustration as she paced back and forth.

'Betty, I'm sure if you have a chat with Tom, you'll sort things out. Why don't you sit yourself down and I'll make you another cuppa?' Olivia cajoled, shocked at the anger in Betty's voice.

'Tom is not a chatty man, as you know. When he doesn't want to chat, you won't get a word out of him. I've dropped subtle and not-so-subtle hints but they're falling on deaf ears. I know exactly what the problem is and it's that Marie one. She's stepped into your place and turned the whole place upside down in a few weeks. She's no good for him at all,' Betty whined, fixing her gaze on Olivia.

'Okay, so ... ' Olivia muttered.

'So, I think you and Tom had a very good marriage for over fifteen years. Marriage vows are a special bond that should be respected. Don't throw your marriage away over some silly holiday. It's time to go back home where you belong. You have a beautiful home in Kildare. You and the boys were happy there. Tom was a good husband and provided a very good life for you all,' Betty harped, cutting Olivia off mid-sentence, placing her hand companionably on Olivia's arm.

'Betty, this is my home now. I'm never going back to Tom. Moving here has made me realise how much I was missing in my life before,' Olivia replied in a slow but firm tone, purposely holding Betty's gaze as she enunciated every word.

'What? You don't know what you're saying. Of course, it'll take a few weeks to settle back into a routine again. Tom will settle too and forget about your little silly foray to the sticks.' Betty pirouetted on her heel, casting a desultory three-hundred degree glance around the humble little cottage.

'The cottage isn't probably to your taste, Betty, but you know, I like it as it is. I like it because I can do exactly what I want here. I don't need your or Tom's approval on any aspect of my life and it's a wonderful feeling. I'm not going back to Kildare today, tomorrow or ever. That's my final decision.'

Olivia felt a mixture of indignation, anger and regret all rolled into one, but felt she had no option but to state her case bluntly. Otherwise, Betty would spend the whole evening trying to railroad her. Past experiences taught her it was often easier to give into her mother-in-law's wheedling and cajoling. But not anymore. She was back in control of her life.

Anger and disappointment flitted across Betty's brow, quickly followed by hopelessness as the realization of total defeat registered in her eyes. She had played all her aces and had to concede to losing this game. Betty was shocked to find that Olivia had become so hardened and bitter in such a short time. She stumbled back to the armchair and slumped into it. All was quiet for a few minutes until the first gentle sobs broke from her. With her head slumped and shoulders rounded and hunched, she was the picture of sadness and despair.

Olivia looked on in shock. She had never seen Betty shed a tear in her life. Betty was strong, confident, glamorous and overbearing. She could be downright rude at times, but never broken like this. Olivia was at a complete loss for what to do next. The silence was broken by further knocking on the door. Olivia in robotic mode switched on the outside light and went to the door to find Sheila.

'Hi, Olivia. It's only out of the oven. I thought you'd enjoy a bit with a cuppa. Stick on the kettle and I'll join you for a cup,' her neighbour said, walking past Olivia with her homemade apple, upside-down cake. Making her way to the table anxious to offload her steaming hot pie, Sheila was completely unaware of Olivia's guest by the stove.

'Sheila, let me introduce you to Betty, my mother-in-law,' Olivia said, giving Sheila a gentle nudge in the arm and a knowing look in the direction of her unhappy visitor.

'Oh, sorry for bursting in on you, Dear. I didn't realise you had company. I can call back later if you like,' Sheila offered.

'Join us for a cuppa,' Olivia replied, delighted for the respite offered by her neighbour.

Now the cold war had set in between herself and Betty, Sheila could prove to be the perfect distraction. Sheila had gotten a short rundown on Betty from Olivia when she arrived. The general gist of it was Betty was quite a formidable character and a true Irish mammy where her son was concerned. Charming as always, Sheila made her way to the visitor, extending her hand in welcome.

'You're very welcome to Roscommon, Betty,' Sheila smiled, waiting expectantly for Betty to take her hand.

The visitor didn't even raise her down-turned head, just sniffed repeatedly, continuing to thrash her sodden tissue into pieces. Seeing nothing was forthcoming with the handshake, she glanced questioningly at Olivia who responded with raised eyebrows and a firm shaking of the head. Mm, she thought, something strange was going on here. This woman was the sort of visitor no one ever wanted. Sheila had a feeling this Betty was hard work all around.

'Sheila, why don't you sit down and I'll make us all a cuppa,' Olivia coaxed, patting the chair beside Betty companionably.

Sheila raised her eyebrows questioningly but obliged.

Olivia made a quick exit to the kitchenette. She felt bad abandoning Sheila but couldn't take any more of Betty.

Sheila observed her unhappy companion. The sobs were slowly receding. Years of experience told her this woman would feel better when she offloaded. Her whole demeanour suggested she had an awful lot on her mind.

'Well, Betty. I'm sorry to see you so upset. I've never met you before, but if there's anything at all I can do to help, just let me know,' Sheila offered, laying a friendly hand on Betty's shoulder.

With a further sniff, Betty raised her head and looked at Sheila intently, taking in all the details from head to toe.

'I take it you're a married woman, Sheila?' Betty enquired speculatively.

'Indeed, I am. I've been married for thirty years. Why do you ask?' Sheila replied cautiously.

'Well, you'd regard marriage as an important commitment in your life. Wouldn't you?' Betty continued as Olivia returned, bearing her tray.

'Of course, I do. I married a good man and thank God, we're still very happy,' Sheila replied, suddenly wary about the direction of the conversation and casting a questioning look towards Olivia. These questions were far too personal for a total stranger.

'Olivia, are you listening to your neighbour? Marriage is a commitment made for life. It's a sacred oath on your wedding day. It's not something to be thrown aside when you get tired of it,' Betty huffed, suddenly confident she had gotten the upper hand thanks to Sheila's speech.

'Betty, will you please accept I'm not moving back to Kildare? I've already explained to you that Tom and I have discussed everything. He is happy with Marie and I have no problem with his new relationship. I wish them the best of luck. To remind you again regarding the marriage commitments and oaths and all that carry on, because you keep forgetting this very simple fact - your Tom is the one that committed infidelity in our marriage, not me.'

Olivia felt embarrassed and annoyed that Betty had tried to sabotage her neighbour in this personal debacle.

'Let's put this argument aside for now and enjoy our tea,' Olivia sighed, filling the mugs and adding milk.

Carefully ladling out a generous portion of upside-down cake onto a plate, she offered it to Betty who grudgingly accepted it. She placed the mug beside her on the nearby table.

'Sorry, for interrupting. Maybe if you fill me in on the problem, I might be able to help,' Sheila offered in her Miss Fixit manner.

'I can fill you in in seconds, Dear. It's like this. I've lived next door to my son Tom and Olivia and their two boys for years. We did everything together. Had our meals together. Went on holiday together. I was involved in every aspect of their lives. We shared everything. I, as Grandmother, was a big part of the family. Then Olivia decided on a whim to go on holiday and didn't return. Of course, my Tom was devasted and felt abandoned, naturally. He is human after all. He was lonely and as expected, a local lady jumped on him at the first opportunity. That Marie has no respect for the sanctity of marriage, I can tell. She's nothing but a home wrecker. A home wrecker through and through, taking up with a vulnerable man like that. Anyway, my son is so busy now that he hasn't a minute to share with me. I don't know when I last had a hairdresser's appointment. If I get sick there's not a soul to bring me to the doctor or care for me. The house is upside down and my washing hasn't been done in weeks. I'm left abandoned with no one for any company. I feel very let down by all this carryon.' Betty sniffed in her best aggrieved tone while pulling out yet another tissue to dab her eyes.

'I see. Is Tom your only family?' Sheila enquired, trying with difficulty to get her head around the situation.

'No. I have a daughter as well,' Betty replied belligerently casting a disparaging look towards Sheila. This woman really didn't seem to understand her dilemma at all.

'Yes indeed, Betty. You have a daughter, Lilly, who lives only thirty miles from you. You could hardly classify yourself as being abandoned. You're in the best of health. This is a perfect opportunity to enjoy your daughter's company again,' Olivia replied, holding Betty's gaze defiantly.

'You know I've always focused my time on you and Tom and your kids,' Betty retorted.

'Maybe it's time to focus on your daughter now and patch up any differences you may have with her. You drove down here today, so you'll be well able to pop over to visit her.

Have a proper chat with Tom and I'm sure you'll sort things out for the better,' Olivia said.

'Don't use that condescending tone with me, Olivia. You know my daughter and I don't see eye to eye. I've given the best years of my life to you and this is how you repay me,' Betty retorted accusingly, the mug and side plate dancing dangerously in her hands.

'Steady on! Olivia is not your daughter and not obliged to care for you, entertain, or amuse you in this life. I think you need to redirect your anger elsewhere. By the sounds of it, your son has ended the marriage. He's started a new relationship and you'll have to accept life moves on and takes many a turn and twist on the way,' Sheila stated, shocked at the bullying manner of Olivia's visitor.

'And that's your answer? I should have known you'd take Olivia's side,' Betty huffed, rounding on Sheila.

'Betty, will you see sense? You've had a great time for years by the sound of it. It looks like you've been tended to hand and foot by your daughter-in-law for years. She's cooked, washed and ferried you about. She's not obliged to do that for anybody, least of all for a mother-in-law. I think you should thank your lucky stars life was so good to you for so long. Thanks to Olivia, you're still a fit woman, blessed with good health. Patch things up with all your family and be grateful you were blessed with one.'

Ignoring Betty's dirty looks, Sheila carried on in praise of Olivia.

'I and my husband Mick are in our mid-seventies and have no children, but we feel truly blessed since Olivia came to live here. She's been an absolute godsend to us. Mick had a stroke and she helps get him dressed and up and about. She walks our dog for us and holds a weekly card game for all the neighbours. She picks up messages and best of all, I can drop into her at any time for a chat. Everyone else around here feels the same about her too. So unfortunately for you, you didn't appreciate how lucky you were to have her. It's our turn now. We enjoy and appreciate her. I'd say, Betty, your loss has been our gain,' Sheila admonished, happy to have her say. There was no point in mincing words. In her short time in the company of this woman, she gauged that subtle hints would be completely wasted on her.

Betty flinched as she listened attentively to Sheila's speech, every word choking her more as the realisation of her words truly hit home. How she'd love to go back in time. She'd savour every minute of her mealtimes, her plate heaving with succulent food and easy family conversations. Olivia dropped her to hair appointments, the cosiness of them all watching telly every evening. Most of all she missed Olivia's weekly delivery of washed and ironed laundry. It was all over and there was absolutely nothing she could do to change that fact.

Betty rubbed her head, the ache of disappointment and loss finally beginning to hit home. With a final defeated slump, she trundled back to her chair and put the wobbling mug and plate down on the adjoining table.

'You're right. I suppose I'll have to accept things as they are,' she mumbled in defeat, lying her head back and closing her eyes in defeat.

'Come on, Betty. You drove here today which shows you're more than capable of driving. Your friends are always off on days out with Active Age. Go and join them or take up a bit of volunteering. Give Lilly and Sean a shout. Offer to visit them. I bet they'd be delighted. It's all completely up to you to now,' Olivia persuaded.

Receiving no response from Betty, Olivia looked towards Sheila for support.

'Betty, you've got to remember life changes for everyone all the time and we've all got to roll with it. You're fit and healthy, but your health can change overnight. You're lucky to have children. Enjoy them while you can. My Mick had a stroke with no warning whatsoever and overnight lost the ability to walk and talk. He's recovering slowly, but it's taken months. Remember, your health is precious. Enjoy the good times and make the most of them while you can,' Sheila added, nodding in Betty's direction.

After what seemed like an eternity of silence, a further scuffle with Betty's handbag followed as she retrieved another tissue, proceeding to blow her nose loudly.

'I suppose I could give Lilly a shout. I haven't seen her kids since summer and I enjoy their company, even though I think they are spoilt rotten. Not enough discipline you know. My friend Maggie's husband had a hip operation about two months ago and I haven't seen her since, as he's the driver. Maggie never took to driving. She's only about ten miles away. I could manage that drive with no problem. Maggie's a great cook,' Betty added wistfully, mulling over different plans in her head, a spark of hope and excitement instantly lifting her features.

'That's the attitude. You drove over a hundred miles here today, so you'll have no problem driving around locally,' Sheila encouraged, mighty relieved to see Betty finally cheer up. For half a second, she thought she might have gone a tad too far with her advice.

'Good! That's settled, Betty. Will I give Tom a shout to let him know you're down here in case he's looking for you?' Olivia enquired, pulling her mobile phone from her bag.

'No, do not, Olivia. He'd have a fit if he knew I drove to you. I never see him during the week anyway, so don't be worrying on that account. I've just remembered there's no insurance on the car. Tom has taxed it alright because he takes it for a spin now and again to keep it ticking over, but I have no insurance on it. Good Lord, what was I thinking today? All this stress has clouded my mind,' Betty muttered, as the realisation struck her she had driven over a hundred miles with not a screed of insurance on the car.

It was by the grace of God she didn't have an accident she thought, echoes of blaring horns ringing through her brain. And what if she had been stopped by the Guards? Oh my God, Tom would have a heart attack altogether. Pulling her handbag to her lap she wrenched it open, proceeding to rummage through its stuffed contents with gusto.

'I knew I had the insurance company card here somewhere. I've been a customer of theirs for years. I'll get them to sort out this insurance first thing in the morning. I hope it's okay if I stay over with you tonight, Dear?' Betty asked, returning the business card to her purse for action tomorrow.

She bestowed a benevolent smile at her daughter-in-law, happy she had the insurance dilemma sorted out.

'Uh. Okay. That's fine. Just to let you know my spare bedroom is very basic and probably not quite up to your standards,' Olivia muttered, taken aback at Betty's decision to stay over and mindful of her fussy standards. She wasn't in the mood for running around after her for the whole night. She was already exhausted from her antics.

'I'm sure it'll be fine, Olivia, once it's clean and tidy,' Betty replied in a conciliatory tone. All the previous bluster and anger had gone as she settled into her chair and kicked off her shoes, well and truly relaxed beside the stove.

'Well, Betty, you're all sorted. It's almost nine o'clock, so ladies, I'll leave you to it. It's been a long day for you both and you'll probably want an early night. I'll see you tomorrow, Olivia,' Sheila said, going to the door and winking discreetly at Olivia on the way.

'Thanks, Sheila, for everything. I'll see you tomorrow,' Olivia replied.

'It was a pleasure meeting you, Sheila. I'll drop into you tomorrow morning before I head back,' Betty said in unison with Olivia.

'You're more than welcome. I'm just two doors up the lane. The one with the blue door and silver Golf in the driveway. I'll see you tomorrow, ladies,' Sheila called, pulling the door shut behind her and making her way out into the night.

# Chapter 35

Olivia turned over as she glanced at the clock. She had completely forgotten to set the alarm the night before and was shocked to see it was almost half past nine. She hopped out of bed, still yawning from the whole drama the night before. Already bone-tired before Betty arrived, the whole episode had left her exhausted.

Jeez, what was the chance of Betty driving over a hundred miles on a mad mission to coax her to return to Tom? It was like a black comedy. The mad mother-in-law on a mission to put the world to right. According to Betty's version of right anyway. Pulling on her jeans and sweatshirt and finding her stray socks from the night before, she donned her slippers and made her way into the adjoining sitting room. Her ears pricked hearing the clink of cutlery coming from the kitchen. Going into the kitchen, she was surprised to see Betty buttering toast and adding milk to two mugs of tea.

'Morning, Olivia. I thought I'd make us some breakfast. It's just ready so I'll carry it through,' Betty chirped as she laid the tray with mugs, a teapot and plates of toast and marmalade, and proceeded to carry them to the living room table.

'Thank you very much. This is lovely. Sorry, I don't have any sausages and rashers in. I don't bother with them much nowadays,' Olivia said dumbstruck. Betty had never in all her life made her a mug of tea, ever!

'Don't worry about the fry-up. Tom rarely cooks me one these days,' Betty answered.

Like a duck to water, she pulled the placemats from the dresser and set everything in place. Sitting down, she tucked into her tea and toast and Olivia followed suit.

'I slept very well last night. I mulled everything over for a while and I think I'll give Lilly a call and drop over.'

'That's good and are you okay about me and Tom going our separate ways?' Olivia asked tentatively, not wanting another outburst with Betty in another couple of weeks.

'I'll have to accept that I do not have any influence in this. As you said, Tom already has made his choice with Marie, so that's that,' Betty replied tightly, smothering her second slice of toast generously with marmalade. 'You never remarked on my new outfit. I was up early and strolled down to Sheila's. She invited me in and I met her lovely husband. She knew I hadn't packed an overnight bag and kindly offered me this pair of trousers and top. I offered to pay her, but she stoutly refused.

She said they no longer fitted her and were destined for the charity shop.  I love the colour and fit. She's a thoughtful lady. What do you think?' Betty enquired, pulling away from the table and standing up for inspection, the whole drama of the night before seemingly completely forgotten.

'I knew there was something different about you this morning. If I'm to be honest, that colour scheme suits you. Much more flattering than green. The style, cut and colour look great. Powder-blue and lilac look fabulous on you,' Olivia complimented, delighted to see she had shed the previous scary purple and green combination. Betty must have been in complete meltdown mode yesterday morning when she had donned that outfit.

'Thank you. I'm dropping into her after breakfast. She has a hair appointment this morning at ten thirty and managed to get me booked in as well. The carer will be with Paddy while she's away, so the timing is working out perfectly. I'll be able to drive us into Boyle so that should make life easier for her. I've also sorted out the car insurance,' Betty added, reaching for the teapot to top up her mug for the second time.

'Wow! I can hardly keep up with you. You seem in better spirits all around.'

'I've accepted things as they are. I was upset yesterday and felt you and Sheila were very harsh with me, but I do know there was truth in what she said. Sheila's right. I am blessed with good health and plan on trying to make the most of it while I can,' Betty said, finishing her toast. Pushing her chair from the table, she gathered her mug, plate and cutlery, placing them back on the tray.

'Don't rush yourself. I'll wash the delph and freshen up. Then I'm going to Sheila's and straight to the hairdressers. I'll drop Sheila home afterwards and head back,' Betty informed Olivia, as she swept into the scullery holding her tray aloft, humming to herself on the way.

Olivia watched in awe, not comprehending the metamorphosis that had taken place before her eyes. She had witnessed a broken, angry woman the night before. This morning, Betty had transformed into a bustling, energetic and almost pleasant version of herself. Finishing her toast and tea, she mulled over the drama and outburst from Betty last night and her impeccable behaviour this morning. She couldn't figure it out. With a contented sigh, she topped up her mug, deciding she believed in miracles after all.

Ten minutes later Betty returned, lipstick refreshed and

ready to set off. 'I'm ready for the road. Thank you for having me. Hopefully, the air is cleared between us. I'll give you a call when I get home. All going well, I'll be back in the Spring and could even bring the boys here if you like,' Betty offered, striding towards Olivia with arms outstretched for an embrace.

'That would be nice. Be careful driving back,' Olivia said in shock as Betty drew her into a bear hug, patting her back enthusiastically and kissing her briefly on the cheek. Olivia's heart was thumping in alarm. Betty had never kissed or hugged her before.

'Don't fuss, Dear. Didn't I drive here in one piece? You've got to take risks, or else life just passes you by. I must be off. Remember, you're at work this afternoon, so I'll be on my way,' Betty chuckled, bonhomie oozing out of every pore in her body.

With a final flourish, she bounced on her way, handbag swinging as she got into her red Golf, Olivia waving her goodbye at the door. She started the car and after a few minutes wrestling with the gear stick, finally ground it into reverse. With much revving and spluttering, Betty eventually mastered turning the car.

Bearing a wide smile of satisfaction she gave the thumbs up to Olivia. With another wave, she started on her trip to Sheila's. The still November morning's tranquillity was broken, filled with the loud cranking of gear changes as the Golf crawled up the laneway in a choking cloud of smoke.

Olivia lost in her thoughts and still in shock at the events of the last twelve hours gave herself a quick mental shake. She raced into her snug cottage to get ready for work, thankful Betty was on her way and she had her snug corner back to herself again.

# Chapter 36

'That was a turn-up for the books! I bet you never thought it would turn out like that,' Sheila laughed, enjoying a nightly cuppa with her neighbour and snuggling closer to the stove, her cup expertly balanced on her lap.

'That's the truest thing you ever said. She gave me a call a few hours ago to say she was home safe and sound. She gushed about how she enjoyed her visit and said she would ring soon. How things changed all in the space of twenty-four hours! When I think back to when I opened the door last night, I nearly collapsed in shock finding her on my doorstep. She was in such a manic state. I didn't know whether to call the guards or the doctor, she was so wound up. She's gone home transformed. A new woman. I'd nearly say we might become friends. Imagine that! We even had fun and she gave me a big hug and kiss when she was leaving. She has never hugged or kissed me. Not on my wedding day or when I had my two boys. For that transformation, I have to thank you for your tough-talking, finally making her see sense regarding Tom and me and making her see I was a decent daughter-in-law.'

'You're more than welcome. I wasn't trying to be cruel to Betty, but she needed to hear the truth about her reality. She's quite a manipulator. Because it worked in the past with you, she was completely floored when you refused to comply this time. And you know, because I'm not a part of the family, I think she appreciated my unbiased opinion. Another thing, I'm around the same age as her, so she probably could relate a bit better to me,' Sheila replied.

'With a forceful personality like Betty's,' Olivia continued. 'I was beginning to ask myself if I was letting her and Tom down and having second thoughts about my hasty exit to Boyle. Thanks to your timely visit, for listening to her, motivating her to take control of her life, being kind to her, being harsh with her, sorting her hair out and finally, convincing her to shed that horrendous knobbly green and purple outfit. Most importantly convincing her to go home and patch up things with her daughter and Tom. For a while last night I had visions of her moving in with me for weeks on end, while she converted me to her way of thinking and dragging me back to Kildare. I'm grateful, on behalf of both Betty and myself, for all your help,' Olivia gushed, hugging her neighbour tightly.

'Steady, Girl. Don't spill my tea. I'm enjoying this cuppa,' Sheila joked. 'When the facts of her previously indulged lifestyle were stated hard and fast, it finally drove home that she'd had it good but hadn't the sense to be grateful. Now that part of her life is truly over, she has no option but to decide to move on and take responsibility for creating a new more positive lifestyle for herself.'

'My God, Sheila. You've left me speechless. You're so right. You should have been a life coach. You're practical, but positive too,' Olivia smiled at her newfound muse.

'I like that title - a life coach. I have been called lots of things in the past, but never that,' Sheila chuckled at the compliment. 'She's gone home with a plan and seems a happier, more contented woman. You're happy she no longer has any expectation of a big reunion with Tom. That in itself must take a load of stress off you. Otherwise, that carry-on could go on for years,' Sheila continued on a more serious note, looking to Olivia for reassurance.

'I'm delighted for her, for me, for Tom and his new partner. The air is cleared and issues are resolved. She's even offered to drive down in Spring when the boys are on mid-term break. Sure, I couldn't refuse. I sure as hell hope she has plenty of driving practice before she drives here again!' Olivia giggled.

'I know! She's very jittery behind the wheel. I'm not a driver, but even I knew she was a bit dodgy. The engine spluttered all the way into Boyle. She kept blaming a dodgy gearstick. To think you allowed her to drive me into town,' reprimanded Sheila, poking her head accusingly at Olivia.

'Don't go blaming me. You and Betty made your hairdresser plans together. I was not involved. You became the best of buddies in no time. Your spin to the hairdressers had nothing to do with me,' Olivia rebuffed.

'You got me there. I couldn't refuse the offer of a lift. Never mind, we got there and back in one piece eventually. Even if we were overtaken by bicycles and tractors. I wouldn't tell you a lie, two tractors and a bicycle overtook us, but I didn't say a word. We were even blared out of it at times, but fair due to Betty she kept her cool. She stared straight ahead and completely ignored them. We just about made the appointment in time. It took nearly a half hour to get there by the time we got parked and everything. It usually takes Mick only five minutes to drive into town. Never mind. She was getting settled into it because on the way back she began to speed up a bit,' Sheila said wistfully, lying back in the chair and recounting the trip to the hairdressers.

Olivia, with her knees curled beneath her on the opposite chair, began howling in laughter.

'I can just see the pair of you crawling along, I'm only sorry I didn't take out my bike for a spin this morning and overtook you to see the look on your face,' Olivia chortled, holding her stomach. She was doubled up on the chair with laughter at the image of Betty's Golf going at a snail's pace into town.

'Enough of that! I was thinking by the time Betty gets back to Kildare, she'll have had plenty of time to ponder recent events and prepare her speech for her son and his new home wrecker. I've got a feeling Betty will have quite a few words to say. Betty's a wild cat at heart and likes to win. She lost the battle with you but I get the impression she'd be willing to start another with poor Marie. I'd say Betty has just swopped sides and joined up with you. l bet Tom's new girl will feel the wrath of her tongue before the day it out!'

'I'd say you're right. Betty is a real Irish mammy regarding her son. He can do no wrong in life and it will always be someone else's fault. I'm sure they'll sort it out,' Olivia nodded in agreement, only too aware of Betty's ways.

'I nearly forgot. Betty left a present for you. She has it all wrapped up nicely,' Sheila said, retrieving her shopping basket and presenting Olivia with a perfectly gift-wrapped present. 'That was thoughtful of her,' Olivia gasped excitedly, tearing open the wrapping paper to find a box containing a delicately, decorated porcelain china cup and saucer. 'I knew she wouldn't be able to stop herself. She had to have her tea here in just a plain old mug, but with this purchase, she's making sure I'll have no excuse in the future not to offer her porcelain china as befits a woman with such high standards,' Olivia grinned, thinking of Betty's self-serving gift.

Wow, she thought, carefully putting Betty's gift in the dresser, Betty was a very impressive forward planner. 'All this carry-on reminds me how good it feels to live miles away from her! Forget about the tea. Let's have a glass of wine to celebrate!' Olivia whooped, bouncing from her armchair and making a beeline for the chilled bottle in the fridge.

# Chapter 37

John nodded at Mark in agreement as they went over the plan again.

'Pass the letter to Suzanne in the morning and get her to drop it into Mum. I think that should work,' Mark replied in confirmation.

'That's right. I'll meet her at the top of the lane tomorrow morning and explain Liz is urgently waiting for it. I'll give it to her when she drops the kids off to school. She should be returning home and going by our place around half-nine and will hopefully call into Liz on her way.

'What happens then?' Mark asked cautiously.

'I'm hoping all goes well. It's not an ideal arrangement but we've got to finally sort it out. I'll give them half an hour and we can join them. What do you think?'

'Tomorrow is as good a time as any. No doubt Mum will be upset tonight. She'll have all the scrapbooks and old photos on display tomorrow. She'll be in shock when Suzanne walks in. I think you're spot on with this idea. Mum has tortured herself for years trying to figure out how to approach her. In all that time, she can't seem to settle on a definite plan. You've got to take the bull by the horns and sort it out. I think we'll all be happier when everything's out in the open,' Mark agreed.

'Thanks, Son. I'm glad you think so too. I'll be happier when we can all be honest. All this ducking and diving is taking its toll on us. I'm sure Liz's initial reaction towards us tomorrow won't be great, but I'm confident it'll be worth it,' John said cautiously.

'We'll stick to the plot. Hopefully, we'll be cracking open the champagne tomorrow evening,' Mark winked, patting his father's shoulder companionably.

'Absolutely, Son,' John sighed, smiling proudly.

Suzanne was in a great mood. The sun was shining and today was her birthday. Thirty-eight today! She was doing her usual walk with the kids to the top of the road to catch the minibus that dropped them off at the National School in Boyle. Her friend had already picked up three-year-old Aoife and took her to crèche. She was hoping to have some time to herself for a change. Alan had surprised her yesterday evening by saying he was bringing her out for her birthday tonight. Nothing fancy. A meal in a local restaurant, but she was looking forward to having a date night with just the two of them for a change.

She loved her four kids but there was very little time for herself and Alan. She was thrilled. He told her he had arranged a babysitter. This morning before leaving for work, he gave her strict instructions to put her feet up and pamper herself for a change. She was looking forward to going out and having fun together. She was a lucky girl.

'Happy Birthday, Mammy. You look beautiful today and smell lovely. Your hair's all shiny and bouncy,' announced Suzanne's seven-year-old Enya as she clutched her mother's hand, skipping along contentedly beside her more morose, teenage sister.

'Thank you. That's a nice thing to say,' Suzanne replied, stroking Enya's blonde curls.

'Happy Birthday, Mum. She's right. You are looking nice today,' Allanah, her thirteen-year-old agreed, slowly scanning Suzanne sceptically from head to toe.

'Thank you. I had a luxurious bath last night. I put in a conditioning hair mask and spent a few minutes styling my hair this morning for a change.'

'You should try a bit more often. You're beginning to get bags under your eyes,' Allanah replied dismissively, flicking a perfectly, straightened lock over her shoulder.

'Thanks for the beauty tips. I'll try and make a bit more effort. Prepare yourself, because while I'm busy titivating, I might overlook making your dinner and washing your clothes. I might have to forget about making your breakfast for the next few weeks too while I'm trying to catch up on some sleep, to rid myself of the dreaded eye bags,' Suzanne winked at her daughter.

'Point taken, but you do look nice today,' Allanah smiled, hugging her mum.

'You're right. I was beginning to slip down that slippery slope of not caring about my appearance. The few minutes of effort this morning made a difference. I'm glad you noticed. Thanks for trying to keep me on the right track,' Suzanne laughed companionly with her daughter, rubbing her shoulder lovingly.

'Okay, Mum. I've given you subtle warnings. No slacking allowed. Here comes the bus. See you later,' Allanah quipped, dismissing Suzanne abruptly as the minibus pulled alongside.

Suzanne hugged and kissed her younger daughter before releasing her onto the bus, knowing not to speak or approach her, which would be embarrassing if witnessed by school friends.

The minibus pulled away and Suzanne turned to make her ten-minute walk home. The sun shone and it was a lovely crisp November day. A lot of people didn't like winter, but Suzanne loved every season of the year and her short morning walk home alone allowed her to see and observe the seasons change. She enjoyed the subtle differences in colour, smell and temperature, and even more so on her own so she could see, hear, and smell every small detail of this well-walked path. There was no real frost yet, but the weak morning sun was filtering hazily through the early morning dew, droplets glistening like diamonds on the remaining leaves of the nearly balding trees. The sycamore and beech tree-lined lane was glowing with the last vibrant shades of ochre, orange and red, all blending harmoniously. The valiant, wild fuchsias were giving their final blast of brilliant pinks and purples before the harsh frost kicked in, banishing their blooms for another year.

The autumn air was redolent with the sweet scent of decaying leaves and autumn berries. In the background, the whitethorn hedge was coming into season adorned with an abundant display of red swollen fruits, tempting robins and thrushes to dine on their lavish fare. She took her time, enjoying the crunch of leaves underfoot. In the distance, the twinkle of Lough Key sparkled in the morning sun surrounding

Rockingham Castle ruins rising majestically and proudly in the background. Life was good she thought, happily strolling along.

'Morning, Suzanne. Isn't it a great day?'

Recognising her neighbour John's silver jeep she stepped to the edge of the road to let him by. John rolled down the window and parked beside his neighbour.

'It's lovely, John. I've been enjoying my walk back after dropping off the girls to the bus. How's everything with you?'

'All good. We enjoyed the card game last night at Olivia's. It's a lovely break in the week. A great way to catch up with everyone.'

'Exactly. Olivia's a lovely girl. She's only been our neighbour a few months, but her place has become a proper rambling house, hasn't it? She has a great way of bringing people together and even worked her magic on Conor. I see him very regularly out and about. Before Olivia arrived he wouldn't answer the door to anyone, not even the postman. She's a very welcome addition!'

'Indeed! She must have some magic, alright. Mark is having his dinner with her more often these days than in his own house.'

'There might be more attractions at Olivia's place than just good home cooking.'

'I won't interfere. Mark would be a very lucky fella if he gets Olivia.'

'I couldn't agree more. We'll watch that space.'

'Absolutely! Would you mind doing me a favour, Suzanne? Liz is waiting for this letter. The postman gave it to me but I'm heading out to a job in Boyle. Would you drop it in on your way?'

'Of course. I pass your house. It's no trouble.'

'That's great. Thanks a million.'

John passed a brown envelope to his neighbour and drove off on his way.

Within a few minutes, Suzanne arrived at her neighbour's house. Opening the small, white wrought-iron gate, she admired the two-storey house. Liz and John moved here a year ago. When they moved in, it was a basic, tired two-storey 60s house with little updating over the years. It had sported the original mustard, melamine kitchen cupboards and an olive green bathroom suite. She hadn't been inside the house since then, but the neighbours had raved about the work John and his son Mark had done on it. Certainly, they had done wonders on the outside. Gone were the wildly overgrown, leylandii trees that had taken over the garden. It was now planted with elegant boxhedging and laurel. The drive was laid with beautiful sandstone gravel.

Suzanne approached the freshly painted, cream porch door, adorned with a wrought iron knocker. Gently lifting it and letting it fall, she waited patiently for a few minutes but got no response. She knocked a second time a little louder. Again there was no reply. The door was on the latch and she could hear a radio playing in the background.

Suzanne pushed the front door, gently placing one foot inside the tiled hallway. The inside door was open. She shouted hello while knocking on the inside door. Again there was no response. She felt uncomfortable stepping into her neighbour's house. As the letter was important she decided she'd best make her way in. Walking down the hallway, she could see the glass panelled kitchen door was half open. Liz was seated at the table, oblivious to the sound of the door knocker with the radio playing in the background.

Suzanne continued to the kitchen door and knocked again. Liz was looking at something over the kitchen table, completely unaware she had company. Suzanne moved slowly to the table and placed the letter on it.

'Hi, Liz. John asked me to drop this letter to you. I knocked but you didn't hear me and …'

Suzanne's eyes were instantly drawn to the collage of photos arranged across the kitchen table. Lots of baby pictures of her with her grandad, school photographs. All pictures of her. Liz was holding a large, picture frame in her hand. Suzanne's eyes were immediately drawn to the picture of her Holy Communion Day, her gappy-toothed smile beaming back at her.

Liz jumped in her chair in shock, her face suddenly draining of colour as she stared at Suzanne.

'Oh, my God, What is this? What's going on? What are you doing with my photos?' Suzanne cried, falling into the nearest chair in shock.

'I can explain, Suzanne. It wasn't meant to happen like this,' Liz stammered, leaning her head into her hands and sobbing.

# Chapter 38

Suzanne stared in shock at her neighbour, trying to comprehend the bizarre scene.

'I don't mean to upset you, but what are you doing with my photos?' Suzanne asked, a nervous laugh escaping her as she patted her neighbour's shoulder awkwardly, eager to calm her obvious distress.

Liz continued to weep. Long, uncontrollable sobs escaped her, shoulders heaving with so much turmoil that she was incapable of replying.

'I'll make us a cup of tea if that's okay and we'll have a chat,' Suzanne appeased, hoping the few minutes of distraction might give Liz time to compose herself.

She clicked the kettle into action, searched the cupboards for delph, filled two cups with strong, hot tea and brought them to the table.

Liz gratefully took the tea. Suzanne was delighted to see her neighbour was calmer, even managing a watery smile.

'I'm sorry about that. I didn't hear you at the door. Happy Birthday.'

'How do you know it's my birthday?' Suzanne shook her head, puzzled at Liz's reply.

'Please, come closer and have a look at the photos. I'll explain everything.'

Suzanne inched forward, a mixture of curiosity and apprehension bubbling up within her. Obligingly, she pulled a chair beside Liz and sat down.

'This is a long story, but the photographs will tell it all.'

'You have all these photos of me! What's it all about? Grandad and I are in a lot of them. Did you know my grandad?'

'Yes. Your grandad was my dad. Your mother was my sister.'

'But Mum was an only child. I saw all the old photos and there were no pictures of a sister.' Suzanne stared intensely at her neighbour, suddenly noting her familiar features, the auburn hair and a slight sprinkling of freckles on the bridge of her nose.

'It's a long story that started thirty-eight years ago today when you were born in Liverpool. Look, here's the picture of you. The only picture I have of you as a newborn.'

'Why are you holding me?' Suzanne blinked, confusion etched across her features.

'I gave birth to you. I was sixteen years old. My mother and sister decided it wasn't socially acceptable for me to bring up a baby. They came to England when I was having you.

Between them and the nuns who ran the birthing home, my baby was taken from me and John and given to my sister to raise as her own. She was married for a few years at that stage and had no children. They thought it the perfect solution,' Liz replied in a flat tone. Telling the story was still upsetting all these years later.

'You're my mum! But my birth certificate has Mam and Dad's name on it as my birth parents.'

'I know. There never was a formal adoption. Joan and her husband put their names down as the birth parents. I had no say in any of this. My dad was my only link to you. I don't know if you were aware of the history of your grandparents' home. My mother laid down the law and poor dad had to live by it. After you were born they took you away from me. I was told never to come back again. My Dad was wonderful and sent me pictures of you growing up, your first tooth, first curl, first steps, first shoes, starting school, your Holy Communion. All your little triumphs are recorded in my box of treasures. They kept me and John sane over the years. When Dad died we went to the funeral despite being barred by my mother and Joan. We kept our distance and didn't approach them. We didn't want a scene that might upset you. That was the first time we saw you since you were taken from us at one day old.'

Liz watched Suzanne's face carefully, very aware of the shock this news would cause her.

'Happy Birthday, Love. I'm sorry if this is upsetting. We have been here a year and every day I've tried to muster the courage to approach you and explain all that happened without you hating us both. But I couldn't find the words. John had enough and today he must have decided to take matters into his own hands by setting us up this morning.'

Liz sighed defeatedly as she stared at the photos, unable to meet Suzanne's steadfast gaze. 'I'm shocked this could have happened. Before Mam passed away she was unwell for about three months. She was getting confused because quite a few times she got upset, telling me I was adopted. I put it down to the strong medication she was on for the cancer treatment. I didn't pass any heed on her, but she mentioned it again before she died that I was adopted,' Suzanne murmured.

'Really! I never knew that. It must have been a huge burden for her to keep the secret from you all these years. Dad said she was a good mother and you brought out the best in her.'

'She was generous and caring. They both were. They were never great talkers or huggers, but I know they loved me.

Now I have a new set of parents and a brother,' Suzanne whispered, unsure how to respond to this strange situation.

'I know this is a very odd situation and it's going to take time. I'm sorry you had to walk in on me like this. John had enough of me stalling. He's become very frustrated with me lately.'

'Of course, it's going to take time, but we'll work it out. I'm sorry for all you've been put through. I've always felt uncomfortable with you because I thought you were staring at me. It's good to know it wasn't a figment of my imagination,' Suzanne laughed, anxious to put Liz at ease.

'I'm sorry, Love. I thought I was being subtle. I've sat by the front window every morning and afternoon as you go by with the kids. I enjoy watching you all,' Liz confessed as a flush of colour flooded her face.

'That's heartbreaking but so lovely. Hug me for my birthday.' Suzanne stood to embrace Liz, wrapping her arms around her affectionately. They stayed in their tight clasp; Liz finally enjoying the smell and feel of her newborn who'd been snatched away so cruelly many years before.

'Thanks, Suzanne. That means so much to me. You're such a beautiful girl, in looks and manner. I'm so proud of you.

Let me get a good look at you.' Liz eased out of her embrace, feasting her eyes on her firstborn. She smiled as her eyes rested on her golden auburn hair, now glinting in the morning sun, her lightly freckled cheeks and beautiful, green eyes sparkling back at her.

'Thank you for being so understanding and taking such a burden off me,' Liz sniffed, struggling to hold back a fresh flow of tears.

'There's no denying I get my looks from you. We can't change the past. I'm sorry for the anguish and pain you and John have been through. John's plan today couldn't have been better, and it's all worked out. We have decades ahead to make new happy memories. Let's celebrate the future and leave past regrets, remorse, and sadness where it is. What do you think?'

Liz stared in amazement at her daughter, bowled over by her maturity, understanding and compassion. She felt her heart swell with love. This was proving to be one of the best days of her life.

'I think you've summed it up. I'll put the kettle on and make us a fresh cuppa. I've got a lovely, fresh cream cake to celebrate your birthday. What am I thinking? Am I holding you up?' Liz asked, gazing adoringly at her daughter.

'Not at all! It's the most unusual but best birthday present ever. I've got a new readymade family, a whole new set of parents and a brother thrown in as well. No more worries about babysitters!'

'So true. I can't wait to get my hands on the kids, but I don't want things to be awkward for you or them. How are you going to explain about us?'

'I think the best option is just to tell them the truth. No more secrets or lies to be stumbling over for the rest of our lives. Don't worry, I'll tell the neighbours Thursday night after our card game. I don't want the news to filter out through gossip. I'll take the bull by the horns and put our news out there to our close neighbours as soon as possible. It's simple really. I was adopted and only found out today. I'm dying for that cup of tea and a slice of cake. Do you think we should put John out of his misery and give him a call?'

'Would you mind? He's probably wondering how things are going.'

'Go ahead and make the call. I'll rustle up tea and cake.'

'I'll do it right away.'

Liz picked up her mobile phone, eagerly going into the adjoining sitting room. Excitedly she dialled John's number. He picked up on the first ring.

'Is everything okay? Are you alright?' John asked anxiously.

'I'm more than alright, John. She's just fabulous. I can't say I liked your method, but the final result couldn't have worked out better. We're having a celebratory cup of tea in a few minutes Do you want to join us? What am I thinking? You're out on a job. Will we leave it until later?'

'No need to leave it. Mark and I are parked outside the door. We'll be with you in two minutes.'

'You crafty pair. That's even better,' Liz grinned, suddenly loving her husband even more for his sneaky, yet perfect plan. Euphoric with excitement, Liz rushed back into the kitchen to pass on the good news.

'We're going to have more company, so you'd better fill the teapot. John and Mark will be joining us. I should have checked with you first to make sure you're okay with that. I don't want to overwhelm you with strangers bursting in on top of you?'

Liz stopped in her tracks, mortified at her insensitivity to Suzanne's feelings.

'Not at all! This is the perfect opportunity. After all, I've known you all for the past year and in the last two months we've been meeting weekly basis at the cards night. Now is perfect timing.'

'Thanks again for making this all so easy for me. I know it's a big shock to you. Please, let me know if you need some time and space from us,' Liz whispered, hearing the rattle as the front door opened and excited voices were heard in the hall.

'I'm very direct, so please don't feel you're pressuring me. If there's any problem, I feel we'll be able to talk it through,' Suzanne smiled, hugging Liz reassuringly.

Liz smiled in amazement. For the first time in her life, she sent a silent prayer of thanks to Joan for her part in moulding such a fine, strong character in her daughter.

John and Mark made their way into the kitchen with flowers and champagne, looking uneasily from Liz to Suzanne.

'Well, Boys. Aren't ye going to say hello at least?' Liz urged, anxious to ease their discomfort.

'Hi, Suzanne. Happy Birthday,' Mark said sheepishly, passing her the large bouquet of yellow and white roses.

'Thank you, Bro. What a lovely present. I adore roses,' Suzanne replied, hugging him. 'And Dad, you also come bearing gifts. This is working out well for me,' Suzanne laughed, opening her arms.

John received Suzanne's warm embrace as she took the champagne. 'Hello, Love. This day has been a long time in coming. Thanks for making it so easy,' John choked as Suzanne remained in her father's embrace.

John stepped back and took in the sight before him. Finally, decades later, his family was reunited at last. Overwhelmed with joy, tears stung his eyes as he drank in every detail of his daughter.

'Don't get all upset. This is a happy day for us. It should be awkward and I should be at a loss for words, but I'm not. I have gotten to know you well over the last couple of months. Mark, you've been an absolute godsend taking Jack under your wing and teaching him the basics of electrical work and plumbing. He's such a handful at times. I thought I'd have to bribe someone to take him for work experience. Little did I know it was pure pity for your old sister that was the real clincher. So, thank you, Bro. You're a lifesaver. I will always be grateful to you for taking on my teenage challenge,' Suzanne beamed, her face glowing with admiration.

'He's just a normal teenager, slow to get started, but coming along nicely,' Mark smiled in return.

'Thank you for being so diplomatic. I'll stop talking and let's pop open this champagne,' Suzanne said, returning the bottle to her dad.

'With pleasure. Liz, get out the posh glasses and give them a dust down,' John smiled, as Liz rushed to the tall mahogany display unit to retrieve her cut-glass flutes.

'Well, Suzanne, the 'not to be touched' Waterford crystal glasses are getting an outing today. They only ever see daylight for an hour on Christmas Day and that's it for another year,' Mark joked as they took seats at the kitchen table.

'Mark, don't go showing us up in front of Suzanne. These glasses are one of the few good wedding presents we got and I like to mind them. What's the harm in that?' Liz asked, buffing the glasses before carefully placing them on the table.

'You're right, Liz. They are stunning and deserve to be minded because they mark such an important day in your life. The youth of today have no appreciation for the finer things,' Suzanne smirked at Mark as she took the proffered flute of bubbly from her mum.

'Okay, point taken. Yes, Mum, they're stunning. You have looked after them well. Less of the youth remarks, Suzanne.

You're only a few years older than me,' Mark winked.

'Let's raise our glasses to a happy reunion with our wonderful daughter and Mark's sister,' John said, leaning forward to clink glasses with his family, his face glowing with pleasure.

'Cheers, to a new start for us all. Please remember you're not just taking me on board, there's also a husband and four kids - sometimes moody, whingy and exhausting, but always wonderful if I say so myself,' Suzanne chuckled as she lifted her glass, savouring the bubbles pricking her tongue.

'Bring it on. I can't wait to have them dropping into me. We'll let you break the news in your own time. You give us the nod and we'll be here waiting to meet them. Let's not forget that cake,' Liz advised, savouring the last of her glass of bubbly.

'I have it all sorted. Clear a corner on the table, Liz,' John asked, placing the candle-laden, cream-filled sandwich sponge on the table.

'Pink candles and all. I'm very impressed, John,' Suzanne gasped at his obvious earlier planning.

'Don't be! I've waited a long time for this day,' John answered, carefully manoeuvring the cake opposite his daughter.

'Dad, thank you. I'm going to make a wish, but I think it's already come true for me. I don't think this day could get any better. It's a wonderful feeling to be where I belong,' Suzanne smiled. Tears glistened in her eyes as she reached across and blew out the candles to a resounding cheer.

Glasses and plates were refilled, conversation flowed easily, and the kitchen echoed with the welcome sound of unrestrained love and laughter, of a long-lost family finally reunited.

# Chapter 39

'I'll finish off the evening by saying congratulations again to Suzanne, Liz, John and Mark on your wonderful news. May you have a great life together,' Sheila cheered, raising her glass to the new family.

The room filled with resounding applause as the neighbours joined in.

'Thanks everyone for your good wishes. We're looking forward to making up for lost time. Liz has already booked a family holiday. No time wasted. Before we head home we'd like to wish the best of luck to Mick now he's out and about again and most importantly back behind the wheel. To continued good health and happiness to Sheila and Mick,' John pronounced, raising his glass and finishing his champagne.

'Thanks, John. Like yourself, I'll have a busy few weeks ahead of me. Sheila has my diary well filled up for the next month,' Mick declared, as Sheila gave him a good-humoured nudge.

The empty cups and glasses were gathered, and Liz carried the tray into the scullery. Ten minutes later, with the table cleared, delph washed and put away, the group shuffled into their coats, zips, and buttons closed tight in preparation for the winter chill. Amid much chatter and laughter, the group headed to the door as Olivia held it open.

'See you, folks. Take care,' she shouted, hastily closing the door on the icy blast of air.

All had left except for Mark who lingered behind.

'Do you mind if I hang on for a chat?' Mark asked.

'You never need to ask that question. You know I love our chats. Go and stick on that kettle again and we'll have a fresh cuppa,' Olivia exclaimed, delighted to have a one-to-one chat with Mark.

Adding a few sods to the stove and perking up the cushions and crochet throw on the couch, within minutes the place was cosy and inviting again.

'You're a star. Your mother has you well trained,' Olivia affirmed as Mark returned, placing the tray on the adjoining table.

'Thanks. It's good to know I'm well-trained. I'll be beating women off with a stick next,' Mark jested, taking a seat next to Olivia on the couch.

'What's on your mind? How do you feel about your new sister? You're now a brother and an uncle within the last few days.'

'I'm delighted with Suzanne. She's sound as a pound. All this secrecy over the past year and a half on how to broach the subject with her had been tearing my parents apart. Mam was getting so depressed about the whole thing and Dad had a different idea on how to approach Suzanne, so they had regular rows over it. Living with their secret was like walking on eggshells at times. But now everything's out in the open it's like living with two teenagers again. They're going around giggling like they're on a second honeymoon. They have the kids around all the time and spoil them rotten. It's good to see them so happy,' Mark revealed.

'Why am I sensing there's a but to this story?' Olivia asked tentatively, shocked to hear Mark had carried the burden of the secret around for so long,

'Well, aren't you on the ball today! There isn't a but at all. I felt while Mum and Dad were under such stress at home, I couldn't move out. Now Suzanne's back in the fold, I can move and do my own thing.'

'You're thinking of moving away?' Olivia queried, her voice trembling. She hadn't considered for a second he'd ever move.

'Recently I was working on a house two miles up the road. The owner told me he had another old, vacant two-storey house nearby and hoped to put it on the market. I took a look at it and loved it. It's an old-style farmhouse with no proper central heating system, just an old brown range. 70s décor is everywhere, kitchen, bathroom, the lot. Brown and orange, flowery patterns are all over the place on tiles, carpets and wallpaper. You get the picture. But, it's dry inside with no obvious dampness. It needs insulation and probably a new roof eventually, but I love it.'

Smiling at Olivia, Mark continued.

'I'm going to check out the range of available grants for vacant homes. I've made an offer and he's accepted. In a few months, when the sale goes through, I hope to be able to move in. I'd love you to come with me next week and have a look at it. Give me your expert opinion on the layout and stuff like that because you did such a good job on the cottages. What do you think?'

'Thanks be to God you're only moving up the road because I'd miss you. I'm delighted you're buying your own place. I'll be up to have a nosey around whenever you like,' Olivia said, overwhelmed with relief he was only moving up the road, instinctively throwing her arms around him for a hug.

'Thank you. It's good to know you were going to miss me. It's time for me to move from the home nest. I'm a big boy now, twenty-eight you know,' Mark grinned, delighted to see her initial shocked look replaced by a relieved expression.

As Olivia moved away from her hug, she realised how smitten she had become with Mark.

'I'm thrilled for you. To fill you in on my news. My mother-in-law dropped in unexpectedly earlier in the week. She had a big meltdown, doing her best to convince me to return to Tom. Lots of tears and drama. We reached an unpleasant stalemate. Sheila arrived on the scene and did some hard talking with Betty. Betty stayed overnight and Sheila, the mediator, made her see sense. When she returned to Kildare she was resigned to the idea I wasn't going back to Tom. Sheila can be a tough talker. I was impressed with her influence on such a hard cookie like Betty. It was like a miracle.'

'That's good to know. No regrets about moving to Boyle? No second thoughts about Tom?' Mark enquired, wanting confirmation a reconciliation wasn't on the cards.

'Absolutely none, Mark. I'm happy here. I'm pleased Tom has found a new partner. I've got a new life. A job. I love my house. I have some lovely friends and no plans to leave. I've found my identity and it feels good. I'm not just someone's wife or mother. I'm back to being me and it's great,' Olivia enthused, fixing Mark with a big smile.

'I'm delighted for you. Good news all around. I'm staying and you've no plans to leave, so it's a win-win,' Mark crooned, relief and excitement rushing through him. 'On that note, I'm going to make tracks. I've got an early start tomorrow morning.' He placed his empty cup back on the tray and zipped his coat up.

'No problem. I'm thrilled with your good news,' Olivia stated, opening the door.

'I'm thrilled you're here to stay too,' Mark replied, reaching forward to plant a peck on her cheek before going into the darkness.

# Chapter 40

'That's a fine job you did on those two old cottages, Olivia. It's amazing what a bit of tidying and a lick of paint can do,' Paddy remarked, studying the final photos and descriptions of the revamped cottages.

'It did take quite a bit of work, but you're right. Most of the work was tidying the garden and getting rid of rubbish. All that was done in two days by the three of us. The hard graft does wonders in a short time. The curtains came from the charity shops, so no big expense there either,' Olivia agreed, appreciative of Paddy's acknowledgement.

'You did a good job. I'm very happy with the photos and revamped description. That's a great idea to put in the viewing times for Saturday and Sunday week. Between one and three should suit most people. Mass will be over and there'll still be daylight to have a look around the cottages.'

'If we put them on sale today, that'll give ten days for punters to view them. It'll minimise time wasters too. Experience has taught me that if you're interested in buying a house, you'll make a point of being there to view it.'

'That's a good plan and you'll be there to show the cottages next week. Great job. So, we're ready to go live on the websites?' Paddy enquired. The excitement at the prospect of finally offloading those cottages after two years was making him giddy.

'I was waiting for your opinion. I'm all ready to go ahead and have them on the market within minutes,' Olivia replied, delighted to have the hard work behind her on these previous unsellable properties.

She was confident they'd get good interest from buyers. Scheduling a weekend viewing would attract a bigger catchment of buyers and the properties would be snapped up in no time. Olivia was as eager as Paddy to offload them at this stage. She wanted to get back to her routine of two days per week in the office and finish her own cottages.

'That's good. We'll sit back and hopefully get a few enquiries. I'm off for more viewings this morning. I know you're finished today, so head off home whenever suits you. Will you forward calls to yourself tomorrow? I have a lot of work on and I've got a feeling the phones will be busy,' Paddy asked, with his most charming smile.

'No problem. I'll be here till five because I have a bank lodgement to do. I'll put those two new sites and two-storey houses on our website. Trust me, I'm as eager as you to offload those cottages. Fingers crossed this ad will do the trick.'

Olivia pressed the key on the keyboard, putting the two spruced-up cottages live on the national property sales websites.

'Good. I'm off now. Give me a shout on the blower if there's anything urgent,' Paddy added, grabbing his overcoat and bustling out the door at lightning speed.

He had the shifty look of a schoolboy going on the mitch for the day. His exit was completed with the resounding bang of the office door completing his great escape.

Olivia shook her head and smiled as she contemplated Paddy's exit. She had known him only a few months and his weekly tales of how busy he was never ceased to amaze her. Without a doubt, he was going into the pub up the road for a long and leisurely lunch, as he did most days. Invariably one customer or another would tell her they had bumped into him in the pub, sharing lunch and a couple of pints with him. For a local man living in a small town, he didn't realise how fast news travelled. There was no such thing as sneaking in for a leisurely lunch and a few pints without bumping into someone from the town. Every week she was amazed at the little stories he concocted to justify his absences. Didn't he realise he was the owner and one of the privileges of being boss is you don't have to make excuses to anyone for your absences! He was a pretty good boss, maybe not politically correct in many ways, but a sound, decent chap.

An hour later, Olivia stared at the page of enquiries she had already taken; shocked at the response to the ads. She had taken over twenty enquiries between emails and phone calls. They all wanted to see the properties straight away. After a call to Paddy, he felt with such momentum the only option was to strike while the iron was hot. It was agreed Olivia would arrange the viewings for the following day. Olivia updated the websites advising that due to unprecedented demand, walk-in viewings were being rearranged for the following day at eleven and twelve o'clock. With the short winter days, an early property viewing was essential. The website advised potential buyers that due to great interest in properties, the sellers were anxious for a quick sale. They recommended viewers have proof of finance in place as deposits would be taken within days of successful bids. Paddy insisted on adding the finance bit. With previous bad experiences, he felt there were too many nosey time wasters out there with, 'Not a pot to piss in and too much free time on their hands.'

Fizzing with excitement, Olivia filled in the city callers on directions, advising them to avoid disappointment by making sure to attend on time for first viewings the following day. The rest of her day flew by in a haze of phone calls. In no time she was finished. Grabbing her coat and putting both sets of keys for the cottages in her bag, she pulled the office door shut and headed for home.

The following morning Olivia was up early and had a good breakfast, knowing she had a busy day ahead. She was eager to sell and was aware first impressions of property made the difference in making a sale or making the customer walk away. She had made a checklist in her diary the evening before and nodded her head as she went through it. A bag of turf and firelighters, a few spare light bulbs, two new doormats, an air freshener, duster and polish, and another notepad and pen to take potential buyers' details. Happy all was on the list, she loaded them into the car and arrived at the first cottage within ten minutes.

Opening the door she was greeted by the cold, dark emptiness of the cottage. Immediately she lit the fire. The firelighters ignited the clods of turf and within minutes flames were dancing behind the glass doors, making the cottage a home again. Doing a quick tour of every room in the cottage armed with duster and polish in hand, she soon had any stay cobwebs and spiders banished, curtains pulled wide open in all the rooms, and bed covers straightened. Within twenty minutes the sitting room was transformed into a welcoming, inviting room, with the previous owner's knitting and crammed bookcases adding to the appeal.

Olivia smiled with pleasure as the early morning sun lit the room with winter sunshine. The cottage spruced up very well dressed in charity shop finery. She topped up the stove to the brim, confident it would warm the radiators in no time. Happy to leave the snug cottage behind, she made her way to the other one a few minutes' drive in the opposite direction.

Letting herself in she turned on the oil, relieved to hear the burner kick into action. Next, she lit the fire in the stove and going through the cottage repeated the routine from the first cottage, dusting and fixing second-hand covers and cushions on the way. Half an hour later with the place feeling warm and spruced up, she locked the front door, confident it was looking as good as possible for this morning's viewings and drove to the office.

'Morning, Olivia. I'll put the kettle on. Are you ready to go this morning?' Paddy asked, going into the kitchenette.

'Yes, Paddy. The cottages are warm and look as good as possible. I'll just have a cuppa before I return for the first viewing, but first I want to check if there are any more enquiries

I need to follow up on,' Olivia replied, turning on her computer.

'You've done a great job with them. The photos look fantastic. With a bit of luck, we'll get a few decent punters today. You might be run off your feet and not have a chance to get lunch,' Paddy supposed, placing tea and her favourite sandwich of chicken, and stuffing on the desk.

'Thanks, Paddy. You're probably right. I'll have it now because I'm starving already. With all the enquiries, I'm sure there's bound to be a few genuine viewers. They're both on the market for offers above seventy thousand. Good value in the current market. They're old-fashioned cottages but sound houses and it's a sellers' market. There's very little availability out there. I think it'll be great,' Olivia alleged biting into her sandwich, enjoying it even more since Paddy had bought her one for the first time.

'That's the attitude! You're a born saleswoman. I'll leave it in your good hands. Let me know how you're getting on. I'm off to meet a man about a valuation,' Paddy winked as he walked to the front door, saying a silent prayer of thanks to the man above that he'd had the good sense to employ this girl. She truly was a little topper!

Olivia waved him goodbye and began replying to emails. Forwarding the office number to her phone, she returned to the cottage for the first viewing. Parking her car, she glanced at her watch to see it was twenty minutes to eleven, pleasantly surprised to notice two cars waiting. Topping up the stove and giving an extra spray of air freshener in all the rooms, she opened the front door at five to eleven. Three couples made their way in, two elderly couples and a young couple in their twenties. She took their details and gave them a brochure each, inviting them to ask questions as she gave a tour of the house.

She gave a detailed commentary on the house, its locations and facilities in the area but didn't get much feedback from the viewers. Ten minutes later, another two elderly couples and a professional-looking woman arrived. Olivia repeated the process. With the increased number of viewers, the group relaxed a little and tentatively asked enquiries here and there. There was a low hum of conversation among the couples. They all chose to keep cards to their chests, with nobody voicing any particular interest in the property.

The single lady didn't engage at all and seemed happy to disappear into the back of the tour. However, Olivia noticed her discreetly taking notes in each of the rooms. Olivia advised the viewing would finish shortly as she was showing another property at noon, up the road. All the group nodded and politely made their way outside except the lady who insisted on having another look before joining the rest of the viewers as they all piled into their cars, following Olivia to the second cottage.

Olivia was pleased to find another three cars waiting outside the second cottage when she arrived. On the dot of twelve, she opened the door. This time she counted fourteen viewers in her notepad. She repeated her earlier routine, pleased to hear the satisfied murmurings of viewers discussing the merits of both cottages. Very quickly the hour flew by with varying questions regarding schools in the area, internet access and the most common question, the availability of a tradesman. Olivia was happy to oblige with answers and had a supply of Mark's business cards to hand.

As one o'clock approached Olivia thanked them for attending, reminding the group the viewing was almost over. If they had an interest in either of the properties, they should advise her as soon as possible. With a folder and pen in hand, she moved within the group, passing out the auctioneer's business cards. They discreetly eyed each other but again nobody was willing to voice their interest. Instead, they duly nodded to Olivia and made their way back outside. Fortunately, Olivia had the benefit of many years of auctioneering experience and knew not to interpret a viewer's apparent lack of interest.

She had learned most potential buyers weighed up the competition and never showed their cards at a public viewing. She locked up and made her way outside.

'Excuse me. Can I have a quick word please?' enquired the professional lady from the first viewing, jumping out of her black Audi.

'Oh, hi. Teresa, isn't it?' Olivia smiled.

'Yes. I have a few questions about the first cottage. Firstly, have you received any offers today? How quick of a sale does the owner want? Is this handyman you recommended reliable, punctual and honest?' Teresa queried, clutching notes in her hand.

'Perhaps we should step back inside to discuss things,' Olivia answered, mindful of the curious glances from the last few viewers, who didn't seem in a rush to leave.

'Okay,' Teresa replied impatiently reaching into her car, retrieving her handbag and mobile, and stalking a path behind Olivia.

Reopening the cottage door, Olivia ushered the woman inside, aware of blatant stares from the audience outside.

'Have you an update? What's the current offer?' Teresa questioned impatiently, stalling inside the front door.

'Do you mind if we sit down?' Olivia suggested, pointing to the nearby couch.

Teresa dutifully obliged, just about managing to sit on its edge, impatience bubbling over.

'I need to know the situation as quickly as possible. I'm from Dublin for the day and would like some answers before returning this afternoon,' Teresa asked testily.

'These cottages have been updated in the last week and only just readvertised yesterday. Today is the first viewing. At this minute I have no offer in yet, but I'm very hopeful to get offers on both cottages before the week is out.'

'I need answers today. I need to get sorted before I go back,' Teresa insisted, clenching the edge of the couch, white knuckles bared in exasperation.

'I'm sorry, Teresa, but I'm not going to have an answer for you today. I see you are very stressed. Why the urgency?' Olivia asked, baffled by the woman's outburst.

'I work in the West one or two days a week and need to start down here as soon possible,' Teresa emphasized, her face flushed with exasperation.

'Okay, but it's a small, rural cottage with just two bedrooms, quite old-fashioned and tucked away on its own. It would be very quiet. Would it suit you being here on your own?' Olivia probed tentatively, looking pointedly at the beautifully dressed, city slicker in her pinstriped, grey suit.

'I usually stay in a busy hotel nearby for two nights a week. I've had enough of it. I'm craving solitude! I want something more homely, calming and peaceful. I would be able to work here with no problem at all. At this stage of my life, I cannot wait for some me time. I can't wait to escape three stroppy demanding teenagers who are never happy and never clean up after themselves. To top it off, I have a wonderful husband who tells me every day to, 'chill out' as he disappears every evening for an hour on his bike in fluorescent Lycra. He returns afterward, all zen-like and smiles, ready to sit down to his dinner, spouting about the merits of exercise and how I should take up some sport while I can. None of my four seem to acknowledge the picking up, cleaning, cooking and listening to them I have to put up with. I've hit a wall. If I have to listen to another person telling me to, 'calm down', I think I might do something I might regret.' Teresa enunciated every word of her tirade, for full effect.

'You're obviously a single woman. I'm sorry for my rant. You just wouldn't understand,' Teresa sighed, forcing a broken smile.

'I can understand your dilemma more than you think. I had a similar situation but escaped here to a lovely, old country cottage and must admit I love it. So, yes. I totally sympathise with you,' Olivia laughed.

'Okay! You moved here and love it. I know I'd love it too. I'm not planning on leaving them. Mostly I do love them. Right now, I need somewhere to work away from home one or two days a week, enough to give me head space. My husband is now working from home four days a week and I think a bit of a distance would do wonders for us all. The kids are teenagers so probably wouldn't notice my absence once the fridge is stocked, mobiles topped up and clothes are washed. I've received a €50,000 inheritance from my mum who passed away last year and can arrange a loan for the balance. That cottage would be just perfect, small, cosy and blissfully quiet. Exactly what I need at this moment in my life!' Teresa declared earnestly, pleading her case.

'Teresa, all I can say is the seller is looking for offers over seventy thousand. You can put your offer on the table today and we'll work from there. I can tell you the seller wants this sale to close as quickly as possible, so you won't be messed about with delays.'

'I can offer seventy today and can go up to seventy-five. I have proof of funds with me. You can keep that copy. My phone number and email details are on the other sheet,' Teresa added, pulling her bank statement from her bag and passing it to Olivia

'That's fantastic. I'll hold onto this copy for the owner. I'll pass your bid to him today and keep you up to date on everything. And Teresa, I'll do my very best for you to get that cottage,' Olivia pronounced, shaking her client's hand as she stood to leave.

'Thanks, Olivia. I appreciate your understanding as only another woman could,' Teresa smiled as they went outside.

'I'll be in touch as soon as possible,' Olivia reiterated, getting into her car.

# Chapter 41

'That's good timing,' Mark acknowledged as he strolled towards Olivia, who was locking the office door at five o'clock.

'Hi, how are you?' Olivia answered wearily.

She was worn out from the last few days. After spending the day staring at a computer screen, her eyes were burning and tired. When the viewings were finished, the phone continued to hop with interested parties putting offers on both properties. Olivia was thrilled to secure Teresa her cottage for seventy-four thousand. The following day she received her deposit and solicitors' details. The prospective buyer was thrilled to hear the sale should be closed within a few weeks. The other cottage was sold to a cousin of the seller who was retired and loved the history and character of the place. He was looking forward to a long and happy retirement there.

'Well, I'm great. Thanks to you I'm getting plenty of work. The ad in your office window and recommendation in Paddy's publicity launch in the newspaper last week are doing wonders for my workload. I've got four jobs lined up directly related to you and another six requests for job estimates. So, thanks very much for putting in a good word for me.'

'That's great news. I'm delighted for you. But without giving you too much of a swelled head, you are a good tradesman and deserve it,' Olivia smiled, slipping keys into her handbag.

'Thank you,' Mark responded, absently wiping his dusty overalls, releasing a cloud of dust into the evening chill. 'You're off work tomorrow, aren't you? Why not take a well-deserved rest?'

'I am off and certainly intend to take it easy. For once, I've no painting or decorating lined up,' Olivia exhaled turning away from the office and began walking to her car. She turned up the collar on her black woollen coat to keep out the November chill.

'I'm off tomorrow myself. I've checked the weather and it's promised a little cool, but sunny all day. I wondered if you'd be interested in going for a spin. We could have a lovely walk and afterwards have lunch somewhere nice,' Mark asked, his hand tentatively placed on Olivia's shoulder.

'I don't know. There's no need to thank me for the extra business. I knew you were an excellent tradesman,' Olivia said, surprised at Mark's suggestion, unsure what response to give.

'It's more than the extra business you've put my way. I want to thank you for looking after me with dinner the last few months and being a good listener and a good friend,' Mark uttered, putting his arms on Olivia's shoulders and gazing at her steadfastly.

'There's no need to thank me for that, Mark. You know I enjoy your company. You have been a great neighbour and friend to me,' Olivia declared, flattered by Mark's earnest comments and patting his arm companionably.

She was acutely aware of his dark, handsome looks, chiselled jaw and dark curls peeping out under his navy and yellow, beanie hat. A Rossie supporter to the end! There weren't many men who could sport a grimy-looking beanie and overalls and still look gorgeous.

'Will you just say yes, please, Olivia,' Mark begged, inching closer and drawing Olivia into a bear hug, tucking her head into the crook of his shoulder.

'Okay. Yes,' Olivia laughed, inhaling the musky scent of his aftershave and succumbing to the pleasure of his hug. The warmth of his strong, muscular body seeped into hers as he pulled her tight against him. It felt so good after all this time, to feel the warm embrace of a man. To feel desired and wanted was such a powerful feeling. Wrapped in this euphoric state, Olivia tightened her arms around Mark and lay her head contentedly on his shoulder.

'I'll take that as a definite yes,' Mark grinned as he bent forward. Clasping her face, he gently kissed her on the lips. Olivia responded eagerly and reaching up, wound her fingers in his dark curls, the beanie falling to the ground. After a few minutes, he reluctantly withdrew from the embrace, holding Olivia at arm's length so he could feast his eyes on her. He had fancied her from the moment he first saw her. Months later, they were still just 'friends' and Mark despaired he left it too late to ask Olivia on a proper date. For once, he listened to his dad and took his advice to, 'Stop dithering and arrange a date.' He couldn't believe it was working out.

'If you want, I could head back to your place now and start the date straight away?' Mark suggested cheekily, pulling the beanie back on his head.

'I don't think so! I'm off before we become the talk of the town cavorting on the main street. I'm starving and must go home and make dinner. See you tomorrow at ten,' Olivia said, waving Mark off and rushing to her car to get out of the cold evening air.

Sitting in her car, shaking her head momentarily to clear her thoughts, Olivia was aware every nerve in her body still tingled from the pressure of Mark's body. Smiling broadly and taking a few deep breaths to steady herself, she finally started her car and headed for home.

Twenty minutes later she had the stove kicked back into life, its amber flames dancing. Within seconds she was flopped on the couch sipping tea, considering the simplest and quickest dinner to make. Her thoughts were disturbed by the thump of the door knocker. Making her way to the front door and opening it, Olivia was surprised to see Mark on her doorstep.

'Mark is all okay?' she enquired.

'Sorry. I knew you were tired and starving, so I thought fish and chips would make life easier?' Mark asked, passing his vinegar-smelling bounty to Olivia.

'That's the best timing in the world. I'm starving. Come on in and we'll have them in front of the stove. I'll grab two plates and make you a cuppa,' Olivia replied, taking the mouthwatering gift into the kitchen.

Half an hour later, well-fed and watered, they sat back on the couch, legs outstretched. In companionable silence they watched the sputtering flames dance in the stove. Seeing Olivia's look of sheer contentment, Mark reached across and gently took her hand.

'I couldn't wait until tomorrow to see you. Whoever thought fish and chips would save the day for me,' he chuckled, moving closer to Olivia.

'I must admit I was shocked to see you again this evening, but it was a pleasant surprise, made all the better with the gift of free dinner,' Olivia giggled, gazing back at Mark.

'Does this mean we're officially a proper couple now?' Mark enquired, tilting her chin to look directly at her.

'I suppose it does. However, I think we'll take things easy if you don't mind. I'm still officially married and only out of a fifteen-year relationship. Of course, I get lonely and enjoy companionship, but I've realised I love my freedom. I love the choice to come and go as I want, make my own decisions, and not be accountable to anyone. I've no experience of casual relationships and know I don't want that, so maybe this arrangement won't suit you. Also, I'm mindful that you are twenty-eight and I'm thirty-five. You may want children and want to marry and settle down. I don't think I want more children. Seven years younger is a big gap, don't you think? And finally, I've also got two thirteen-year-old sons who are going to be visiting during the holidays. Do you think you could cope with all that?'

'Wow! You've given this a lot of thought. Seven years' age gap is nothing. It's all about attitude. After all, your husband was years older than you and not mature enough to hang onto you. So no, I don't think the age gap should make any difference. You're full of enthusiasm and get up and go. I love that about you. I've been on a few Tinder dates, but they're not for me. We'll take things very slowly. Right now, you'll be glad to hear I'm not hoping to become a father soon. As for your marriage offer, I think we should take things slowly to start,' Mark howled, as Olivia lunged at him with the nearest cushion.

'Hey, I'm being serious. Because I'm married there are more complications. I don't want us to start a relationship without you first considering my extra baggage,' Olivia laughed companionably.

'Of course, I've considered all that. Sure there's bound to be some aggravation at times, but all relationships have their ups and downs. I like to think we're already good friends. We talk about everything and anything and get along well. If we disagree I'm sure we could talk things through and sort it out. It's worth taking the risk, isn't it? We're mature adults. I'm sure if either one feels it's not working out we'll talk it out and if we can't agree, we'll have the sense to part ways on good terms.

Besides all of that I fancy you an awful lot, which is very important,' Mark murmured moving closer, his lips grazing Olivia's teasingly.

'Is it worth risking our friendship? I like to think we're good friends too. I'd hate to jeopardise that friendship. I can talk to you about anything. You've been a wonderful support to me. I love our chats and …'

Olivia's words were cut off by Mark moulding himself next to her, his hands sending tremors through her entire body. Reluctantly pulling away from him, Olivia smoothed her hair down and tried to continue her debate.

'So, you see Mark, we are the best of friends now. Why risk all of that for a whirlwind romance?' Olivia blurted breathlessly.

'Because it's just as you said. We are good mates already. The basis of any good relationship starts as a friendship and builds from there. I've read all the books on it. We've already done the friendship bit and now we're getting to the pleasurable bit. I fancy you and I get the feeling you might have a mild attraction for me too,' Mark teased in return, stroking Olivia's hand. 'I respect you, Olivia. If you don't want a relationship, that's fine. I won't pressure you. But life is short and a bit of romance could make it all the sweeter. Don't you think?' Mark crooned, removing a stray curl from her face.

'Maybe you're right. Sheila said something similar to me this week. She told me I was too young to stay single and not to judge all men by Tom's behaviour. Something like, 'Life's too long without romance.' Maybe I am over-analysing it,' Olivia murmured, her head muddled with her dilemma.

'Oh my God, Sheila! Is she calling to you tonight?' Mark asked, suddenly stricken at the prospect of Sheila bursting in on top of them. He knew she was a very regular visitor to Olivia's.

'Your face has turned ashen. Steady on! She's not around this evening. She's gone out in the car with Mick, so I won't see her until tomorrow evening,' Olivia giggled.

'Thank God for that. She's a sound woman, but God, you'd have no privacy with her knocking in every ten minutes.'

'Ah, just to correct you! Sheila is a godsend. She's been so good with advice and sorting a job for me. She even gave me your number when I was looking for a plumber, so don't knock her. And, she was the one to encourage your mum to work in the charity shop and was responsible for dragging Conor back into the land of the living. She calls around most evenings at the same time for about twenty minutes or so. We always have fun.

I agree she might be slightly nosey, but I think she's just a little lonely at times,' Olivia replied defensively.

'Okay, sound! Apologies to Sheila. I didn't realise she was such a decent character. I don't want our relationship to be under constant scrutiny by Sheila if you know what I mean,' Mark said humbly, surprised to hear Sheila was the driving force behind his mum's job.

'Don't worry about Sheila. I'm sure we'll manage to outmanoeuvre her. I'll be giving you lots of interior design advice at your new house and now Mick is motoring again, Sheila's already planning to travel far and wide to visit relations. She'll be doing her best to catch up on lost time. She probably won't have as much free time for calling to see me. I regard her as a good friend and neighbour,' Olivia stated reassuringly, snuggling closer to Mark.

'That's good. So, we're going to give this romance a chance then?' Mark asked, his eyes dancing with pleasure as he clinked his mug against Olivia's.

'Why not? I know there are no guarantees for success with any romance, but we'll give it a shot. Maybe Sheila's right, life is way too long without romance.'

Olivia set her cup down as Mark reached over and pulled her into a tight embrace. Feeling the strength and heat from his body, Olivia relaxed against him, the stresses of the day beginning to melt away.

'Sheila is so right. Let the next chapter begin,' Mark laughed, pulling away from Olivia.

Reaching gently, he held Olivia's face between his hands and tenderly kissed her lips.

THE END

Printed in Great Britain
by Amazon

52285686R00239